BLISS
RIVER

THEA DEVINE

BLISS RIVER

BRAVA

KENSINGTON PUBLISHING CORP.

http://www.kensingtonbooks.com

BRAVA BOOKS are published by

Kensington Publishing Corp.
850 Third Avenue
New York, NY 10022

All Kensington titles, imprints and distributed lines are available at special quantity discounts for bulk purchases for sales promotion, premiums, fund-raising, educational or institutional use.

Special book excerpts or customized printings can also be created to fit specific needs. For details, write or phone the office of the Kensington Special Sales Manager: Kensington Publishing Corp., 850 Third Avenue, New York, NY, 10022. Attn. Special Sales Department. Phone: 1-800-221-2647.

Brava and the B logo Reg. U.S. Pat. & TM Off.

ISBN 1-57566-801-7

First Kensington Trade Paperback Printing: July 2002
10 9 8 7 6 5 4 3 2 1

Printed in the United States of America

BLISS RIVER

Prologue

The Bliss River Valley
Murthagorda, South Africa
Spring 1897

There she comes, one of the children of Eden. Even as she walks, there's a restlessness about her, a discontent.

And I'm not the only one who has noticed.

No, it is obvious to those of us who know her best.

We've talked about it; we agree: She is the snake in the garden, the thing to be most feared. We've agreed what to do.

It won't be difficult.

She's gorgeous. A creature to be envied, to be worshiped. All the men want her, even if she pretends she's not aware of it.

But she's been part of the fabric of the Basin for all the years of her life.

Or was that a mistake?

Sometimes I think it was a grievous lapse in judgment to keep her in Murthagorda, but I have no proof, no proof.

It's just that restlessness—and something in her eyes. Maybe it's something only I can see . . .

And maybe I'm imagining it.

Everyone else sees heaven in those heavenly eyes . . .

And that was the whole point. Everyone agreed. And what to do about the children, too. Inevitable whelps. Keeping a person from the kind of life that mere mortals only dream of . . .

No—there's no going back.

Once she's tethered, she'll come to understand. Everyone does. Everyone wants it, once they understand the concept.

After all, everything's taken care of, and there's never a price to pay.

If that isn't heaven on earth, then nothing is.

It's so seductive, she will want it, too. She'll grab for everything she can get with both hands, just as we all did.

And then we'll have her.

And the threat will be no more . . .

Chapter One

The Nandina Club
The Bliss River Valley
Murthagorda, South Africa
Summer 1898

He didn't see a glint of recognition in her eyes, and it both pleased him and irritated him.

She had no idea who he was. But there was no reason that she should, not after all these years.

All she needed to know was what the pleasure-seeking members of the expatriate colony lounging on the shady club veranda knew: that he was a top-ranked breeder of polo ponies who had come to display his first crop of bangtails to the newly inaugurated team on the newly built playing field at the Nandina Club in Murthagorda.

As he had planned. Every step he had taken to bring him to this moment, with him astride his prize pony and swinging his way down the field, had been planned with excruciating attention to detail.

It was his way. Deliberation. Penetration. Know the enemy before the attack. Lessons learned too young, too soon, and only implementable because he had moved in two worlds for so long, it was second nature now.

But there was a ferocity in him that he held rigidly in check, the part of him that raced his ponies over the sands of Saffoud and the greensward of the Nandina playing the field with the recklessness of a sheikh.

He was all of that and more, and a good fellow besides.

He drew his pony to a thundering halt beside the veranda, and the admiring crowd immediately burst into applause.

One man separated himself from them, his hand outstretched. "Charles! Fantastic beast. Excellent show."

Charles swung down from the pony, tossed his mallet, tucked his hat under his arm, and grasped the other man's hand. "I'm gratified you're pleased."

The man shook his head. "They're beauties. Worth any price." He clapped Charles on the shoulder. "Let's drink to it. They should be ready for us inside."

The crowd accompanied them, including *her.* He made it a point to be within visual distance of her. *Her.* The wife of a man who had a hundred thousand pounds to spend on a string of polo ponies to while away the idle hours of the idle rich in the sultry heat of a country thousands of miles from home.

He despised them.

But he wasn't averse to taking their money. To moving in their world. To making himself indispensable to their pleasure.

The heat was stultifying and it wasn't much cooler in the dim recesses of the club. But he was used to the deep bone-seeping heat of the desert, and the piercing, burning caress of the sun.

This was nothing to him; this was an oasis. He accepted a drink from a passing waiter—they all did—as Moreton Estabrook led them to the rear of the gathering room to a porch overlooking a cool fountain shaded by a stand of trees.

Perfect here. The group sank exhaustedly into a dozen or so wicker chairs arranged in a circle around a large wooden table. The women immediately pulled off their hats and gloves and summoned waiters to bring wet towels and someone to operate the fans.

Charles watched the bustle with a cynical eye. Spoiled aristocrats they were, and petulant, deliberately never getting used to the suffocating heat, and then using it as an excuse for their dissipated, self-indulgent excesses.

Indigent second sons could live like a sultan on the cheap here, and if there was money, a man could be king, if not God.

What was Moreton Estabrook, with his free-handed ways? King—or desert rat?

He had called for more drinks, and the waiters were just setting them on the table.

"Charles," he boomed, taking a glass. "Good job. Ladies. Gentlemen. To Charles Elliott and the new polo club."

They all lifted their glasses. *She* lifted hers tentatively. "Hear, hear."

"How soon can we make the arrangements?" Moreton asked. "And can you stay on until we're properly established? We'll pay for your time, of course."

Of course. Charles felt a spurt of anger at the assumption he could be bought, but he let nothing show in his face. It was going just as he had planned, but he wasn't sure he could tolerate Estabrook's smarmy condescension for more than another five minutes.

He reined in his natural impulse to squash the fleshy bug that was Estabrook, and lifted his glass. "I am at your disposal for as long as you need me," he murmured. *For as long as I need you.*

He sipped his drink. Vile-tasting liquid. He watched *her* out of the corner of his eye. She had the good sense to pretend to drink and then to set her glass aside.

She was inordinately quiet—or maybe that was just her way. She didn't look too much older than the younger women of the colony, the daughters of the patriciate of Murthagorda.

She didn't look like one of *them*.

Dissolute fools. She was very much one of them, rich, idle, indulged and loose-living. He lifted his glass once again, just grazing his lips with whiskey to hide his disgust.

Voluptuaries, the lot of them, pigs in heat. The women, casting covert glances his way, flirting with a fan, a look in the eye, the wriggle of a hip, a moue of the lips.

Wild. Willing. Untamed. Just ask me. Just touch me. Just come for me.

Painted whores. They knew nothing of love and sensuality. All they wanted was a body to feed on and toss away. They thought him like any other man in the Valley, every other man they had ever known who was easily seduced by a wanton woman with the morals of a goat.

There wasn't a man alive who wouldn't fall into their beds.

Except him.

And he was well aware that his reserve was too enticing, too much of a challenge. He was an enigma, a novelty, fresh blood; they liked what they saw and nothing else mattered.

Moreton rubbed his hands together. "This is excellent, most excellent. By God, we'll be national champions before you know it. We'll hold tournaments, we'll bring in youth and . . ." He stopped abruptly, catching a sharp look from the woman lounging across the table next to *her*.

"Well, you know what I mean." He snapped his fingers

and immediately a servant brought him another drink. "Again, Charles," he lifted his goblet. "Welcome." Everyone followed suit. "Good. Well. Dinner, of course, and then— well, there's much for Charles to learn about Bliss River if indeed he is to be among us for a while."

"All in good time," the woman sitting beside *her* murmured.

"Nonsense," Moreton said. "Charles has been here several days now; it can't have escaped him how we live here. I tell you, man, the longer you stay, the more reluctant you will be to return to Argentina. There isn't anyone who has come for a visit who hasn't decided to stay. Fair warning, then." He tipped his drink again, and Charles acknowledged it just as another servant presented Moreton with a huge handwritten billet of fare.

Moreton scanned it quickly. "Ah, dinner. Excellent. Tonight, my friends, we dine informally on lamb kabob, rice, lentil salad, and biscuits. Perfect after such exertions, my friend. And then after, with our brandy, we'll talk"— he winked, as if he and Charles already shared some secret—"man to man."

They didn't move, not an inch from where they had settled themselves after the demonstration. There were endless rounds of drinks, a confusing babble of gossip and discussion of current affairs.

Charles found himself pulling back even farther, just watching them all edgily, with an air of polite attentiveness that totally belied his boredom.

Hedonists, all of them, drowning in food, drink, and orgiastic pleasure. Especially pleasure. He was an expert at that in every form imaginable, and Moreton was naive to think that he hadn't immediately perceived the whole moral underpinning of the Valley.

But that had nothing to do with his purpose. His purpose still sat across the table from him, aloof, tense, and wary. Aware of him?

But he sensed no curiosity about *him* whatsoever. Rather, her attention was focused on Moreton, and the woman who sat beside them. The one who'd sent Moreton that warning look. The one who reminded him of a bird of prey, sharp, rapacious, merciless.

Dinner was served—chunks of marinated lamb and vegetables on skewers over a large firepot that fit into an inset in the table. Rice bowls. Lentil salad redolent of vinegar, oil, spiced tomatoes, onions. Flat biscuits to scoop the meat and vegetables. And wines and liqueurs, free-flowing, a servant assigned to refill every empty glass. Finger bowls full of cool water and floating petals. Servants to wield fans for their comfort as they ate.

Conversation slowed and petered out into an awesome concentration on the food. Their appetites were boundless, their enjoyment close to ecstasy.

There was no such thing as moderation.

"Help yourself, Charles, please," Moreton invited. "There's always more, and even more after that. And dessert is yet to come."

So he helped himself, pacing himself to give the illusion of eating more while the others swamped themselves in gluttony.

Dessert was an anticlimax. They were too full, yet no one turned down the small cakes, fruit, and cheese that removed the main meal. There was coffee and tea, and claret and brandy to accompany that.

There was silence and complete absorption in the food, as the sun went down and twilight rose. Charles estimated they had been at dinner for close to three hours by the time Moreton rose, spread his arms, and indicated the meal was done. "Come, Charles, let's walk."

He had no choice but to follow. *She* did not give him a

second glance, but he felt the interest and attention of every other woman on him as he gracefully withdrew from the table.

There was a palpable excitement in the air as they walked through the clubhouse, and then out onto the grounds in front, where a knot of women and girls were milling around.

Or were they?

"So this is our little village," Moreton said. "Pennyfield vetted you so I know you're a right one. I know you like what you see."

Ah yes, Pennyfield. The connection. The conduit. The licentious bastard with his hints and smirks and allusions to life before the serpent struck. All too clear now what he meant. Charles was repulsed. "What exactly have I seen?" he asked finally, impassively.

Moreton waved his hand. "Freedom. For everyone." He nodded at a group of women coming toward them. "And another night of voluptuous expectation. This is our life in Bliss River Valley, dear Charles. This is as close to heaven as a man can get. Look at those beauties trolling for a lover for tonight."

Charles went rigid, and Moreton sensed it. "Do I shock you, Charles? Because of Lydia? But we've been married for years. This is our custom, and it is understood Lydia will find her own partner for tonight as well."

Yes, Charles thought, his hands clenching, Lydia was very good at finding partners for the night. And she had recanted everything she had attained to be the wife of *Moreton Estabrook?* It was almost laughable.

Except that Moreton was as serious as a priest as he elaborated further. "Vows and commitments mean nothing here. This is the Garden of Eden, my friend. This is where all things are possible, every fantasy is permissible, every desire can be met. For everyone, male and female.

And without regrets, without recriminations. Take what you want. Candy in a shop, my friend. Choose one piece; choose three. Whatever your wont, whatever your need.

"And surely you have needs after all the time you traveled to come to us, Charles. Choose one luscious morsel for your bed tonight. Look around you—the way the women are swinging their hips, the way they watch you, the way they lick their lips. They want you, the beauties. All of them with tight young bodies and hard-tipped breasts. Take one, Charles. Any one you like. Take two. They'll burrow all over you and make you feel like a king.

"It is the way here. From age sixteen on. And we teach our children from the time they can talk that everyone belongs to everyone, and no one belongs to just someone. It's a foolproof system. It readies them for their coming of age under the peacock fan; it primes them to participate in the daily pleasure as they come to learn what pure guiltless pleasure means. And thus we perpetuate heaven on earth, my friend.

"But, all this talk of pleasure has stiffed me to the root. And you need a partner for tonight. You know, you need not be particular. You need not be shy. Our women are eager to spread their legs and let you nuzzle inside them. Look around at all this prime flesh, my dear Charles. You can have any woman who takes your fancy."

Moreton was watching him closely. It was abominably clear the pasha was offering him his choice of the harem, and he had better make a selection. Moreton was no better than a whoremonger, showing off his stable.

They were all of a piece, these women, similarly dressed, educated in lust, alike in their movements, their blandishments, their lewd, practiced smiles. One was no more enticing than the other.

Except that one—

Far on the edge of the crowd, he saw her, aloof and removed, her ramrod posture immutable and proud. *She* was not engaged in a mating dance, far from it. She seemed disdainful of it, above it. She looked like she was trying not to be noticed.

And yet, who wouldn't notice her? She moved like a queen, her pure profile silhouetted against the waning light, her dark hair tumbling in curls down her back.

He watched her for another moment, curious. And then she moved into the crowd, obviously lusting, as they were, for a lover. She was no different than the rest of them: a child of paradise, educated to fleshly pursuits.

Goddamn. He didn't want to choose, not a one of them, and he would not perform on command, and so where would that leave him with his coy mistress in the morning? Probably the object of the pernicious gossip the colony loved to feed on.

There was no way around it. Someone would share his bed tonight whether he wanted it or not.

He shrugged. "You choose for me, Estabrook. I have no preferences."

Moreton eyed him consideringly for a moment. "I know the very one," he murmured. "She is much more suited to your obviously refined tastes. She will come to you within the hour, my dear Charles." He clapped him on the shoulder. "You have only to take yourself to your bungalow and relax, and then prepare to spend yourself until she sucks you dry."

If there was anything Georgiana Maitland had learned in all her years in Bliss River Valley, it was the potency of her femininity. That, and the power of the word *no*.

"But my dear," her mother would chide her, "there's absolutely no reason to deny yourself. You've been amply prepared. You know everything. You are merely fulfilling your destiny. What more could any woman desire than to be a vessel for a man's pleasure? But even better than that, any man *you* want. *Every* man you want."

"They're all pigs; who would want them?"

"They want us," her mother would say, "and that confers power."

But her mother had it all wrong: submission led to dependence. Refusal, withholding what was most desired, gave you the power.

She had watched for years as her mother danced a quadrille of passion with dozens of men in the Valley, yearning and hoping that Moreton would abandon his duty to her sister and come to *her*.

How often had Georgiana heard about the debutante days of the wild Wyndham sisters who had had the whole of London at their feet. Olivia and Lydia, walking all over the men who wanted them, rejecting proposals and marriage, status and wealth, and stubbornly going their own libidinous way. And look at where they were now: stuck in a sultry swamp of lust and concupiscence, yearning for lovers they could never have and a stability and order they denied they wanted.

And herding their children into the morass with them.

Her own father had abandoned them his second year out in the Valley and returned to England, Aling, and the countryside that he loved, believing in his soul that her mother, Olivia, had already poisoned *her*.

But it wasn't too late—it *wasn't*. She didn't want this life; she wanted to get out of it, to get away somehow and join her father in England. It wasn't too late. The initiation meant nothing. And she'd kept herself as pure as she could, rebelling, demanding to choose, and then making as few choices as possible, enough only to satisfy Moreton that she was conforming, that she was one of them.

Never.

She didn't often do the twilight promenade. It was a nightly ritual that everyone knew was meant to precipitate a night of voluptuous promiscuity. It was never talked about; it was just done. There wasn't a man in the Valley who wasn't up for night after night of mindless fucking. Or a woman who wasn't ready to accommodate him.

The promenade was their meeting ground.

She was the rare one. The one who valued her body and its pleasure. But she was twenty now, and getting too old for games. Moreton had warned her.

Moreton, the bastard, the high priest of penetration.

She shuddered whenever she thought of it. And that her mother wanted him, still. Forever. For all the years her mother had known him, for all the years she wallowed in hatred when he chose Lydia, and for all the years after she went on the rebound and married Georgiana's father.

And then what transpired but that Lydia ran away with that Oxford-educated Bedouin prince, Ali Bakhtoum, and immured herself in the desert.

So there was her mother, Olivia, firmly married and fuming, ensconced deep in the English countryside, and there was Moreton haring off to Africa and establishing an expatriate colony at Bliss River to feed his debauched fantasies. Because he certainly wasn't going to take on Ali Bakhtoum for the love of Lydia. At least the way her mother told the story. Olivia followed him to the Valley over her husband's objections, and never left.

And meantime, incited by a distraught letter that Lydia had somehow smuggled out to him begging him to save her, Moreton stormed the desert stronghold of Ali Bakhtoum and rescued her, leaving Bakhtoum and his entourage dead in the process.

And Olivia brokenhearted once again.

Because then Moreton went and married Lydia. And

Olivia never divorced her father. And here they all lived in a haze of hedonistic harmony, educating their children to follow in their ways.

Dear lord. She never got used to it. And her obdurate father never believed that she could be saved.

But for the past few days, there had been a stranger in their midst, and that was the thing that compelled her to walk the twilight promenade, that gave her a small surge of hope.

A foreigner. Someone from outside who wasn't used to their ways. Someone who might revile them. Someone, she thought, she might somehow coerce into helping her get away.

Coerce . . . She knew one way of doing that. Only one thing to barter for his help.

So it all came down to that, she thought mordantly. It was all about sex all the time; there was no escaping it, and she was never going to get away.

Chapter Two

She had to try. There were so few visitors to the Valley. And those who came went through a rigorous scrutiny to be certain they were the kind of people Moreton wanted there.

And Moreton wanted this visitor, obviously, so what hope was there, really? The man had passed the test and would be here for the foreseeable future. That meant he understood everything, and he was willing to participate in anything.

But even with all that, she was still curious to see this man the women had been gossiping about so endlessly for the past two days.

He would be on the promenade, of course; every man in the colony paraded there every night, hard and hot to fuck. Or they stood sometimes, lounging against a wall, their hands set low on their hips, subtly pointing toward their already bulging crotches, ready to root in the next available orifice.

Sometimes it was quick behind the door, in the club-house on a table, or in a frenzy on the floor. Sometimes it was an invitation for a night of long and leisurely sucking and fucking.

It was the heat; it made you torpid and heavy with arousal, your body languid as honey awaiting the sting of a bee. At night, you could divest yourself of corsets and constraints; you could flash a bare ankle, or the thrust of a tight naked nipple against a thin lawn dress. You walked slower, undulating your hips. You felt your body liquefy with an unnamed yearning. Your body stretching toward something hot and filling you with pleasure. Just the thought, just to imagine . . .

All the juicy women along the promenade, all with the same yearning, the same tight wet place between their legs lusting to be mounted and driven to mindless oblivion.

And the visitor had his choice of any of these women and more . . . willing wanton women who wanted that hot space filled and their bodies satiated with whichever penis was available for the night.

She skirted around the crowd as the women twitched and switched and provoked the men who had lined up to make their choices.

He was not among them. No, she could see him exactly where she expected him to be: at Moreton's side, with Moreton eagerly explaining the process of procuring a partner for the evening. Moreton with his hundred mistresses casting for yet another, not hesitating to fondle and feel each of the women who passed his way.

Women she knew. Women who never looked at each other as they swayed and sashayed and played the coquette, shimmying up against any hand that burrowed down their bodices or against their buttocks.

How could *he* not be like those men? And did she really think she was *not* like those women?

And yet, from afar, there was such an air of restraint about him. He reacted to nothing, which must have frustrated Moreton to no end. Nor did he ogle any of the women flaunting themselves along the clubhouse promenade.

Moreton talked earnestly and the stranger listened, a tall, dark, well-built, paragon who stood aloof in the midst of the usual ruttish display of naked pandering that appalled her still.

After all these years, with all her experience. All she knew. All she'd done. She was not exempt, much as she might try to justify it.

She moved into the crowd, still watching him. People were pairing off. He said a few words to Moreton. Moreton responded and clapped him on the back, and off he went, in a long, lean, efficient walk, down the main avenue toward his bungalow.

With no one on his arm for the evening.

Interesting. So how likely then was he for the role of savior?

She was being naive, she thought as she moved into the shadows and removed herself from contention this night. There wasn't a man in the Valley who did not love the freedom, the women, the life.

There wasn't a woman who didn't respond to the attention, the pleasure, the liberation from guilt and social censure.

There was something for everyone in paradise.

But what about her? What was there for someone like her, who had been inculcated from birth, who had played the game, and still rebelled? What about her?

"Georgie! *Georgie!!!*"

It was Moreton, chasing after her as she tried to hide. But you couldn't hide from Moreton. He had his fingers everywhere, literally and figuratively.

She stopped, feeling weary to her bones. "Yes, Moreton?"

"My dear. Don't sound so jaded, so tired. You need to be bright as a tuppence tonight."

"And why is that?"

"I noticed you made no choice tonight. But then you know my concerns about your stubbornness on that score. So you will show some respect for me and our Valley life by entertaining our guest this evening."

She was jolted. That was the last thing she would have expected Moreton to say to her. "I'm not in the mood."

"You never are. And that's no excuse anyway, even though I've been letting you get away with it for months now. It's time to perform, Georgie. Our guest is a man who will appreciate the difference between you and the succulent sirens in our little Eden. You'll do him tonight, Georgie, because that is how it is and that is what I want you to do."

She bowed her head. She could *perform*—they all could perform—it wasn't a matter of that. It was a matter of whether she could get something from the guest in return. If he could help her—*would* help her—it would be worth spending an evening on her back.

"Georgie."

That tone brooked no resistance. And it was nothing she hadn't done before. Sometimes she thought that for all his protestations about her defiant nature, Moreton kept her in reserve for the more particular guests who came to the Valley, and that was why he did not force her compliance to his rules.

"Go to him in an hour, Georgie, after you change into something more appropriate, and inform Olivia where you'll be. I want to hear a full report in the morning."

"As you wish," she murmured. Nothing was different about this assignation. Everything was the same. The visitor would be just like the others. He would take his piece of her and then move on, and all Moreton wanted was the assurance that his trust in the stranger was not misplaced, and that his little house of cards would not crush them all in the end.

Charles could not imagine what kind of trollop Moreton would send to him this night. And in this stultifying heat where it took as much energy to breathe as to move, he did not need a hot sweaty body to cater to. The thought made him shudder, and he rang for his manservant to bring him a ewer of cold water.

That, at least, made sense. In his own place, a man could divest himself of his clothes and keep his body cool and refreshed. He had had enough of those people for today in any event, and all he felt like doing was washing away the stench of this promiscuous Eden.

But what the hell he was going to do with the perfect whore and her expectations was beyond him at the moment.

He needed to think. He needed to plan. He needed to reassess his feelings about *her*.

Her. Lydia. His mother.

By the creator of all things, he had not expected to find a woman so beautiful, so ill-used, so morose as she. She had traded one desert prison for another, and neither choice had served her well. She was deeply unhappy and deeply scared. She was not—if Charles gauged her at all properly—one who would indiscriminately take partners or willingly live out her own lover's debauched fantasies.

What to make of all that then, after all his preparation, after all the years of festering hate for the woman who had abandoned him and caused his father's death? The woman in pursuit of whom he had come to England to live, to be educated, to learn how to walk among her people so that he could sit beside her and slice his knife through her perfidious heart?

She, who knew not who he was, and didn't care.

Nor had she cared that he, the child, had also been left for dead. How many days had he lain there before the carnage was discovered? How many days before his uncle beheld the truth of what had been done and swore his revenge? How many years beyond that until he had taken an oath in his uncle's blood to become the instrument of that revenge?

But she knew him not, and he found that the strangest thing of all. Her whole focus was Moreton. Lecherous, dissipated Moreton, her savior. What had he saved her from that she seemed so distressed, so much in pain? And why, in the name of all that was holy, had she stayed?

Ah—sympathy, the devil's tool. He mustn't let a chink of it pierce his armor. This woman had married his father in a calculated way, had willingly chosen the nomadic life, had borne his father a son, had professed her love for him over and over, and in the end, had pleaded with the carnal and perverted Moreton Estabrook to liberate her from her prison at the cost of many lives, and nearly his own. This litany of sins he must not forget, must not let the anguish of this one woman, who had given him life, turn him to stone.

Things were never what they seemed.

He stripped off his shirt, almost as if he were stripping away the noxious ideals of the Valley, and immersed it, rinsed it, wiped it all around his broad shoulders and upper torso and tossed it aside.

The wet felt good against his heated skin, but it cleansed away no sins. The heat of the Valley was a different kind of heat—a kind of oppressiveness that was compounded of lust and desire. There was something unholy about it, something nauseatingly perverse and offensive. A poisonous fever in the blood.

For one long moment, he wished he had never started

this quest. It had cost him far too much already, and he was fast losing his edge, and in danger of losing his soul.

Especially after tonight.

There was a knock at the door.

The woman. Moreton's choice for him.

Unimaginable. Tempting to just not answer the door. But he had committed himself to playing the game, to getting close, to doing what must be done.

He eased himself out of his chair, just a little curious but not in the least aroused.

Opened the door.

Her. The dark curly hair. The defiant posture. The blazing eyes. The diaphanous gown. Even she. *Even she.*

Her husky voice: "May I come in?"

Damn, damn, damn—he had so hoped there was one among them exempt from this obscenity of an existence—

Damn Moreton to hell . . .

He'd sent him the queen.

She stepped into the room, closing the door with an unobtrusive flick of her hand. Her heart pounded wildly as she met his indifferent gaze. This one would not be easy. She couldn't read his desire at all, and she felt as if she had stepped onto a ladder and the first rung wasn't there.

But he was shirtless. That meant he expected something, didn't it? Or else why had Moreton sent her to him?

Words weren't necessary; she knew that from experience. She lifted her chin and untied the ribbons around her neckline. Not that he couldn't see everything anyway. Her gown was designed for just that—to reveal and conceal. She had only to move one way or another and he would see the shadow of her pubic hair, the outline of her taut nipples, the curve of her tight, round buttocks.

It was hot in the room and his aloofness made her uncomfortable. She saw none of the signs, none of the signals she was accustomed to seeing. She saw only that impassive face, those opaque eyes. The sheen of perspiration on the sun-dark skin of his bare broad shoulders and flat belly. She saw no evidence of arousal or desire. She saw nothing but a man watching her with the distant curiosity of a scientist.

She shrugged her shoulders and subtly worked the gown down her arms to the vee of her breasts.

And watched him, seeking cues.

He wasn't moved, when normally other men would be salivating to see more, and it made her feel just a little off-balance.

But all men were the same. Perhaps his threshold was higher—he needed to see more, he needed for her to do more in order to respond.

She pulled the gown over her breasts and let it slip to the floor, and then slanted a glance at him. She knew exactly what he saw: her naked body, curvy and beautiful; her legs, long and made for wrapping tightly around a man as he pumped the essence of himself into her; the enticing black bush of pubic hair between those legs; and her lush full breasts with their bulbous aureoles and tight rosy nipples. She knew he knew that she came to him ready for him to plunge himself into her.

She saw it in his glittering gaze. Nothing escaped him, from the tendrils of her hair caressing her shoulders, to the way she licked her lips, waiting to see what he would do.

Just like every other man. He'd tried to be so above it all, and there he was, tight as a fiddle, elongating against his trousers as she watched, with not a little thrill of triumph, until he was towering and erect.

He watched her watching him, as his body betrayed him. Who could resist her? The queen with the body of a concubine. With the morals of a harlot. Looking for a diversionary fuck.

Well, not from him, not his penis, not his body, not his soul. It would cost him nothing less to mount her and pump her, and that was all she goddamn wanted. The length, the hardness, and the vigor of his penis.

And to bend him to her voluptuous will.

She was just like the rest of them, damn her to hell, and he would never succumb. He alone had that strength of will.

He turned away abruptly, turning his back on her nakedness, rejecting her so forcefully she took a step backward.

This wasn't possible. She knew the beauty of her body, the extent of her sensual allure. He was playing games with her. There wasn't a man to whom she offered herself who didn't want her. Not *one*.

And this one, curse his eyes, would be no exception. She would make this one get down on his knees to her, make him moan and beg. Make him regret he didn't take what she offered.

She came up behind him and slipped her arms around his hips and pressed just the tips of her nipples against the hot skin of his back. Just the very hard tips, rubbing them lightly back and forth so that he felt the softness of her breasts in contrast to those hot hard tips.

She felt him stiffen, and smiled to herself. All men were alike. A hard nipple, her questing fingers . . . yes, that was next—find him where he lived: she slipped her fingers into the waistband of his trousers, working them against his hips, all the while keeping her nipples just touching his back.

His muscles rippled, tightened.

Her fairy fingers slid all over him, inch by inch, over and under, squeezing him and teasing the thick ridged tip that poked out his trousers so deliciously.

He could not be so immune to her touch. She grasped

him hard and tight with her one hand, and slipped the other between his legs to take hold of his scrotum. It was taut, ripe, full in the palm of her hand.

"*Let go of me.*" His voice was barely a rasp.

She was affecting him, she knew it, and he resisted her. How could he resist her?

She slid her hand up to the bulbous tip of his penis and held him there, stroking them there, rubbing her fingers all over the ridge, stroking him there, stroking them there.

"Let *go* of me."

She shimmied her breasts against his naked back and pumped his shaft. "I don't want to," she whispered. "I love your size. You're so long and strong and hard. I'd love to feel that much penis inside me."

"Let *go.*" There was steel in his voice now.

"I'm naked for you, wet for you, ready for you. Just poke your gorgeous penis where we know it will pleasure us both . . ."

"Damn you—" He grasped her hands and wrenched them away from his body. "Damn you . . . Get dressed."

She hated him. "That's amusing. I *am* dressed. So why don't you just fuck me?"

That did it. That question he could deal with. He felt himself coming under control to the point where he could face her. "You're a whore."

She was taken aback by the virulence of his tone. No one had ever characterized any woman in the Valley as a whore.

"And you're a *man* . . ." She put as much venom into the word as she could. Not that it fazed him.

"So we understand each other. Get dressed."

"This is as dressed as I get when I'm in male company." There, that angered him again. He didn't like bold women, bad women, insolent women.

Naked women.

Did he require a woman to be dressed when he came to her bed? Did he like burrowing and furrowing before he embedded his naked penis in her naked sheath?

The thought was intriguing—to be wholly covered except for those two naked parts wet and hot slipping and sliding one into the other. She went hot, imagining it, imagining his hands seeking, stroking, wriggling into her cleft, parting her labia so that he could insert himself, fit himself just there, just . . .

She edged toward the sofa. This was the challenge now. To have him. To have that long hot length of him inside her and to bring him to moaning groveling surrender.

There wasn't a man she knew who was immune to a woman strutting her nakedness. Nor was he by the look of his straining penis. He was just in better control of his animal nature. And he didn't care that his lust was obvious or that he was perversely in command of it.

She perched on the edge of the sofa, her back arched, her legs spread, her breasts thrust forward, her nipples tight prominent points of enticement.

"Your penis tells me you want my body even as you scorn it. You want to bury yourself hard right"—she fluttered her fingers between her legs, grazing her bush and then poising them there—"*there,* as deep as you can root into me. Your penis wants my pussy. And I want your penis. So let your penis fuck me and you stay out of it altogether."

"Bitch." He wheeled away. So now he had a naked mouthy bitch of a whore sitting on his couch displaying every inch of her body to him and demanding he fuck her.

Not likely. No matter how his body was reacting to her blatant nudity.

He picked up her gauzy gown and tossed it to her. "Cover yourself."

"Unlike most women, I never dress for a man," she said

with that maddening insolence. "I don't play games with a man whose penis I want. I come naked and ready to fuck."

He turned away again. There was no way to keep watching her and not want to fuck her. She was as tempting as Eve, as gloriously sexual, as intensely seductive, her body, the apple. He had only to bite to wholly lose his soul.

"Fuck me," she whispered, cupping her breasts. "Just come over here and rub your penis all over my nipples. Let me lick it and suck it even longer and harder. You let me fondle it an awfully long time, you know. You liked my hands on your penis. You loved how I fondled your head like that. You liked it too much. So now let me fuck that penis until there's not a drop left. Until I squeeze you dry. I want it all inside me . . ."

Her voice was hypnotic, the images seductive, mesmerizing, too voluptuous and real; his penis spurted urgently; he stepped toward her, ready to strip himself and abandon all the foreplay to jam his throbbing head tight and hard into her hot wet hole.

And she smiled.

And in that moment, he perceived that every word had been memorized, and had been practiced on dozens of men dozens of times solely to make them submit.

And that even the most meaningless coupling was more meaningful than this paltry show, if he surrendered the most valued part of himself to this soulless woman who valued nothing.

"*Get out.*"

She heard him through the foggy haze of escalating desire. "What?"

"Get out. Just get out."

"But—you . . ." She shook herself. How could he move from pure naked lust to this righteous coldness in the space of minutes? Her fingers flexed, aching to touch him, he was that close, his penis so close she could touch him, she could convince him, seduce him, make him want what they both wanted, and make this night, in Valley terms, a success.

"OUT . . ."

There was no emotion in him. It was as if he were encased in ice, and she knew it was futile to try to entice him. Futile to try to reach him at all.

She felt engulfed by futility. This man was different, and she had tried to coerce him by Valley rules and standards, and now any chance she might have had of enlisting his help was futile as well.

She reached for her gown, the heat of humiliation washing over her body. She had never been rejected before. Never. And she had always been able to persuade the most recalcitrant men to the Valley point of view.

So why was this one different when all men were basically the same?

"He'll want details," she said abruptly. She was gowned, although she felt even more naked in the gown than she had without it. And she was at the door.

He shrugged. "I don't care. Give him details."

"He'll send me again tomorrow."

"Will he indeed? What a thick obtuse man. What will you do?"

As if she had a choice.

"What will *you* do?" she retorted, and swung the door closed in his face.

Chapter Three

"Shhhh—I just heard her come in."

"It's too early, my darling. She should not be back this early. I don't like this. I wasn't sure about that man . . ."

"She'll tell you all in the morning, my dear. Come, we're not nearly finished."

"Why didn't he keep her there?"

"Moreton, my dear, my pussycat is hungry for your cream. Forget about her and concentrate on me."

"So easy to do, my darling. *Uhhh*—there . . . I hope you felt that."

"*Ummm* . . . oh, oh—"

"Exactly . . . let me give you more . . ."

"Yes, yes—"

"Can't get enough?"

"Never . . ."

"There, my darling . . ."

"Yes—yes . . ."

"Just this, until morning . . ."

"*Shhhhh—shhhhh* . . . till morning—"

* * *

Hot. It was that heat that suffused the body and leached into the soul. The heat of righteousness, rejection, the knowledge that someone had judged her and found her wanting.

And it was heat like cotton batting, surrounding her, exhausting her. She couldn't outrun it; it was a wall. It was a blanket smothering her. It was a thousand recriminations beating like native drums in her heart, her head, her mind.

She was a pawn, and a fool. She'd always known that. But it had always been so much easier to give in to Moreton's rules than to fight them.

Because he had always been perfectly willing for her to go.

Just leave, he'd say. *Take your things and go and see indeed if you will be better off far away from our little Eden.*

Go—go without clothes, without money, without transportation, without protection. A woman alone in the jungle, in the veldt—Moreton would not make it easy, by any stretch of the imagination.

What abject fool would want to leave, anyway? Not those whose every obscene fantasy was satisfied. Not those who could have the luxury of choice every single night of their lives, and not have to mind their morals. Not those who wanted to live like a pasha on pin money, and rut through a harem besides.

Moreton was a master at divining the blackest desire in the soul of man and making it seem as if attaining it would be the equivalent of finding the Holy Grail.

How had he done it? Did it matter?

He had founded the swamp that was Bliss River Valley, and they had all waded in after him. And baptized the children as well.

Oh God . . . and she was the worst sinner, racing from redemption to the quagmire, to lay naked on her bed, and resisting redemption yet again.

They were all lemmings, all of them, and she had to get out of there, she had to, before she wholly lost her life.

But even as she tossed and turned in her bed, she felt the rising tide of desire, and the legacy of Bliss River. Heat. Nakedness. Unslaked need.

It was like a sickness in the blood, the desire pumping through her veins. She had been well and truly taught: If you are naked, you fuck. And you fuck whoever is available whenever you want whenever he wants.

And that need was not mitigated by her abject failure with the stranger. She had only to prowl the gridlike streets of the Valley village to find a willing penis. Or go out to a country house party where the sole purpose was to find and fuck as many partners as possible, all day long, all night long.

No, the need was something that had been escalating for some time now, as she came into womanhood. It was like a rushing wave, catching her when she least expected it, crashing over her now, when she was regretting how she had handled the stranger, how she had rebelliously lived this bizarre and craven life.

Her body stretched and liquefied, heating up of its own volition, and apart from anything she desired intellectually. Even in the close stifling heated air, she felt the molten swirl of desire pulling her down.

Why hadn't he just taken her? What kind of man refused a woman's most intimate offering?

He would never help her. Never. He'd spend the month or two here that he contracted for, and he would teach them to ride and swat little balls across a big field, and in the end, he would leave and nothing would change.

Or . . . was it that *her* body was not acceptable to him, and someone else might be?

There was a thought that dashed all desire.

It wasn't possible. She was too experienced. Too beautiful. Knew too well just what to do.

Or thought she did.

But this time, the seduction of her hands had not worked. This time, her nipples had not whipped a man into a frenzy of wanting her. This time . . .

Whose hands, then? Whose nipples?

She sat up abruptly and cupped her breasts. There was no one who had nipples like these, hard, jutting, prominent, provocative. Easily excited. Nipples that loved the touch, the tongue of a man.

And still he resisted.

She could not get it out of her mind. He didn't want her. Even though he'd been aroused and his penis had been stiff as a pole, he did not take her.

That engorged penis—oh yes—inside her throbbing body *right now*—that would be heaven . . . in a place where such things were fully and completely permissible . . .

She wanted it . . . *she wanted it*—

That was the thing she couldn't outrun: that she wanted it, that she'd been so completely inculcated that nothing mattered at this moment but someone jamming his penis deep inside her and sating her billowing need.

Her swelling body shimmered with it; her nipples ached to be touched, to be sucked. And the wet between her legs— she fantasized a thick long penis probing and pounding and just exploding inside her.

Just that . . . just that—

Why, *why* hadn't he fucked her?

She turned on her belly and succumbed to the heat.

"How long have we been together now?" Moreton asked the next morning, as he and Olivia lay in bed, covered only by sheets and sweat. "Since just after Georgie's birth, by my count."

"That could be so, and I wonder that Lydia hasn't caught on yet."

"She knows nothing about us, my darling. You know that. She plays by the rules in any event. I made sure of that, and she is still completely engulfed with gratitude that I got her away from Bakhtoum—even after all these years."

"That's a good thing. And yet, you are uneasy about something, and I don't think it's Georgie."

"It's indeed Georgie, and the early hour she returned. And it's also the reaction of the stranger as we came to promenade last night. And it's the letter from Henry asking for the divorce . . ."

"Oh, that . . ."

"And—" Moreton let go of that point quickly, " it's how tired I am of spoon-feeding these babies their rules and rights of community when everything is so perfectly obvious."

"And so, the serpent," Olivia murmured. "My Georgie."

"Things have to change. We grow older, less vital; there's no one to take our place. Occasionally even *I* yearn for a more sedate life back in England."

"Where you would fuck the parlor maid every morning just for a diversion," Olivia said.

"Only if she feather-dusted the furniture in the nude."

"Don't be ridiculous, Moreton. What could be better than this? And it's of your design."

"Well, it was nothing more than the fantasy of a second son in his twentieth year to soak himself in sex," Moreton muttered. "Never mind. Forget I said that. What will you tell him about the divorce?"

"I will. I've wanted to for years."

"But if you do," Moreton said carefully, "you might lose everything."

"Georgie's grown. What more?"

"Aling, should he die."

"My dear Moreton. Were you even serious about a country house yearning? *You?* You'd turn Aling into a brothel in a twinkling. Besides, it's so deeply in debt, it isn't worth having. I'd rather pounds sterling frankly than a decaying country house."

"A brothel is not a bad idea—to pay off the debt. You could be its mistress. Hire the girls. Fuck the clients. And put money in your pocket to boot. It's Bliss River on a paying basis. Do think about it, Olivia. It may profit you not to leap into the bucket on this."

"You may have a point," Olivia said. "Indeed, I think you do have a point, if only you would position it where I can feel it."

"How much would you charge for a morning fuck?" Moreton asked playfully, as he mounted her and stuffed himself into her.

Her breath caught. "Ahhhh—*now* I begin to see . . ."

It was another bright, scorching, sticky day, the relentless sun pouring down on the playing field like molten glass.

Down at the far end, four of the eight players crowded against each other, swiping at the ball and jostling horses for position. Spectators crowded around the perimeter, umbrellas bobbing to keep off the sun, Georgiana and her mother at midfield, watching as Moreton wheeled his horse, broke loose, swacked the ball, and took off down the field with Charles Elliott shouting instructions in pursuit.

"He'll kill himself, Moreton will," Olivia muttered. "What a god-awful sport—grown men killing themselves over a stupid ball."

A moment later, Moreton swung the ball through the goal posts and everyone cheered.

"Oh, that was good," Georgie said, clapping. "He probably cheated. Mr. Elliott doesn't look too pleased."

"Indeed." One of the onlookers turned at Georgie's comment. "He was to have veered off and given Smythe the ball. Not a cheerful team player, our Moreton."

"I see," Georgie murmured, as the two teams lined up again at the half mark and waited for the referee to roll the ball.

Immediately Moreton went off after it, as if it were his toy.

"Doesn't like ceding power," Olivia said. "But then, who does? Come walk with me, Georgie, and tell me how last night went."

Now what? Her instinct was to lie. But what if Olivia wanted details? She could do details.

"It went well," she said heavily.

"Yes, he looks like he would be excellent in bed. Those thighs—have you been watching the way they grip the horse? And those hands . . ."

"Yes," Georgie whispered.

"And yet you were home surprisingly early. Or could you not sustain his interest?"

Georgie stiffened. Her mother never pulled punches, but there was something in Olivia's tone that was off-putting, as if Olivia were suggesting she could have serviced him better.

"Believe me, Mr. Elliott was well and truly aroused. He is a man of magnificent proportions, Mother, which only a younger woman could truly have the stretch and the honey to accommodate." She had an excess of both—and still he had turned her down.

Would he have turned down Olivia?

"And yet—you were home early."

And now, the most injudicious lie of all, one that would hold Olivia for all of an hour before she checked it out. "It is Mr. Elliott's custom to sleep alone, and it isn't for me to gainsay what a guest might wish."

"*Hmph,*" Olivia snorted, by which Georgie inferred *she* would have. "So you will fuck him again tonight."

"It is what he most desires."

"Good. Moreton was worried."

"There is nothing to worry about. He is just like every other man—he enjoys forbidden fruit and he adores the knowledge that there is no snake in Eden."

Her lies would come back to haunt her, Georgie was absolutely certain of it. Her mother had already spoken to Moreton, probably she had said something lewd to Charles Elliott, and the end result would be her lies would catch up to her.

But, as the day waned, and the polo players gathered for a classroom session and dinner subsequent to that, neither Moreton nor her mother came to accuse her, and Georgie debated going to Charles's bungalow again.

It would be expected of her. Especially after what she had told Olivia. Moreton would expect another report. Another assurance.

It would be humiliating, because Charles would turn her immediately away. But it would give her another shot at seducing him. Another chance to fondle his penis and try to coax it between her legs.

Just the thought of it made her wet with yearning. It was a fever seeping into her bones, making her languid, supple, weak with desire.

She could never survive like this outside the Valley.

This was the tether; this was the thing Moreton knew that the others did not: Once you chose Eden, you were lost to the outside world.

How could she face Charles Elliott again?

"It's time," Olivia called up to her.

"I know." She had dressed as she was expected to dress—in something easily removable and visually enticing. Her nipples were already tight with anticipation and straining against the gauzy material of her gown. But she was shaking. It was one thing to think about approaching Charles Elliott, quite another to be on the verge of risking still further mortification.

"I envy you your breasts," Olivia said, as she came down from her room.

Georgie let out her pent-up breath. Nothing about Charles or her spur-of-the-moment lies. Now to distract her mother. "Where's Moreton?"

"On the promenade. Apparently hours of riding and whacking each other with sticks did not dull anybody's anticipation for the night's fucking."

"Even you?" Georgie murmured under her breath. "How nice for them. I'm off then."

"How nice for *you*," Olivia said. "I do envy you, you know."

"Don't—"

"Of course not. You should go . . ."

Olivia was watching too, as she crossed the broad avenue that bisected the village. Watching as she passed the rows of bungalows on either side of the street, each with a deep veranda, and each screened from its neighbor by trees and fencing.

All Moreton's vision, lapped in luxury, open to everyone, convenient to all.

Night sounds accompanied her—animal and human. No restraint here, everything sexual for common consumption.

But Charles's bungalow was dark. She felt a stab of hope that he might have made some other choice for the evening. That the lights were out because he was in bed right now fucking someone else.

No. The thought of that made her even more crazy, because she had felt the size and the heft of his penis. Because she had wanted it. Because *he* had said no. And by rights, he should say no to everyone.

It was clear to her in any event that Olivia was suspicious. She probably had her binoculars out already, following Georgie's every move.

Dear God, why had she lied like that, why had she let herself in for another painful half hour with this unobtainable man?

Because you've never been rejected by any man you set out to seduce? Because just holding that rock of a penis almost made you convulse? Because you want him to fuck you and you'll do anything to make him?

She felt the fever rising again just imagining what it would take to make Charles Elliott break. What it would take to make him lose all restraint, all control. The thought was so arousing, she almost couldn't bear it.

She had to go to him naked. Not that that had been any inducement. But surely, she had a better chance of getting inside his bungalow if she were naked.

She tore off her gown and tossed it in the shrubs, and then boldly knocked on his door.

And now . . . and now—

A light flashed in the window. The door swung open, and his voice came at her, disembodied as a ghost: "Get inside. God, you have no shame."

She sauntered over the threshold and into the light, which was set on a low table just by the door. So he could see her, all of her.

He stood just beyond it, a broad-shouldered shadow of the night, radiating hostile disapproval.

She felt her body shudder; he was fully dressed, except that his shirt was unbuttoned, which meant he might just have been lying down, resting. Probably there was no other woman here.

Good. Maybe. She couldn't lose her nerve now, even with that damning, discouraging look in his eyes. She took a deep breath. "But, Charles, this is Eden, where everyone is equal and no one needs to be ashamed of anything he feels or wants. I'm just here to give you what you want."

"We settled that last night. You know nothing of a man's wants. Especially mine." Liar. God's hell, he was a liar. The queen knew too well his wants and needs.

He ripped off his shirt and tossed it at her. "Put it on."

She let it fall softly to the floor. *What will it take?* There was not a glimmer of interest in his opaque gaze as he looked at her. Through her. Even after his rousing response to her hands last night. It was her nudity that wasn't seductive to him.

Rather, he stood with his arms akimbo, with the light playing over the tight musculature of his shoulders and belly, and waited for her to do his will.

What will it take?

She bit her lip. He'd toss her out again, once she complied, and she'd never be able to get her hands on him again. And then what? Back to her mother's house, and questions and judgments, as if she had failed her mission.

A mission? A mission of what? Sin and sacrifice? But she was trained to do that. Educated to want, to need what a man could most fulfill. What only a man could fill. What this man could fill to the depth and hilt of her.

What was expected of them both.

She let out her breath in a hiss. She had to make him let her stay to save them both.

"*Put—it—on—*"

That tone brooked no resistance. She picked up the shirt. "I let them think you were pleased with me, that you wanted me here tonight. They expect me to stay."

"I have no sympathy for a whore. Put on the shirt and then get out."

"I want to stay."

He turned his back on her.

She slipped her arms into the sleeves. It hung on her as long as a robe. Protection from sin. What could she say to make him pay attention to her? "They wondered why I came back from your bed so early last night."

He slammed his hand down so hard on the little console table that the kerosene lamp wobbled and wavered. "By the hounds of hell, what kind of place is this?"

He wheeled on her. "They, they, they. Who are they? Why the hell do *they* care whether I fuck you or fifty others?"

"That is the way it is."

Her matter-of-fact tone stopped him for a moment, and he looked at her, really looked at her. The queen. The proud one. The one who wasn't like them. And yet here she was, abasing herself to a man she didn't even know. Offering her body without restraint, without recriminations, without value.

That is the way it is.

No. That was the way Moreton Estabrook conceived it: an isolated valley so far away from morality that he could give in to every randy impulse, and excuse his excesses by the fact everyone else had license to do it, too.

Including the heirs to the kingdom he educated to follow in his dissipated path.

And this one—with her knowing eyes and her facile hands that knew just where to touch, just what to say. He'd spent a restless, sleepless night trying to get the feel of her hands caressing his penis out of his mind.

What was it but the practiced touch of a harlot, and the spurious words of a trull, a litany of enticements spouted solely to excite and provoke. Nothing about it was real ex-

cept the hard points of her nipples against his bare back.
That was real, fomented by a simulated desire that would
play itself out because that was what was expected of her.

The debauched soul. He could have no sympathy for
her. She was not stupid. She knew what she was.

"Exactly," he muttered. "How else could Moreton get
away with this? How *has* he gotten away with it?"

"Everyone stays," she said, pulling the edges of the shirt
tightly around her, almost as if the covering would ward
off his anger. "Why wouldn't they?"

"Lesser men would. And women are weak, and everyone succumbs to the lure of the flesh."

"Except you," Georgie muttered daringly. "I just wanted
to save you."

God, of all the things he ever expected to hear anyone in
this Valley say . . . The queen was delusional. *Save him!*
"I'm overwhelmed by your generosity. Save me. By fucking me? Save me from what?"

But she didn't know. Was there ever anyone who had rejected the Bliss River way of life? Why would they? What
would Moreton do if the Valley were endangered by some
self-righteous interloper? "I don't know, since everyone
does it."

"And you do it. Without a thought, without a qualm.
Just give your body over to some dissolute stranger to penetrate and pummel."

A faint smile played over her mouth, a smile that said
she was certain of her course, sure of his response. "No.
No—I'm offering myself to *you.*"

Her presumption floored him. "Bloody hell . . . whore!
Strumpet! Bitch! Get out. *Get out* . . . GET OUT—"

She cringed, she turned, she ran. There was a fury in
him that was all out of proportion to the deed. All she
wanted was his erect penis; it would have been perfectly
easy for him to insert himself, pump her, and take them

both home. She couldn't understand his anger, and his antipathy, or why he would want Moreton to question his motives for coming to the Valley.

So she couldn't save him, and he wouldn't save her now. The thought made her shudder. She felt humiliated all over again, and she wondered why she even thought she had to try.

This was the truth of it: She would never leave here, ever. She was destined to be a slave to the Valley's needs forever.

Chapter Four

Lydia had always lived around the edges. Even in the halcyon days of her youth and subsequent debut, in those heady times when she and Olivia did all those wild and daring things that got them into so much trouble and were known as the bad girls in their set, even then, she had always thought that she was somehow removed from the events in which she participated, and not really *living* them.

It was Olivia of course. She was so vibrant, so voluble, so beautiful, so bold and adventurous. So full of flagrant disregard for all constraints.

Everyone adored Olivia; everyone wanted to be in her orbit. Lydia had always felt like a limp dishrag next to her, felt like the scolding companion, the colorless sidekick who provided doses of unwelcome common sense and comic relief.

Olivia did whatever Olivia wanted to do, while Lydia held back and fussed. There was nothing forbidden, as far as Olivia was concerned, but there were bridges Lydia eventually discovered that she would not cross.

For Olivia, morality didn't exist. Society's mores were brushed away. In an era of rank and sustaining propriety, she slept with every man she wanted to, drank like a sailor, smoked cigars, and experimented in other ways that Lydia did not care to be privy to.

Lydia hesitated, on the edges, while Olivia *lived*.

Until Moreton. There came Moreton, tall, handsome, blond, as soulless as Olivia. Two of a kind they were. And Olivia wanted him.

So was it any wonder that the one *he* wanted was Lydia? Lydia would be the crown of all his conquests, the wild, virtuous virgin. If he could topple Lydia, he could tumble anyone. It was all a matter of charm and perseverance, and a trunk full of lies that the Queen would believe.

Lydia believed.

Moreton was the love of her life, she was sure of it. He saw her true self. He would mend his ways. He yearned for nothing more than a pure heart to tend his happy home. Their pasts didn't matter. Not when they were mates in their souls. He put her on a pedestal, worshiped at her feet, and fucked Olivia while he was doing it.

And so, in revenge, Lydia succumbed to the lure of the East, and the exotic attentions of Tellal Ali Bakhtoum, a Bedouin prince from Syria who was completing his studies at Oxford. Later, she did not know whether she was really attracted to him and the anomaly of his civilized persona versus his sensually barbaric lifestyle, or whether it was she just wanted to cut out Olivia, who was fucking him while she was bedding Moreton.

But Lydia won. Lydia was the virgin still, something Bakhtoum prized; and she had had no qualms at all about snapping him up right under Olivia's nose and eloping with him in the dead of night.

It was a decision, in the first year, she did not regret. The nomadic life had its compensations, not least the fact that she was always on her back at the service of her virile and vigorous husband's demands.

It was when the child was imminent that she began to feel the limitations of her life, and the traps beyond the sand dunes.

No nannies in the deserts of Saffoud.

And she was expected to breed every year thereafter so her husband might prove his manhood by siring many sons, by which he would acquire much prestige.

And she would be relegated to the next tent to spend her life behind the veil. It was like going into a nunnery.

The second year, there was still no child. Bakhtoum was still kind to her, but there was no doubt what was in his mind and heart and what her place was in his life. She was the vessel that would carry his sons. The English lily whose honey was nectar to his seed.

To that end, he visited her once and twice a day, and sometimes more, until her body was wrung out from his constant penetration, his endurance.

The pleasure was sublime. She was truly living life now, and not on the edges. He was energetic, impassioned, intense. Demanding. Lusty. Forcible.

Her exotic desert lover whom she had stolen away . . .

Who knew nothing about the ways of Englishwomen and all the little tricks of prevention they kept up their sleeves and under their pillows. Never gave a thought to pills and potions, and herbs and internal barriers to a man's potent seed.

Judas kisses to keep him on point. A hot wanton body to keep him enthralled. Even she had never understood the depths of her carnality, and he rewarded it richly, in that first year.

When had he become suspicious? During that barren

year, after she had already conceived and borne a son? After every coupling failed, every thrust and stroke brought further disappointment and the inconceivable conclusion she might now be barren?

In Ali Bakhtoum's world, this was not possible, and Lydia knew her evasions and lies would not persuade her husband much longer. Nor could she stand it much longer. The isolation, the shunning, the anger, the violence with which he now took her to prove that there was the seed of sons in his passion, in his blood.

Then, and only then, when she was in danger of being caught, in danger of being condemned to death for her treachery, only then did she resort to the most desperate plan. She smuggled out a note to Moreton, begging, hoping, praying, he would come to her rescue.

And Moreton came. Moreton and his mercenaries. Moreton, her knight, her beloved, took action and one sandstorm-blinding day, their camp was set upon by an enemy, ravaged, savaged, and plundered, and utterly destroyed, everyone murdered, even her son.

Only she was saved, she who lived around the edges and cowered on the sidelines as the wholesale slaughter began. She walked away from the carnage into the libertine world of a man whose sole purpose in life was fornicating. And willingly agreed to marry him, his mistress forever, along with every other woman he wanted.

On the edges, as always. He still wanted her. She was enduringly grateful for that, especially after all that time. Nothing else mattered, anything Moreton wanted he could have, as long as she could just obliterate all thought of the desert—and her son—from her mind.

It was easy when you drowned yourself in an excess of sex. Moreton's needs were no different really from the heavy demands of Ali Bakhtoum. It was a matter of being on her back all the time. And when he got tired, he focused his attention elsewhere for a while, and eventually he came back to her.

He liked her fawning gratitude. It was easy to do, and she liked the security of fucking one man, and not having to worry about anything else.

But she was worried now. The stranger in their midst upset her for some reason. She felt the intensity of him; she felt uncertain around him. His dark good looks aroused something familiar in her. There was something about him that unsettled her.

But because she liked living around the edges, she said nothing to Moreton. She had nothing to say anyway, nothing concrete, no reason she could give Moreton to expel the stranger from their fleshly paradise.

And yet . . . and yet, she was uneasy.

She would watch him, she thought. Carefully. Covertly. He would be here such a short time as it was, and he was providing a much needed respite to the jaded colony.

Anything else she felt was the product of her overcautious imagination.

Anyway, she didn't know what she was thinking.

Yes, she did. She was thinking he moved like the men of her husband's tribe . . . Except they were all dead. Moreton had made sure of it. None of them could follow and exact retribution.

And anyway, the money had run out a long time ago, if that was what anyone was after. All those jewels that her husband's people set such store by. All meant to be worn only by her. All gone now. All of them that Moreton had found he sold to pave the way to paradise, which had been the impetus altogether for the daring rescue.

She shook herself. All he had *found*. She was over that now anyway, that Moreton had had another agenda when he'd invaded the camp. And she ought to have known that anyway, that Moreton did nothing for the love of anyone but himself.

But she had caught on quickly, in the rapid evacuation after the slaughter, enough to save something for herself, and Moreton never knew.

The rest was nerves, and that was all. Moreton was with some other lover, a relief to her, and she ought to be relaxing instead of looking for ghosts in the shadows.

But still, shadows lurked. And there was a stranger in their midst who walked with a familiarity that was disquieting.

And so, she would watch. And stay on the edges, until the stranger was gone.

Olivia was intrigued. Aling, a brothel. How delicious. How perfect. And Henry somehow gone.

They could go home.

Did she want to go home?

She thought she liked it perfectly well in Bliss River Valley. It was aptly named. *Bliss. Pure unadulterated, uncomplicated fuck-your-brains-out bliss.* She would never get tired of it. Never. All those stallions willing to paw her and pound her, and Moreton still hers.

If this wasn't paradise, she didn't know what was.

But Aling—she hadn't *hated* Aling, she'd just hated Henry. Henry had no juice, no life. He would have been a better match for Lydia after she found her conscience, but it was too late by then.

Henry was willing to take her on, to be the calm waters in which the violent storm of Olivia Wyndham tossed and turned. She hadn't had much choice: her parents damned well clipped her sails. And handed him the keys to the money box besides.

Anything to get her off their hands.

She didn't like thinking about it. She was well on the

way to being on the shelf by the time Henry offered. Or they bought him. They bought him, she was certain of it. Poky old Henry wanted an heir, and after that she was free to go her own way.

So while Moreton continued to poke her, she pretended there was even a chance at a child because she wanted to convince Henry to come to Bliss River Valley, to the enchanted hedonistic life that Moreton so explicitly described.

A flood of sex, he'd called it. Hot and cold, spilling, streaming, flowing sex, all day long, all night long. Whatever she wanted. Whenever she wanted. A place they could be what they were without censure or rules or hoity-toity deacons of decency preaching at them.

What are we? she'd asked him.

Adam and Eve, he'd said, and we are going back to the garden.

He'd gone first, she and Henry followed later. She couldn't stand to be without Moreton, who was always at full staff and ready for duty when she wanted servicing.

But she didn't dive headfirst into the salacious life. Henry was appalled for one thing, and she was pregnant for another. Henry wanted to go home to Aling, when she began to show.

She wouldn't go; she couldn't go, not before she'd explored every nuance of this lubricious life that Moreton had created in his Eden.

And so Georgiana was born in Bliss River, Henry went home to England, and Moreton suddenly had another complication on his hands. What would they do with the children?

What *could* they do with the children?

Olivia thought they had made an excellent compromise. Witness Georgie. As intractable as she could be sometimes, she was still the most beautiful, and the most desired of all those who came to age in the ceremony of the peacock fan.

Ah, the youth. They were taught to embrace sex, taught nothing was forbidden, everything was accepted. They watched their parents change partners night after night; they yearned for the moment they would be initiated into sex under the peacock fan.

Sixteen was the age they determined the girls would be most ripe . . .

And Georgie was twenty now. And Olivia was starting to feel her age.

Oh no, oh no—oh, she didn't want to ever think about it. Ever. No one grew old in Bliss River Valley.

No one . . .

Moreton was king. Moreton was still a stallion, with his long tactile shaft.

Some things never changed.

Some things did. Her body. No sag there, but the stamina . . . the strain of accommodating all those stallions . . . she was dry sometimes, she was tired sometimes, but that was not for Moreton—or anyone—to know.

So maybe she, too, sometimes thought about Aling and the English countryside and respite from her life of unremitting sexual pleasure.

Sometimes it wasn't a pleasure. Sometimes it was a damned chore.

Don't tell Moreton . . .

. . . a brothel . . .

In the posh English countryside, surrounded by all those wealthy nobs running like lemmings from London.

It was a thought to be considered. A stable of beautiful young things. A horde of hot young bulls with pounds sterling in their pockets and stiff hot rods, not a bad way to spend their ensuing *middle* years . . .

Delicious thought. She'd still have Moreton *and* all the pricks she could handle.

So it wouldn't be caving in to her middle years. She would be spending them more creatively and lining her pockets besides.

So. So . . . Aling.

No divorce, then. She wasn't prone to giving Henry anything he wanted after all these years. After he'd abandoned her and their daughter. Damn his soul. Why should she make things easy for him?

But of course, he wasn't making things too easy for her either. The old male bag was still alive and she didn't know what she was going to do about that.

They were rechalking the lines, a half-dozen men painstakingly measuring the 300-yard length and 200-yard width, and making sure the center line was precisely on, and the 30-, 40-, and 60-yard lines were exact.

Charles was among them, dressed in a light shirt, jodhpurs, and helmet, pointing his mallet this way and that as the horse-drawn apparatus moved slowly across the field and filled in the scuffed lines with a crisp blow of white chalk.

"Too damned by the rules, if you ask me," Moreton muttered, as he waited by the pen. The horses were getting fretful. They were all getting restive waiting for the day's instruction and the ensuing match to begin.

Georgie shaded her eyes. But it was really just an excuse to catch a glimpse of Charles. Oh fine, and what did she think that would tell her?

"They're almost done."

"And it's almost noon and it will be too hot to play."

It *was* hot, but that might have been the wash of heat she felt, as if *she* had failed somehow last night. One thing she hadn't done was return to her mother's house before morning. She'd hidden out in the club, curled up in one of the banquettes in the bar, and it had saved all the awful questions and embarrassment of admitting she had failed with Charles Elliott once again.

There were no questions at all as she crept in that morning dressed in Charles's thoroughly wrinkled shirt. No comments. No requests for a report.

The evidence was clear: she had spent the night. He had ravaged her gown and given her something to cover her nudity. Just the way every gentleman was expected to respond.

Charles was proved a right one, and so he qualified to stay on in the Valley.

The deceits. The lies.

"Put on your hat, Georgie." This from Olivia from under the depths of her wide-brimmed straw.

But then she couldn't see him, couldn't watch him as he leaped onto his mount, and rode at breakneck speed down the course and toward the goal. Couldn't admire the flexing of his thighs, the control of his horse, the steel in his body—

What was she thinking? That somehow the degradation of the previous night would be wiped away by day? That her cheers would encourage him to change his mind? That he'd come to his senses and somehow make it known to her that yes, he'd been a fool not to fuck her when he'd had the chance?

She jammed her hat on her head. He *was* a fool, and he knew nothing about what he had gotten into here, or what was expected of him. So if it wasn't her, it would be someone else, but sometime during his sojourn here, he would have to spend his cream.

She couldn't bear to think of it . . . that thick heavy

penis pumping into someone else . . . not her . . . damn it, the man was a hammerhead, and she was wasting her time.

She felt a presence behind her and turned. Lydia, an umbrella in hand, said, "Oh. Georgie."

"Welcome to polo, Lydia. Isn't it fun? According to Mother all that hard riding does not drain the juice from the plum."

"They're addicted to hard riding no matter what form it takes," Olivia said acidly. "And balls. They could be doing more interesting things with their balls . . ."

"Feeling like a little goose and duck, Sister dear?"

"Always, Sister dear."

"That Charles person . . . quite stunning. How *is* he in bed, Georgie?"

Georgie cringed. Of course everyone knew. Even Lydia who seemed to be in her own world sometimes. "Like *nothing* you could ever imagine," she murmured, which waffled over the truth, without telling an outright lie.

"I expect everyone will want to take him on then," Lydia said. "Is his dance card full yet?"

"Oh, he's a particular one," Olivia intervened before Georgie could answer. "Moreton made the choice, so stop salivating."

"I wondered about that. And I'm not salivating. He's far too young for me, and definitely not the kind of bangtail I prefer."

"Darling, he's a pacer if ever there was one. I'd ride him to a lather if I had the chance . . ." Olivia's sleek head followed his movement as he raced down the field. "Look at those legs, those loins . . . the way he moves—"

Lydia was looking. Lydia looked horrified, but Olivia wasn't paying attention to her.

But Georgie was. She touched Lydia's arm. "Lydia?"

Lydia looked faint. She shook herself. "I'm all right, Georgie dear. Just a touch of the sun, I think."

Just a touch of hallucination, rather. It cannot be; it just cannot. They were all dead, all of them. I haven't felt a moment of regret for that, not even for my son.

Well, maybe for him.

But they were savages, after all. Barely civilized. Tellal Ali Bakhtoum had been the best of the lot. And even he— raising his son to follow in his footsteps, his nomadic barbarian life . . .

I don't want to remember the rest . . .

Besides, the stranger's name was Charles, Charles Elliott, as English a name as there was. And he was from Argentina. He had a ranch. He raised polo ponies and came highly recommended.

Moreton would never let anyone into the Valley who hadn't come highly recommended. Who wasn't willing to play their games.

He'd been willing. Hadn't Georgie said so?

So there. I am imagining things.

Maybe.

It was the way he handled his mount: the line of his body, the hard line of his chin and cheek . . .

She turned away from Georgie, turned away from the sight of *him,* had purposefully stayed away from him these past few days apart from at dinner. But of course, formally dressed and with the veneer of manners, his hair slicked back, and his skin bronzed from the morning's play, he looked and sounded nothing like the desert brigands from whom she had escaped.

It was on horseback where the ferocity of his nature was defined by the game that she saw it. With the sweat pouring off his face, his eyes shaded by the helmet, his arms flexing, and his legs controlling the every movement of his mount, it was then she saw the truth about the man—and she felt a tremor of fear.

It could not be. It would not be. Everyone was dead. Everyone. Moreton had made sure of it.

She felt cold as stone. She couldn't move. She had to know; she was utterly terrified to know.

She waited with Georgie and Olivia as the game came to a thunderous conclusion and the players rode along the fence to accept the congratulations of the onlookers.

Only Charles hung back, to remove his helmet and wipe his face.

And his gaze locked with Lydia's, his eyes dark as the devil's, hard, judgmental, unforgiving.

No. No! She would not acknowledge the possibility. It was the only way. *Never give him leverage. Never let him see her fear. Cut him dead whoever he was.* If she had the courage to do it.

She had to. It was the only way.

She held those eyes for a long cold minute, held her breath to calm the furious pounding of her heart, and then lifting her chin, she disdainfully turned away.

It wasn't even for Olivia to know. Olivia had her own secrets, after all. But Moreton—she had to tell Moreton.

Moreton would think she was crazy. That was the thing. He wouldn't believe that after all these years the boy could be alive, could have transformed himself into a vengeful adult. Not after all these years. And so many thousands of miles away.

But Lydia knew: She'd read death in those glitteringly opaque eyes. He'd searched the world for her; he'd sworn to avenge his father's death. It was the way of his people. And somehow he, of all of them, had survived, had hunted her down, and would make her account for her sins.

She felt like death already. Instantly she understood why

she had been so removed from everything in the Valley. There was no bliss for a woman who had tacitly conspired in the murder of her family. No life for one who counted her comfort above her commitments. No way to outrun a past that had never had a future.

Her son. Dear God. She hadn't said or thought those words in so many years. He was dead; he'd been mourned. But she'd never missed him, because, in the end, had she remained with his father, he never would have been hers anyway.

And she knew she was unnatural, thinking like that, dead herself after she countenanced all that Moreton had done in the name of delivering her from the heathen.

Who was the heathen now?

She had to find Moreton *now*, to tell him that a viper had invaded Eden.

Chapter Five

He told her she was imagining things. He told her the boy had died; he was certain of it. But he didn't tell her why: that he had made sure of it himself, so that there would be no witnesses, no evidence. So this Charles Elliott, whoever he was with his exotic dark looks, his ever-so-English name, and his precise clipped accent, couldn't possibly be the boy.

"What if he's the boy?"

He was in bed with Olivia after a very strenuous coupling, and they were side by side, staring at the ceiling.

The boy had invaded the bedroom. But this was the first time Moreton had mentioned him because he had been weighing the consequences and ramifications of Bakhtoum's only son and heir turning up in Bliss River Valley.

Especially in light of his unexpected yearning to go back to England. Especially since he had been thinking for a while now that Lydia had quite outlived her usefulness.

And here came her long-lost son, obviously bent on revenge. He could not have shown up at a more opportune time.

What could be better? He could use that. He had a list

of grievances against Lydia pages long, not least that he had always suspected she'd withheld some of the jewels from him. The jewels of Ali Bakhtoum, the riches of the desert that Lydia had disingenuously tempted him with in her desperate letter begging for salvation from the heathen sun.

Why else would he have taken such a risk? He'd rescued her for the jewels, he'd appropriated the jewels, and he'd always had the feeling that she'd withheld something. But he'd never been able to find anything, not for want of searching, and he'd had to raise money for the entertainments of the Valley in other ways once that initial stash had run out.

And that was the other thing: somehow he had become the director of amusements in the Valley. People got bored too easily; once they signed on, they expected too much, and even unfettered sex was not enough to keep them amused. A man could only get it up so many times a day, after all.

As he had good reason to know.

Damn, but he was tired.

And now the boy—

He pondered it some more, not wanting to jump on his first thought. But it was a bolt of inspiration; it was a *fait accompli* the moment he conceived of it.

God, he had a black soul. And he didn't care. What was life but a tightrope walk to put yourself in the best position possible when you had little or nothing in your pocket.

Look at what he'd accomplished. He'd made real the wet dream of every horny man: an isolated society of sex-crazed voluptuaries who wanted nothing more than to spend every moment of their lives fucking.

That was an accomplishment, one for which he would never get credit in the history books.

No matter.

The reign of every king eventually came to an end. And rather than wait for the assassination, he would step in the line of fire.

"If it's the boy . . ." he said tentatively.

"It's not a boy," Olivia said sharply. "It's a grown man, vetted by the right people for the right reasons. Lydia is hysterical. Or feeling guilty. Or something."

"But if it *is* the boy . . . think—"

"I thought the point was never to think."

"Olivia, I beg you. Mind your serpent tongue for a moment, and think—Aling. England. You and me. The brothel. The money." He waited a moment while she absorbed that. And then: "The boy is the solution to the problem of Lydia . . ."

"What—How—? Oh!" Light dawned. And then a moment's hesitation: "Oh . . . my sister?" Weighing every angle now, seeing every side, particularly hers, and the price she would pay to have a future with Moreton.

And then she shrugged. "You unconscionable son of a bitch."

"Do you care?" he asked carefully, stroking that part of her body that was already hot with need.

"Not when you do that," she purred. "When you do that, the whole world can go to hell for all I care. Including Lydia. I will leave it, as I leave everything, in your capable hands . . ."

The lies. The deceit. Her mother never questioned it when she left the bungalow that evening. Olivia just assumed—they all assumed—that she would be with the guest, the stranger.

She ought to go to Lydia's, Georgie thought. She ought to find out just what made Lydia look like a ghost this afternoon. The problem was, they were all too entangled.

They had absolutely no recourse for any problem that came up. It was Moreton's fantasy, Moreton's creation, Moreton's rules.

If you wanted to play in Moreton's world, then you allowed Moreton to be your judge and jury.

And they all wanted to play, even poor Lydia who'd been gullible enough to marry him. Why? Or were the reasons of no moment to the freedom of the Valley?

Georgie felt a supreme desperation to find a way out. There had to be a way out, and she had resigned herself to the fact it wasn't going to be Charles Elliott.

God, she had so hoped . . .

Even so, she left her mother as if she were going to spend the evening with him.

She'd deliberately timed it. The promenade was over; they were all paired off. A whole group was on its way to a farm for a long weekend of debauchery, drunk on lust and whiskey. They were already fornicating in the lorry as they drove down the track out of the village, their laughter and shrieks trailing like a comet.

Was there ever a place like this?

This, she'd been taught, was the norm; that was how Moreton had sold it to them all those years ago. All that repression and depression with which they'd been raised, trying to constrict themselves into suppressing their perfectly natural needs—that was abnormal.

And Bliss River Valley was the answer, a place where man, woman, child, could be totally, naturally, as God made them, free.

Only they weren't free. They had no more freedom than any society; there were rules and strictures here, too. Even if the governing precept was *feel free to lie with anyone.* You made your bed and then, if anyone had any reservations about it, if anyone didn't want to, he or she was censured, shunned, shamed.

Not one of them.

Moreton's vision. Moreton's Valley. The man was depraved.

She had to get away.

But how many times, for how many years, had she yearned for that, tried to plan for that, only to wind up exactly where she had always been?

Well, she was older now, more self-sufficient, more aware of the yawning future that awaited her as a vessel of lust in the Valley.

Her own mother had sold both their souls for that—

And her own father had self-righteously determined she could not be redeemed.

Maybe she couldn't. Charles Elliott made her feel as if she were branded, as if she were the spawn of something vile, born in Eden, destined to die in the Garden, forever in service to any man's lubricious desires.

Not tonight. She would spend the night on the banquette in the club. No one would ever know, if Charles Elliott didn't tell them. And he wouldn't tell them. He hated this more than she did. He wouldn't last more than another few days in the Valley as it was. Her secret would be safe.

Unless they found him out.

Her jab about saving him, saving them, had hit a nerve.

It just wasn't enough to save her.

So now Lydia had really *looked* at him, and now she knew. And had probably told Moreton, and between the two of them, they'd probably murder him where he slept.

Moreton wasn't above anything, as Charles had good cause to know.

Hadn't Moreton sent him the queen? By the sacred heavens, the queen. He couldn't get her out of his mind, couldn't push away his insidious craving for her by sheer force of will.

The naked queen, flaunting her body with a fluid certainty that every man wanted her. That he wanted her.

So right. Yes, he wanted her. Yes, he could have rutted like every other goat in the Valley. Yes, yes, yes. He could have treated her like the whore she was. And he should have, since everything in the Valley was for the taking.

She belonged to them all. That body, those breasts belonged to every man in the Valley. And for all he knew, every man in the Valley had spread those legs and shot his seed into her. For all he knew, they had all suckled those luscious breasts, fondled her silky skin, and buried themselves so deep and hard inside her that she couldn't tell one from the other and didn't care.

That was the kind of woman she was.

Regal as a queen, dirty as a pig.

Ah Moreton, you are a worthy adversary. And now that Lydia knows, I wonder what you'll do . . . The queen won't distract me, you know. But I don't think she told you that. I don't think she told you anything about her abortive seduction: about how she came to me, naked, about how she stroked and played with me, and about how I refused to root myself between her legs.

Not that I didn't want to, Moreton. Just this once, I will confess to you: I wanted the queen on her knees, sucking at my vitals. I wanted to spew all over her breasts and rub it into her nipples. I wanted her to eat it and love it.

You have no idea, old man, how hard I had to control myself to keep from just mindlessly ramming myself into the queen's parlor. She was an excellent choice, old man, more than you knew.

But it's not going to stop anything. Lydia's fate was written in time, blood for blood, blow for blow. I'd kill the whole colony for vengeance's sake, but I swore only this one reprisal, and so it shall be.

On the blood of my father, my father's brother, and on my father's son, I now take my mother's life into my hands . . .

She could outrun nothing in the Valley. That was her fate. Even after concealing herself behind the bar at the Nandina Club until the last patron left, even when she thought herself safe under the reassuring cover of darkness as she settled herself into a far corner of the dining room where no one could find her, she still couldn't hide.

Someone bumped into the table, someone tripped over her ankle. A light flared in her eyes, blinding her.

"Georgie—is that you? I thought—"

Never ever safe. Never ever alone. Never to escape . . .

She leaped off the banquette and ran.

"*Moreton!* . . . Georgie's back . . . I just heard the door latch—just the faintest click; she doesn't want us to know."

"Perfect. Let her get settled, my dear. I don't want her to know we're awake. . . . I can't believe our good fortune. I couldn't have planned it better if I tried. I never thought the moment would come so soon. Shhhh—it's almost time to go . . ."

Moving surefootedly in the darkness was second nature to him. The night held no fear. He knew every trick of using it to his advantage, no more so than now when the streets were empty and ghosts walked the shadows.

It was time, finally, to scout out the enemy. Time to bring all his plans to fruition and escape this hellhole.

Time for the wrath of the heavens to fall.

The simple plan was always the best: a quick strike in the dead of night, and gone before dawn.

He edged his way along the back alleys of the houses on the avenue.

Her house was set slightly apart, at the end, more grandiose than the rest. A fitting throne room for the king of this universe, and his wife.

His mother . . .

It still sat odd in his mind. He still felt that shard of pity for her, more so after having spent these days in her husband's wicked paradise, and watching what her life had become.

But that did not negate her sins. Nor did it wash away the blood oath he had taken. He would bathe his hands in it, exactly the perfect vengeance he had promised all those years ago. He would cut out her perfidious heart and bury it in the sands of Saffoud, so she would dwell in the tents of his father's people forever.

But there was blood everywhere—

And Lydia, on the floor, drowning in it.

Lights, suddenly, blasting into the darkness.

People. A buzz of words, around him, incomprehensible.

And Moreton, triumphant, standing over him, a kerosene lamp held high, revealing the brute violence of the scene.

And Lydia, in a flood of blood, stone dead on the floor.

Olivia was inconsolable. "Of course he did it, Georgie. He was *there*. He didn't deny it. Oh, my beautiful Lydia— all those years, everything we went through, everything we shared . . ."

Including Moreton, Georgie thought balefully, not in the least moved by Olivia's tears.

"We should have known," Olivia wailed. "We should have protected her."

"And how exactly would you have done that?" Georgie murmured. Her mother didn't normally dramatize things to this extent. If anything, she reacted with little or no emotion to everything.

But then, it *was* her only sister. It had to be such a shock, especially because someone they'd let into their secret, someone who had been vouched for, someone they had trusted had come in their midst with murder in his heart.

These things were not possible in the Valley. It was one of Moreton's guiding principles, and it only proved how clever, how insidious the stranger truly was.

"I don't know," Olivia sobbed, in answer to Georgie's question, "but we ought to have done something."

"But did you even *know?*"

Olivia raised her sodden eyes to her daughter, gauging the depth of her indignation, her commitment now that she knew the full story of Lydia's misbegotten past. A past that could have been her own, Olivia thought mordantly, had *she* succumbed to the fascination of Ali Bakhtoum. "Of course we knew. We just didn't know the boy was still alive. It was thought the brigands killed everyone."

"Except Lydia."

"Would that she could have been that clever this time . . . the ungrateful bastard, coming after his mother like that— oh my God, Lydia-a-a-a . . ." And Olivia collapsed on the settee, tears streaming down her cheeks. "I just can't conceive of a world without Lydia . . ." She put out her hand, a futile gesture commanding sympathy, demanding contact.

Georgie didn't know how to give sympathy. Olivia had never asked that of her, but then, there had never been a violent death in the Valley.

And Georgie didn't even know how *she* felt. This wasn't someone she had felt was family. Even though Lydia was her mother's sister, they were never that close: There was some great divide there, probably because of Moreton, probably because Lydia had been much more restrained than most of the women in the Valley, probably because she hated Olivia and her wanton ways.

Probably. But what did Georgie know?

And yet Olivia cried, the incessant tears blurring her features, contorting her pretty mouth. Olivia pounded her chest, rent her clothes, threw herself on her bed, her keening cries cutting like shards of glass through the air.

A gray cloud settled over the Valley, almost tangible in its presence.

They'd taken Charles Elliott to the Fawzi house a mile out of the village, constructed a makeshift prison of the outside shed, and incarcerated him there.

The following day, they buried Lydia, the first grave in a cemetery they had to mark out in a hurry, not far from the Fawzi house.

Everyone was in attendance. It was thought that Charles Elliott could view the interment through the one window in the prison.

Olivia cried. Those who had known Lydia from the beginning wrung their hands, and murmured words of solace to Moreton, and then they went on to the Nandina Club to celebrate Lydia's life.

"What life?" Olivia muttered.

"A life clever enough," Moreton whispered, coming up behind her, "that in the end it left the legacy of *this*—" His arm snaked around her, and in the flat of his palm was a diamond large enough to make Olivia gasp.

"Oh yes—I knew there was more—I knew it. Lydia was always one to hedge her bets. And Bakhtoum was infatuated enough with her to have given her something like this in their first days. Well, she left it to us, my darling. To the one who was clever enough to figure out where she was hiding it. In the place of life, Olivia"—he clenched the stone in his hand, squeezing it as tightly as he could have wrung Lydia's neck—"and you know exactly where I mean—"

Olivia shuddered. Clever Lydia. Too clever for her own good.

"A gift to fund another dream. In my hand, my darling Olivia, the key to England, to Aling, and—our new life . . ."

"And so, we must decide, what do we do with him?" Moreton asked at an impromptu meeting of the Valley elders that evening after dinner.

"An eye for an eye is what," someone said, to immediate approving murmurs.

"I mean, who'd know? It's not like he's got family." A titter at that comment.

"And consider this: Do you want the nuisance of calling in the authorities and everything that might derive from that?" Moreton asked. "People, this is no simple matter. Nothing we could have planned for all those years ago. This was meant to be a colony of like-minded people living and sharing minds and bodies, in harmony and with mutual consent. And I promise you, people, just the idea of that will impede any reasonable investigation. They'll sit high on the gallows with that and how we live our lives in our Valley. So I ask you to think about all of that, as we try to determine just what to do with this murderer in our midst, and if you're still of a mind to bring in outside authorities, then so be it. Or, if you're of a mind to execute Valley justice on a man who used our good will and our money for his own nefarious purposes, so be that too."

*   *   *

"You scared them," Olivia said admiringly, as they huddled in a corner after the meeting. Everyone had gone, except a few stragglers and Georgie, who looked a little lost. But Olivia couldn't concern herself about that now. A moment later, Georgie slipped away, and Olivia turned her attention back to Moreton to give him his due.

"You absolutely put the fear of God into them over outsiders spoiling their party. You're a damned genius, Moreton, my darling. I don't know how you do it."

Moreton waved away the compliment. "Everyone's afraid to be sexual. Sex equals the forbidden. They still haven't excised that rattlebrained foolishness from their heads. It's like they're still in England, and just sneaking around here. But they don't want anything to be forbidden, and that is all the better for us, my dear. They're much easier to manipulate when there's a little undercurrent of fear."

"You managed it beautifully, my darling, eliminating two impediments with one strike. It could not have worked better."

Moreton smiled. This had been child's play. And now his subjects, his lemmings, were playing right into his hands.

"How long do you think, before they vote to hang him?" Olivia asked.

"I'll make sure it's as soon as possible. We don't want anyone to reconsider. Two days—no more. And to put the cap on it, I'll keep pounding them with the idea that any authorities we allow in the Valley will take away all their fun. They don't want anyone to take away their fun." He patted her hand. "And we have only just begun . . ."

They had killed Lydia? They?

Dear heaven, she knew Moreton was capable of anything, but her mother? *Who had cried a river of tears over Lydia—her mother complicit in Lydia's death?*

It was inconceivable. And it was utterly believable. More-ton, the man with no feelings; cold-blooded, amoral, and utterly rapacious; king of his kingdom, ruling with an iron fist that would wipe out any opposition to anything he wanted ...

A monster ...

And her mother—his consort, his queen—

She had never in her life been so terrified. If they had no compunction about killing Lydia, what wouldn't they do in the name of preserving their secrets?

Now, for certain, there was nowhere for her to hide ...

Chapter Six

A ct natural ...
Oh, she knew how to act. What had she done with
Charles Elliott? What had she done every day of her life in
the Valley, with Moreton, with her mother?

Act as if you heard nothing ...

She could do that. She would take her cue from her
mother. She would immerse herself in hypocrisy, pretend
sorrow and rage, and support the verdict of the death of
Charles Elliott.

Yes, that would do it; that was what they wanted to
hear, and it would reassure Moreton and her mother that
she was still one of them.

One of them—while she plotted to make her escape.
This was what it took to galvanize her—the anarchic justice of Moreton Estabrook.

Georgie sat staring broodingly out her bedroom window until the early hours of the morning. From that van-
tage point, all she could see were the rooftops of the
houses in the Valley and the purple mountains ringing it
just on the horizon. But she knew full well that hundreds
of miles of desert and flat plains with brittle scrub grass,

palm trees, and little else lay beyond, a barrier as hard to breach as a maidenhead for someone who had never gone beyond the mountains.

Moreton had planned it so: Bliss River was a very hard place to get to. And equally as hard to get away from, even discounting the practical things you needed just to travel.

So just how did she think she was going to manage to leave?

Well, Charles Elliott would soon leave and in a most ignominious way, with the stain of blood on his hands.

She closed her eyes, envisioning him. Not one nuance of emotion in his face when they sentenced him. Not one shard of regret that his mother was gone. Not a word or a gesture of remorse.

What kind of man was he, this man from away, whom Moreton had welcomed, encouraged and taken into the fold?

He was not a murderer, by evidence of what she had heard. But it didn't mean he hadn't had murder in his heart . . . so what was she thinking?

She was thinking, she was wondering, how exactly Charles Elliott had come to the valley. By caravan, by night? He must have, because of the ponies . . . a dozen of them for which Moreton had paid a sultan's fortune. They'd come by ship from the south and then by caravan to the Valley.

It just seemed that suddenly one day the ponies were there, and Elliott too, and the arduous trip, the stultifying heat didn't seem to faze him: he was chalking the field and lining the ponies almost from the moment he arrived.

He was a seasoned traveler, obviously.

She wanted to believe that, to believe that he knew his way around, and were he able to leave the Valley, he would know exactly where to go and how to get there once he was beyond the mountains.

Even England.

And *she* knew how to get him away from the Valley.

How desperate was she?

Where would she go?

England. Not a moment's hesitation there.

But then what?

Aling?

Her father would set the dogs on her.

Aling . . .

Child of the desert, transforming herself into a proper English lady?

There was a nightmare, for herself *and* her father, even if he were to let her in. There would be things hard to give up, proprieties to be observed. Rules and structure for the first time in her life . . .

She felt a wave of longing for it, as a part of herself, that she might never know. Olivia had told her stories, all of which could be fairy tales for all she knew, painting a picture of a life so unlike the Valley that she wanted it to be true, and she yearned to be part of it, too.

Her father, at least, was true. And for all that he had abandoned them in the Valley, surely after all these years he would show *her* some mercy.

He would, she knew it. He would enfold her in his arms, tell her he was sorry he'd left her; he'd welcome her and tell her how courageous she was to escape them.

He'd tell her she'd come home.

Home . . .

She'd never had a home. She'd had a room, she'd had meals, education, companionship—of a sort. But she'd never had a home.

Her father would give her a home. He couldn't turn her away, she thought, not after all it was going to cost her to leave the Valley.

But every sacrifice would be worthwhile, she thought, if only she could get to England . . .

*   *   *

Elliott . . . her best chance, her last hope. She made the decision sometime in the early hours of the morning, after she'd fallen asleep and dreamed of castles and country houses in England.

She had something to barter now. Knowledge, money, admittedly her father's money, but how could he not offer a reward to the intrepid adventurer who'd rescued his daughter from the gates of a hedonistic hell?

Or, barring that, her body. There was always sex, and Charles Elliott was not immune. She could seduce him: The trip was probably long and onerous. He would have needs, and it would be one way of compensating him for taking her on. But that was all for later. She had much planning to do before she even approached him with the scheme.

She had but this day to put it all into place.

"Georgie! Georgie!"

Oh dear heaven, Olivia.

She slipped on a loose-fitting housedress and hurried downstairs.

"Yes, ma'am?"

"I thought we might take breakfast together."

They never "took" breakfast together. Georgie obediently sat herself at the table, and Olivia rang for the serving girl, who came with a steaming pot of tea and a plate of biscuits to start. "The usual," Olivia told her, which meant eggs, toast, bacon, oranges and pineapples, some fried eggplant and marinated beans.

"Well then," Olivia said. "Tomorrow morning, the evil man will pay for his crime. An eye for an eye, as they say. And I will feel that Lydia has been avenged."

Georgie said nothing. Olivia slanted her a look. "Don't you think, Georgie?"

"What?"

"That Charles Elliott's death will avenge Lydia's?"

"Absolutely. You can do no less."

"So everyone agrees," Olivia said placidly, pouring the tea.

One of them . . .

"I hate that this must usher in a new era in the Valley," Olivia went on, taking a pair of tongs and delicately setting a biscuit on Georgie's plate. "Everyone's loyalty to our way of life must be vetted. If a viper like Charles Elliott can find his way in, then who knows what might arrive on the next camel. Don't you agree, Georgie?"

She felt a chill flitter down her spine. "I . . . what are you getting at?"

Olivia helped herself to some eggs and toast, which kept her busy enough so she didn't have to look at Georgiana, and thus she could speak in that flat tone of hers that was meant to convey honesty.

"I'm getting at the fact that you haven't enthusiastically embraced the life here. That you think you own the word *no,* and that you even have the right to say it. That sometimes it seems as if you'd rather be someplace else. But that isn't possible, and you know it. What I want to see, what Moreton wants to see, is you participating more fully, and your servicing your share of the men who want to cork you."

The chill turned to ice. "What if I don't?"

Olivia turned a cold eye on her. Georgie was ever resistant to her duties as a child of the valley. Never could fully engage in the life of a voluptuary. Georgie was and had always been a problem, and she had to be brought to heel *now.* "But you will, Georgie. Because we must do everything we can to preserve our way of life here, and let nothing take it away from us. And you know there are people who would want to take it away."

"They'd never find us," Georgie muttered.

Oliva snorted. "Charles Elliott found us."

"He only wanted to take Lydia away."

"Georgie!"

"I don't see why I have to lie on my back for just any lob-cock in the Valley."

"You never listen. This is your power, my dear girl. They want what's between your legs. It's nothing for you to give, and they always want more. They'll do anything to get more. So use that power. Show your loyalty. Tell me you won't fight me anymore on this."

No, I won't; I'll be gone.

"I won't fight you anymore on this," Georgie parroted obediently.

"Well, good. I thought we'd come to blows on it, given your usual obdurate behavior. I'm satisfied you understand what's at stake," Olivia said, ferociously buttering a biscuit. "You *do* understand what's at stake?"

"The whole world as we know it," Georgie said with a trace of irony in her voice.

"Exactly," Olivia said, biting hard into the biscuit. *"Exactly."*

What did one need to travel in the desert? Two fleet horses. A supply of food? Dates, nuts, oranges, beans, rice, coffee—anything that wouldn't spoil. A pot of some sort, something to eat and drink out of—she couldn't think; she had to think.

What did she know about traveling in the desert? Knives. Water. Robes. Boots. A tent. Dear heaven, where would she find a tent in the Valley? Sheets would have to do. Blankets. A compass. Were there even such things in the Valley?

She hadn't yet propositioned Charles Elliott, and she was racing around like a dervish trying to gather everything together before she approached him. There was no time, either, to think or to plan. Spur of the moment. She would die if she stayed. And she couldn't be certain he'd agree to go—of course he would agree to go; he wasn't ready to martyr himself to the hypocrites of Bliss River Valley.

But would he take her?

Well, the practicalities first, just in case anyone even saw her going into the Fawzi house. Not that it was heavily guarded. But Charles Elliott was securely contained, and it would take some doing to even get him out, let alone have to explain her presence there.

Don't think about that. First things first.

Just get everything together you can think of . . . time is running out . . . it's nearly the witching hour when everyone gathers to drink, dine, and debauch . . .

She felt stupid. She knew nothing about subsisting anywhere but in the Nandina Club. Her ignorance of other ways of life was chilling, but she had no time to even think about that. She still had to barter with Charles Elliott.

The best time would be when they were all occupied at the Club.

"I'll be a little late," she told Olivia, feigning a certain enthusiasm she knew Olivia wanted to hear. "I want to soak in a tub and really get ready for this evening."

"That's the spirit," Olivia said approvingly. "Throw yourself into it, my girl. Enjoy it. Feel your sex, your power. We'll expect you at five, then, to have dinner and promenade."

"I wouldn't miss it," Georgie murmured, while she mentally ticked off everything she needed to do in the ensuing hours. First, Elliott. Then the rest. And the sooner they got out the better.

Dear heaven, make him willing . . . And the horses. She'd have to get them in place. Where? And how much could they carry in their race to freedom?

She waited until the gong sounded that signified the Club was open for dinner, and then she made her way to the Fawzi house, a considerable walk in the opposite direction.

Still. Thank heaven for that. There would be no guards either, since it was assumed everyone would be at the Club in preparation for the night's dissipations. So Elliott could well be bound or chained. All she knew was that they had no fear he might escape.

The shed they'd made over was at the back of the Fawzi house. A hundred feet beyond that, in a grove of palm trees, was the newly laid-out cemetery and Lydia's freshly dug grave.

Georgie averted her eyes and pushed her way into the shed. Lantern light glowed; they hadn't left him in the dark. What they had done was build a wooden cage on one side of the building. Then they'd laid him on a wooden platform and tied his splayed arms and legs to the base.

Nevertheless, it was dim and dank, and Charles Elliott was twisting and turning in a rage until he sensed her presence.

"You! *You!* Get *out!*"

Georgie stared at his rope-burned wrists. The emotion he hadn't shown throughout the episode was evident there. He was like a wild animal, writhing, tortured, out of control.

His fury was utterly daunting.

"Listen to me," she finally managed.

"Listen to you? *Listen* to you! By all the prophets . . . listen to *you* . . ."

He was laughing, a raw scraping sound that grated all along her nerve endings.

Now what? She'd never thought he wouldn't listen to

her. She never would have predicted that he wouldn't hear her out, especially when his life was at stake.

"You're a fool, Mr. Elliott," she said sharply, cutting into his mirth.

"And we know what you are," he shot back. "This is a fitting punishment for someone who denied you. You're here to gloat."

Her fists balled in frustration. This was not going the way she'd envisioned. "You arrogant beast, I'm here to save you."

That stopped him. His body stilled, his head turned toward her, and his flat black gaze sharpened. "You?" As if it were totally inconceivable. And then suspicion wiped away that intentness in his eyes. "Why?"

Now. How to broach it—"So you'll take me with you."

He ruminated on that for a moment. "Where?"

The *coup de foudre.* "To England."

He stilled. England. Where he had planned to flee after having done the deed. She wanted to go to *England?* By the fates, this was too good, too fortuitous. A trap? "For what? So you can fuck every manjack from London to Leeds?"

The telling heat washed over her. She couldn't let him provoke her. This was too important; this was her *life.* "My father. You'll take me to my father."

Dear bloody hell. This promiscuous piece of mutton had a father in *England?* And she wanted to *save* him?

She caught the faint look of interest in his expression and pressed her advantage. "Even if you could escape, you couldn't get out of the Valley without help. I'll get you out; you get me to England. That's the bargain."

"What bargain? I could abandon you in Sefra once we were free of the Valley." And he would, for that matter. Why had she thought he would leap at, and honor, her proposition? Why was he even arguing? She girded herself. "Without my help, you won't leave the Valley at all."

She let him chew on that for a moment, then added, "Without my help, you'll be buried in the Valley. There's no way you can get out that Moreton won't have guards in place to prevent you. And since you'd be an escaped prisoner, they'll have orders to kill on sight. Valley justice, Mr. Elliott. Since they're going to kill you anyway."

"I'm beginning to see," he murmured. *Yes. Let her help, let her get him out, and just take over and flee. What man ever kept his promises to a whore anyway?* "But you—why you?"

"Let us just say, it is time for me to leave the Valley, and if you need further inducement, there are other things I can offer you for the duration of the journey that I need not elaborate and that *you* may have cause to *need*. And then, perhaps, at the end," she crossed her fingers, "my father will be so grateful for my return, he will reward you as well."

So there it was—agree to her terms, she would deliver him from hell, and then she would be a millstone around his neck for thousands of miles while offering her body up in sacrifice for his enduring it; and in turn, that might yield a thousand pounds in gold, her slave market, her *mahr,* her bride price in England.

Something to keep him going, as it were.

Clever. Naive. But he wasn't above using her. Not in the least.

Bloody, bloody damn—how the hell had he gotten himself into this?

"There's not much time." Her voice was low-pitched, flat, without urgency.

"When?"

"Tonight."

He closed his eyes. *Good, excellent even*. He made his decision and took control. Time was of the essence now. "Two horses, in the cemetery whenever, however you can get them there. In my bungalow, my gear, in a roll in the closet. In the chimney, high above the damper—you'll need a stick to prize it out—a pouch with my papers."

"They'll have searched there," she cautioned. They would have taken apart the whole bungalow, to find what, she didn't know. Everything was self-evident and they had convicted him on that alone.

"Not that far up the flue. I trusted no one in this hell-hole."

"But we'll need so much more . . ."

"We will travel as light as possible. You'll need a robe, boots, some food if you can gather it without arousing suspicion. Water. There should be some *guerbas*—water skins—with my gear. Make sure whatever you do, you fill those skins. Leave everything else if you have to." And she might have to. It might be too much for her, too much for the ponies. But that would come later.

For now, she offered the one thing he needed and wanted: hope.

"And the rest," he added, pinning her with his burning gaze, committed now, "we'll leave in the hands of fate . . ."

She got out of dinner, no easy task when she had pledged her body to the community, because Moreton and her mother couldn't be everywhere in the Club. She would tell them, if they asked, that she had dined on the verandah with friends.

That bought her the time she needed to get to Charles's bungalow.

No guards there, fortuitously. But then, no one was contesting the fate of Charles Elliott; they were all in it together, and he was safely locked away.

Into the bungalow by the back door. Georgie lit a candle she'd had the forethought to bring.

In the closet. There was one in the parlor, one in the bedroom downstairs, one in the bedroom upstairs. Upstairs first, escorted by long shadows in the narrow staircase, jumping at every noise.

In the closet—not much else here but a bed and dresser. Or else Charles Elliott lived like a monk. Nothing in the closet.

Downstairs then, her footsteps resonating on the bare treads. Light waning outside. Lights twinkling from the Nandina Club, echoes of laughter drifting across the boulevard reminding her that time was tight.

A perfunctory search of the kitchen and the parlor, and then into the downstairs bedroom closet. There, on the floor, the *roll.* And next to it, the two water skins. He was precise, if nothing else.

Up onto her shoulder and onto the settee in the parlor. Not too heavy, the roll, and no time to investigate its mysteries. She piled the water skins next to it.

Now the fireplace. A poker would do to dislodge the pouch . . .

All that scraping against the brick. Too much noise? She couldn't feel anything at the tip of implement. Push harder then.

Wait—there!

Damn! Was that a footstep on the gallery? A light?

She sprawled on the floor, slanting her gaze at windows. She'd worn black, but still—if someone were deliberately searching, or sent to guard the house—but why would they? They'd trussed Charles Elliott up like a turkey; he couldn't possibly escape.

She still didn't have the pouch. The footsteps came ominously closer. The door opened. A shadow peered within.

Hold your breath. Oh, heaven—the roll . . .

"What's this?" A light flashed, the shadow paced into the room. "Looked like a body on the couch. Wouldn't put it past the bastard. It looks like he'd planned to abscond the minute he did the dirty."

A voice outside responded. "Not our problem."

"We should take a look at this stuff . . ."

Oh, good lord—if they come in . . . if they . . . They won't; they can't . . .

"Hell no, man. We've got ten minutes before promenade. You really want to spend good time with this shit?"

Hesitation, duty warring with desire.

"Well, we can tell Moreton we checked. Who'd touch the stuff anyway?"

"Right. As opposed to who's going to touch our stuff. Come on."

The door closed, the voices trailed into the distance, the light diminished, disappeared.

Breathe . . .

Crawl to the fireplace. Take the poker. Don't think about what just happened. Just . . . Just poke the damned flue . . .

They could have caught you . . .

All right—so what?

Explaining to Moreton is what—

She'd have thought of something. She was facile that way—

She shoved the poker, felt resistance at the point, and knelt down on the hearth to lean into it with all her strength.

What strength? Her bones felt like water; her heart was pounding so hard, she thought she'd have an attack.

One last thrust. *Plop* . . . An oilskin-covered oblong packet fell onto the brick. And no time to examine it and discover his secrets.

Okay. Tuck it into her dress, grope for the roll and the damned water skins, get them on her shoulders. *Jesus, what was in the damned roll?* And wobble off into the sunset.

Wobble into her mother's arms more likely.

They would effect this escape by the skin of their knuckles, at the rate she was attending to things.

But there were things to be attended to first. Things she had to take the time for. She wasn't stupid, and she knew the fallacy of her plan: he'd said it himself. He could abandon her at Sefra. He could overpower her here, for that matter, and leave her for dead.

So she knew she had to preserve some power. And that lay within the possessions he was so avid for her to bring. At the very least, there might be a tent and some supplies she might never have thought of. At best, some money, which, if he abandoned her, would still give her some leverage to get away.

And so, in the shadow of his bungalow, her heart pounding wildly, feeling as if eyes were watching on all sides, she groped to discover his secrets, the blind seeking the blind.

In the roll, a small tent, poles, pots and utensils for cooking, a change of clothes. Things mundane and necessary. She couldn't believe that was all. There was no light. The darkness and the press of minutes ticking by faster than sound made her edgy, determined.

She'd pick his things apart seam by seam if she had to. A man didn't walk into the Valley with no money, no protection. And someone like Charles Elliott, bent on murder. He had to have other components of a plan in place, if the knife had been dull, if Moreton hadn't wanted the ponies, if they found him out . . . Elliott looked like a man who left nothing to chance.

Wait now . . . wait. She was running her hands over the canvas cover and felt a lump. Not inside the roll, outside.

Outside? Clever. Oh so clever. In the wide straps in the underneath part of the roll where it lay across the pony's back . . . in the seam on the underside . . . She was amazed at how much more acute her touch was in the dark, and how much more terror she felt.

Concentrate. You can't leave the valley with just a knife in hand. You've got to disarm him too—

Definitely an opening there. She took a deep breath and inserted her fingers. Definitely a small gun tucked deep inside. About as big as her hand.

Power. He wouldn't abandon her now.

Loaded? She slipped it into a pocket.

Now . . . to get that thing back into a semblance of the way he had rolled it . . .

Well, she could buckle it together at least. The rest he'd find out when they were on their way.

And now the pouch. Slick. A buckle here, too. She ripped it open and felt inside. Paper. Maybe money; she hoped it was money. She lifted out a handful of sheaves and folded them into her pocket.

And he had thought there was honor among thieves.

Nothing was that simple. Everything had a price, and now she had the wherewithal to pay it. He had just thought she would never think of it.

Well, he'd pay dearly now for underestimating her and rejecting her. They were on an even footing now, and she had a fighting chance, whatever his plans might be.

And then, she was later than she wanted to be for the promenade. Late for everything, suspiciously late, and scared to death that her mother would demand to know where she'd been.

It took more effort than she'd imagined to get those

things and some food and the water to her hiding place. More time to put herself to rights, more time inventing heart-pounding excuses for not being where she'd promised Olivia she would be this evening.

And in the end, she had the best luck—she was far too late to be chosen as someone's bed partner for the night.

Chapter Seven

She had everything piled up near the pony pen. How she had managed that, she would never know. It was her hauling each piece one by one under the cover of darkness; it was that everyone was occupied in their self-indulgent excesses, and that Moreton and Olivia assumed she was, too.

And it was the fact that Moreton trusted no one would come the aid of Charles Elliott, which didn't mitigate his checking earlier on to make sure the prisoner was down for the night.

Thank heaven, she hadn't set him free sooner.

The water skins were the worst. The skins were exponentially heavier filled, and Georgie wasn't sure the skittish, delicate ponies could carry that much weight. In addition to Charles Elliott's bedroll, and the sack of food she'd managed to appropriate: dates, oranges, bread, cheese, nuts, tea. She wondered how Elliott had been clever enough to make her do all the work.

She'd stolen a pair of Moreton's boots as well, and sheets and twine, and a large knife with enough heft that she could hack through wood and rope.

The first part was done.

And now she waited outside the shed. It was suffocatingly hot, with a thickness and moistness in the air that portended rain. Moreton had come and gone a long time before, but still she waited as the night grew thicker, longer, and suffused with sounds: the humming of the *taubib,* the flapping wings of the night birds, the stamping of the ponies, a faint keening noise in the distance.

The night had a silence all its own, full of mystery, heat, and allure, covering her like a cloak, making her feel secure.

Dear heaven, was she really going to do this?

Slowly, slowly, the time slipped away. Time meant nothing in the Valley, except insofar as nighttime meant the onset of pleasure. Nighttime was a lover in and of itself.

She was so aware of it; she'd counted on it.

The time was almost right. She stood poised, watching, waiting. Everything was in place, everyone was in partner, no one was sniffing around.

She took a deep breath, felt for the knife, waited for that one sweet moment of surety—and slipped into the shed.

So after all his careful planning, he'd put his life in the hands of a capricious flat-back. Insane. And gave her access to his kit and his money besides. God, heat stroke. It had to be. Something dire, because if he were in his right mind, he wouldn't have been so desperate.

In all probability he *could* have gotten away.

For all he knew, *she* was gone. The hours since she'd arrived to bargain with him had been pure torture, endless, broken only by the appearance of Moreton who had not been above coming to gloat.

"You did me a favor, actually," Moreton told him. "I could have sworn I killed you, but now—well, the fates had something else in store."

"I *will* kill you," Charles spat. Never cower, even when you're tied hand and foot and the enemy could run a stiletto up your ass. "Nine lives and all that. You can't be sure I'll die tomorrow. You were so certain before, and look what happened."

"Oh, I'll make sure of it, my friend. Just as I'm certain you survived to see this day because you were meant to hang for the murder of your mother, and save me the trouble. In the morning, Charles, we shall each go to our destiny."

God, he wanted to take Moreton down. It was good to think about vengeance. It fired a man's soul; it corrupted him, kept him moving, dodging, feinting, wary, always in fear for his life.

It would be the same for Moreton, if he escaped. Moreton would forever be looking over his shoulder, forever wondering where Charles would turn up and when he would die.

Where was she?

Time had never moved so slowly. The lamp wick burned down, guttering, flickering, sending eerie shadows on the walls.

He was flat on his back, bound hand and foot, helpless, useless, with no control over his life, and a great shearing grief that his mother was dead.

But praise the prophets, not by his hand. Of every sin he could have committed, this would have been the worst. Not by his hand. And only because when the wheel of fate turned, his plan and Moreton's greed had intersected, and the deed was otherwise done.

He would avenge her death, now that he knew the depths of Moreton's depravity. The circle would be unbroken. From the heavens, she would smile upon him, reunited at last with his father, and finally at peace.

Goddamn—where is the whore?

He couldn't stand it; he would almost rather die than be helpless. He had to trust; he *had* to. She wouldn't have come to him otherwise. She needed him, and she knew he needed her.

That was the way of conspirators. Each had a hold over the other; and maybe she was trusting a bit too much, to think he would keep his promise to get her to England.

England. God, he loved England. His heart belonged in England—but his soul yearned for the wanderlust of the desert. Which was the truest part of him, after all these years, he still did not know.

It would be easier to go back to Argentina. There, in the freedom of the pampas, and the elegance of society, both sides of him could coincide without conflict.

But they would look for him there. They could find him much easier there. So all along, he had planned to decamp to England where he could lose himself on the moors and brood on his sins.

Dear heaven, his uncle could not have known what he set in motion when he sent him to be educated in England.

Walk among them, his uncle had told him. Learn their ways. Hide in plain sight . . .

And so he had, forging an identity for himself he now did not wish to disclaim. England . . .

Where the hell was she?

He could die now. Just will the spirit out of his body, let himself go to a place where he would be truly free . . .

He couldn't endure much more. For a man like him, this was hell. This was death.

He needed a plan. He would concentrate on a plan before he went crazy. She couldn't possibly have a plan. Her offer seemed too spur-of-the-moment, probably instigated by the fact that they were to hang him in the morning, and she needed to run away.

So they needed a plan. They had to decide where Moreton would give pursuit, and go in the opposite direction. He would probably figure them to try for Port Elizabeth. Or Capetown. They couldn't go east, blast Moreton and his deep-in-the-middle-of-the-veldt sensibility. They couldn't go much of anywhere from here without the greatest inconvenience.

So they needed a plan. They'd go north and west, perhaps, through the Kalahari Desert and north toward Kabinda and Sierra Leone, a massive trip in and of itself. But someplace Moreton wasn't likely to follow.

North and west—it would be so easy to get to Argentina from Kabinda. Why not? Why not? What would she know, this unschooled, untutored trull in whose hands he had committed his life? If he said it was England, she'd probably never know the difference.

Damn, damn, damn . . .

A scraping noise. The door opening a crack, silhouetted in the flickering light. He held his breath as a shadow slipped in the door, slight, slender, female, an implement in her hand.

"What the hell—?!"

"Shhhh . . ." She moved across the dirt floor and knelt by the makeshift cage. "I can cut through this, I think."

"It'll take a damned long time," he growled, but she was already sawing away at the bars with a gritty determination. Nothing was going to stop her now, especially not six feet of two-inch-thick wood.

At least she'd found a fairly substantial knife. She was not stupid.

"I left the horses for you. I got everything else over by the pens, but I couldn't handle the ponies."

"Can you ride?"

"Yess-s-s—got it!" as she sawed through the first bar. She shot him a triumphant look as she sidled over to the second bar on her knees. "Another five minutes . . ."

It seemed like five hours to him, but at least some of the necessary components were in place. Like the fact she'd even come.

All he had to do was get free and get out and he'd be gone.

Innocent little bitch.

She worked in silence and he studied her in the flickering light. The queen, he'd characterized her, and she had a certain presence, a certain driving tenacity that was regal in and of itself.

And she was beautiful, as a queen should be, with her lustrous hair and profligate body, and she was a wanton. He couldn't for a moment let himself forget that.

It was solely and completely a bargain of convenience. He might have outwitted the noose on the morrow, but he infinitely preferred escape by night, and it didn't matter what he had to promise to achieve it.

She made a sound as she hacked through the final half inch of wooden bar. "Now—" she took a bar in each hand and pulled against the cuts she'd made in the upper portion. "Not quite there . . ." she muttered, and began sawing at the one and the other, this time with a kind of recklessness as if time was running out.

And it was, he was certain. He had no sense of what time it was, just that it had been an achingly long night, and he'd been waiting and waiting. Now, he was inches away from freedom.

She dropped the knife, grasped the bars and pulled.

Cra-a-a-ack . . . She grabbed the knife, dove into the cage, and onto the platform to saw through the ropes. All of four minutes it took to release him, four long harrowing minutes to give him back his life.

And no time for anything but to get out of there.

He grabbed the knife, and they crawled through the broken bars, he on numbed hands and legs. Out the door,

running down the track hand in hand, toward the pony
pen, running, running, running . . . toward their fate . . .
toward the unknown . . .

"Georgie? *Georgie?*" Olivia knocked on Georgie's bedroom door early the next morning. It was almost time to
mete out justice. She could hear the sound of the stanchion
being built even at this early hour.

It remained only to see if Georgie had come home.
"Georgie!" When even that tone of voice didn't rouse her
daughter, Olivia thrust open the door.

The bedroom was empty. Excellent. Georgie had kept
her word, had fulfilled her promise.

"Well?" Moreton, behind her.

"She's not here."

"Good. I'm delighted she finally understands."

"It's almost time."

"Yes. I will have the honor of escorting Charles Elliott
to his death."

"What time did you settle on?"

"Seven. They don't have to be part of this."

"No. Lydia wouldn't want that."

"My thought exactly, my dear."

They walked side by side out onto the Avenue. "Everyone's probably still asleep anyway," Olivia murmured.
"They do like to sleep in."

"They haven't our energy, our style. And they don't like
things that are messy. Charles Elliott is messy. Well. We'll
clean that up fast. In any event, we'll take breakfast after
the disposition."

"That's wise." They were almost to the Fawzi house.
The men who had volunteered for construction duty were
out on the plain just beyond the cemetery. The noise of the
hammering was louder here. The ponies in the nearby
pens were restive.

"Thousands of pounds worth of horseflesh," Moreton murmured. "It does my heart good to think how much money that will bring us. You can tell Smythe to get one ready."

Olivia went off, and Moreton went around to the shed. He didn't have a morsel of feeling for Charles Elliott.

The man would die. Lydia was gone. He would take Olivia to England and rectify matters there. And then, what a glorious future lay ahead of them, with money pouring in, and them taking their ease and living at Aling.

God, he couldn't wait. All the pieces of the puzzle were falling into place. Another half hour and this piece would be done.

He rubbed his hands together in anticipation, and opened the door of the shed.

"OLIVIA!"

And Georgie was gone, too. Olivia felt betrayed and she didn't know why. Yes, she did. Because Georgie had promised. Georgie had agreed to everything, agreed with everything she had said. It was as if she'd crossed her fingers and then aligned herself with the man who could destroy all their lives.

She'd never get over it; she'd never forgive Georgie.

"Oh, but don't you understand, my dear?" Moreton consoled her. "This is better. This gives us a reason and the opportunity to go England sooner."

"How do you know they've gone to England, for God's sake. Maybe he's taking her to Argentina."

"Olivia, be sensible. We don't know the whole story. Maybe he kidnapped her and will hold her for ransom."

"I wouldn't pay a ha'pence for her," Olivia snapped. "No. She's been acting strangely. She never wanted to partake of the pleasures. She was ever trying to deny her nature, and she has now gone in collusion with this murderer. I wash my hands of her, wherever she may be."

"Well, let's pretend she's gone to England—they've gone to England—and give ourselves this opportunity. This is the perfect excuse to leave the colony."

Olivia thought about it for a moment. "Yes, it is, isn't it? Going searching for my wayward daughter who was kidnapped by the oh-so-clever Mr. Elliott. If you're certain this is the right thing to do. And in whose not very capable hands would you leave it all?"

"At this point, I honestly don't give a damn. The ponies will bring us enough money to travel and set up in London, and that's all I care about right now. If we find Georgie, so much the better. If we can come to an accommodation with Henry, we can begin our new life."

An accommodation . . . Henry, the sanctimonious, the patronizing, the righteous, would never come to an accommodation with anyone, Olivia thought, *but why spoil it for Moreton?* He must know that as well as she. He was just refusing, in his usual way, to let obstacles stop him.

And Henry *was* an obstacle, but she had no doubt that Moreton would find a way around it, just as he did everything else.

It was one of the things she liked best about Moreton. He never let anything get in his way.

In the end, things didn't work out quite as Charles had envisioned them. For one thing, the ponies had been difficult to commandeer, mainly because he was weaker than he thought after twelve hours of being tied up and on his back, and the animals were fractious, spooked by shadows coming for them in the dead of night.

And then, Georgiana's plan to get them out of the Valley

involved back roads and narrow tracks out toward the mountains, no easy task by the light of a shrouded moon.

So all his plans to overpower her and get away were knocked into a cocked hat. This part of the journey he could not accomplish by himself. They had to go slowly, both because of his condition and because the ponies were so precariously loaded with their necessities.

But this way, Georgie pointed out, they would be aware if they'd been followed, and there were copses and crevices in which they could hide.

By this route, they swung around the Valley, precariously climbing into the mountains and going west toward the coast. Georgie was positive that Moreton wouldn't think to come looking for them this way. Moreton surely would assume they'd gone south to the nearest port.

Whether Moreton would assume they'd go to England was another story altogether, but it helped to further distance him from finding them.

They walked on slowly until dawn, barely speaking except to figure out the logistics of which way to go. How many hours that was Charles couldn't gauge. He was faint, dizzy, and hungry. They needed to rest the animals and assess where they were and what the next step was.

They were not yet clear of Bliss River Valley. They were high up in the foothills, when they finally decided to stop.

There, they watered the horses and removed the bundles so they could rest, and they had something to eat as well.

"The hanging was to have happened at seven," Charles said, leaning against an outcropping of rocks and finishing off an end of bread. "Is it seven yet? They must know by now I've gone. I wonder what they'll do."

"Moreton will be furious," Georgiana said. "But he is adaptable. If you're gone, and I'm not there, he'll be angry. Then he'll figure out where to come look for us. Or forget about the idea altogether."

Charles slipped to the ground, suddenly unutterably weary. To this point, he couldn't have engineered his escape alone, but he could travel much faster from here on out were she not with him.

In the blazing light of the emerging sun, she did not look too prepossessing. She was dressed impractically, in a light gauzy dress and flimsy slippers, again reinforcing his thought that this was pure impulse on her part. She had no idea what lay ahead, and she hadn't prepared herself for it or for what would be required of her, like restraint, modesty, containment . . .

It was amusing to think about it, really. She was not coming farther than Sefra with him anyway.

This was new territory for him, as far as the terrain at least. He knew nothing about South Africa; he'd come in by boat from Capetown by way of Cameroon and had traveled to the Valley by caravan from there.

But he knew everything about survival in the desert.

They weren't entirely without resources for this leg of the journey. She'd had presence of mind enough to bring food that wouldn't spoil. The skins were full. He had the knife, a useful weapon and a tool, and she'd brought a pair of boots and some sheets. Not bad thinking for someone as sheltered as she.

Sheltered? She? Odd thought.

He was feeling more himself after eating. He got up and moved all the supplies to the midpoint of where they sat. It was now time to take stock.

"Let's see where we are." He unstrapped his bedroll and spread it out, tossing off supplies and feeling for the gun. The change of clothes, the bedding, the tent and poles, the pot, the dishes and utensils, the matches—

No gun.

He steeled himself not to react. *No gun. That lying little . . . Miss Holier Than Fucking Thou . . .*

"Were you looking for this?"

He jerked his head up at the sound of her voice to find his pistol aimed dead at his heart.

"I *was*," he said caustically. He picked up his oilskin pouch and opened it. *Shit. Light fingers there too.* "Aren't you the clever one?"

"We're going to England, Mr. Elliott."

"No doubt about it."

"Or I could just leave you stranded on the mountain, much the same as I'm feeling you might have left me. You know, one of the reasons Moreton chose this location was the mountains. You could get lost in them for days. You think you're going one way and it turns out you're going the other. A man could die in the mountains."

"A woman could die in the desert."

"Indeed, I'm very aware of that. So you see, we do have something to offer each other, Mr. Elliott."

"Oh yes, nothing to it, you'll just coast along in the Kalahari on a couple of sheets and some dried dates."

"It always pays to be prepared," she murmured, but she'd never been prepared for anything in her life except spreading her legs. And the one thing she would never admit to him was that she was scared. She was absolutely pulse-poundingly scared of what came next—the days and weeks alone with him in the desert with no protection but a knife, a gun, and some good will on both sides.

Definitely something secured at the point of a gun.

She was shocked that her hand was still steady, that she could point that thing and that her voice didn't waver and that she sounded as if she knew what she was doing.

In reality her legs were watery and the thought of leaving the Valley was scarier than hell. *Better the devil you know . . .* She ought to just go back and resign herself to the life. That was the simplest thing. The best for them both. And maybe, when she was too old, she would be shipped out, allowed to live in peace somewhere, a reward for time served in the Valley.

Better to be Moreton's whore?

There was no other choice but to go. And Charles Elliott was looking dangerously like he wanted to jump her and wrest the gun away.

"Don't do it, Mr. Elliott. We are going to England."

So she'd made her choice, as much as part of her wanted to run back to the Valley. The unknown was frightening, but what was known was scarier still.

She was wrestling with it: the queen had reigned in but one country, had known only one place. Beyond the mountains, she'd become a commoner, subject to the rules.

The thought was amusing. "England, then," he agreed, "but you'll have to keep your clothes on. That might be awfully difficult for you."

The bastard. "Then I won't," she said insolently. "What else?"

He sized up the thought. The queen, naked, sashaying through another man's manor hall, offering her breasts, her body—she would, too. She had no restraints on her morality, no constraints on her soul.

He couldn't fight her, at least on this part of the journey; her weapons, and his memory, were too potent.

"All right, you kept your part of the bargain. And I will keep mine."

"I expect you will, now. I hope I took all your money?"

He looked grim. "Enough. But we have with us enough to keep going for a week or more until we can get more supplies and find our direction. My *shuldari* is big enough for two. There's food and drink; the horses are fleet and surefooted. We can easily make camp once we're away from the mountains. We can defend ourselves. Don't look so shocked. Did you not think there were brigands roaming the desert? And you leave me without a gun . . ."

"And a knife," she interpolated, holding up the object in question.

Where, in that flimsy dress, had she concealed all that? For one tearing instant, he felt like finding out.

And then he clamped down ruthlessly on his desire. She was counting on that; she was provoking that. It was what she knew how to do best, and it would take every ounce of resolve to resist her.

On every level.

He didn't give her the satisfaction of a retort. Better to act as if it were meaningless. He could make do without a weapon; he had done it before. His expertise was the desert, where she would be but a mewling infant in his hands. And then they would see who had the power

He went on, his voice flat and without expression: "You were forethinking enough to bring those sheets, with which you will fashion a burnoose to protect yourself from the sun. We will travel from sunrise to sunset so as to cover a lot of ground. I assume you want to get to your destination as soon as possible."

"Faster," she said, feeling as if she were running for her life.

But she'd had no life. She'd had the morals and mores of the Valley, and every moment of her time there had been directed toward one aim: to prepare her to spread her legs.

Wasn't it ironic that she was escaping from the valley with the only man who wouldn't want her to.

The only one perhaps that she wished did.

Well, there were many miles to go. They'd be sharing a tent, sharing food. Sharing anything with him couldn't be worse than sharing everything with the self-indulgent, gluttonous men of the Valley.

She hadn't forgotten their abortive encounter. Neither had he, and it didn't take any overt signal from him for her to know it. It was there, simmering beneath the surface, what she had been, what she was, and how he'd resisted her.

She was still what she was, she supposed, and he would still deny he wanted her, but she might seduce him yet.

And that was another kind of power, yet to be tested.

She stared at the gun, and then out at the Valley, so tiny, from where they sat, a village of ants, a village of insects, all of them, buzzing and sucking all the queen's honey, obedient to their king.

Pledging allegiance to their amoral, murderous, debauched *king* . . .

She stood up abruptly; there had never been any other decision she could make. "I will go to England, however long it takes."

Chapter Eight

Curious, the power she felt with a gun in her hand. Five inches of nickel-plated steel that could make six feet of indomitable male pride bend to her will. That was power.

Except she'd probably not be able to sleep for the entire journey worrying about what his next move might be. Charles Elliott was not one to come to heel that easily. He needed her now, and he was clever enough to cede her the upper hand—for the moment.

When they cleared the mountains, it would be another story entirely. Because of that, the farther they got from the Valley, the more wary she became. She was playing a game in which she did not know the rules. It appalled her how much she didn't know.

Like how to deal with someone like Charles Elliott. Which was why he was riding ahead of her, and she had the gun pointed straight at his back.

He seemed unconcerned. Maybe a little apprehensive. Someone unschooled in handling a gun who had an itchy trigger finger was definitely cause for apprehension. She might shoot and actually hit him.

That alone would keep him on the track, she thought. He took her warnings seriously; he did not want to die on the mountain.

No, he wanted to get off the mountain, and leave her to her fate.

It was a long plodding trip, on a narrow track that climbed high above the Valley and then suddenly dipped downward. And the ponies were skittish, uncertain of the footing, the weight they were carrying unsettling them. There were points at which Elliott dismounted and led them both on foot. There were places she couldn't walk with her fragile slippers.

"You could put down the damned gun and trust me," he muttered, as they came through a particularly fraught stretch of the track.

"I'd trust an *arak* faster than I'd trust you," she retorted.

"You might have to."

They went on in silence. He couldn't fight the spirits; they were everywhere, even in the licentious soul of the whore who thought she'd bested him. Little did she know. Much she would soon find out.

They camped for the night on a narrow ledge overgrown with desiccated shrubs.

They cooked some rice, ate it with dates and water, after which Charles fed and watered the animals, and settled them in for the night.

"Let yourself sleep. I would not for a moment try to find my way off the mountain without you."

"But you might try to find your way to taking the gun. That I can't allow because I *will* go to England, and you are going to take me."

She was as determined as the dawn; he knew when he was beaten. He settled down on the narrow strip of grass about five feet from her, crossed his arms, and went to sleep.

This was an ability he had cultivated during his years at Oxford. To snatch that half hour's rest, and to keep moving, moving, moving. A man needed to be alert and refreshed when he was at the danger point.

Traveling with a novice with a gun in her hand was a danger point.

She could not keep up her brave stance much longer. She had to get some sleep. They had to come off the mountain sometime. There would be a breaking point, and then, probably very easily, he thought, he would regain control.

It required some preparation before they could enter the village of Akka. She could not go waltzing in dressed as she was, Charles told her as they camped on a rise about a mile from the village.

The time had come for modesty and restraint.

"And what exactly does that mean?" she asked suspiciously.

"It means you must cover yourself head to foot, and that the most you can reveal is your eyes. And even then, *khanum,* it is too much."

It was inconceivable to her. Shroud herself wholly and completely? Just to pass through a village where they meant only to stop and rest for a night?

"Why do you call me *khanum?*" she asked fractiously. "Do you not know my name is Georgiana?"

Ah, the queen had a name. In all this time, he had never thought about her name. She was the queen—the queen of courtesans and concubines. A lady of *rank* to a certainty.

"It is the equivalent of *my lady.* And no, I did not know your name, nor did I particularly care."

That stung. "Really? My *lady?* You depended on *me,* the whore of Bliss River Valley, not even knowing my name or if I had a shred of honor?"

"We use what instruments are given to us," he murmured.

"Truly? So I am an instrument, a whore, and a *lady?*"

He wasn't in a mood to coddle her. Even with the gun still pointed at his breast. Five inches of barrelhead could do a lot of damage if he set her off. "Be sensible then. We are two desperate people who can help each other, and so you will shroud yourself as best you can in those sheets and you will leave everything else to me."

"I'm willing to cover up to travel in the desert. Why must I do this now?"

"Because, *khanum,* that is what is done. You have a lot to learn, and this is but the first lesson. Modesty in dress. A foreign notion, admittedly, for one who thinks flaunting her naked body is dressing up." He stopped abruptly at the picture his words conjured up.

But he hadn't forgotten, hadn't let himself think of it. Not while the queen—*Georgiana*—had the power to shoot off his balls. But now here they were, on the edge of the desert, and the thing was as tangible between them as the air. He saw it in her eyes, and a certain little gleam of triumph as if she knew, as if she were waiting for him to slip, to slide, to need.

He was stronger than that. Words were just words: they could provoke desire, or kill it. The queen needed a little humility anyway. That much he could give her while the game was in play.

He went on brusquely, "Perhaps we can trade for a proper *abeya,* but until then, the sheets you brought will veil you adequately."

He picked one up and started to drape it over her head. She waved the gun at him. "Don't touch me."

He shrugged. "Do it yourself then."

"I won't do it at all."

"Then we don't continue the journey."

"I won't do this."

"*Khanum,* if you walk into that village clothed as you are, they will kill you."

That was stark enough. She didn't believe him. Maybe.

And she didn't trust him as far as a camel could walk. She kept the barrel of the pistol aimed straight at his heart. "Why?"

"It is ever the lure of Eve. Man cannot resist it. So he suppresses it."

"Or he avails himself of it," Georgiana spat. "These men are no different from the men in the Valley. And I will not kowtow to some ridiculous dogma. I'd sooner walk into the village naked than clothed like a nun."

"Yes indeed, *khanum,* we know you like to walk around naked. But those are paltry words against the doctrines of this culture. You will do what I tell you, and cover yourself or we can go no farther. No. You can go no farther."

It was a pretty potent threat. He could leave her there. And all the money in the world would not get her where she wished to go then.

She nodded. "All right. What do I do?"

"Put down the blasted gun."

"That I *won't.* What next?"

"May I touch, *my lady?*"

She nodded warily, and he began again, taking one of the sheets and draping it over her shoulders and around her arms, making sure it fell precisely to the floor and didn't pool around her foolish slippers, which were now almost in shreds.

The second sheet went over her head. He folded the edges up and around her face and then pulled them forward to obscure everything but her eyes. Then he crossed the tails and tied them to secure it.

"You know too much about this," she muttered.

"I know what I need to know," he answered, and instantly the words hung between them, fraught with possibilities, everything transformed into sexual terms.

He disliked it intensely that she was so unaware, for one who had lived on the Continent from birth. And yet, she'd been as cloistered as a nun in some respects. She'd never gone beyond the mountains. Her whole life had been schooled to the philosophy of the Valley.

She would never be able to live elsewhere. She couldn't even bear to have a makeshift veil over her head. She was stamping and shaking like an agitated mare, her hands tight around the pistol, which made him as nervous as a stallion about to be gelded.

The boots were the hardest. Smart as she was to have thought of bringing them, she could not make herself put her feet into them.

And they weren't all that big on her. It was just they were so confining. So *heavy*. Hard to walk in.

"You'll get used to it," he said, unmoved. "You'll have to get used to all of it to make this journey."

"I don't have to like it."

"Ah, but who does, *khanum?* We do what we can with what we are given."

"Exactly," she murmured, and she meant it, literally.

Everything in sexual terms with her, he thought acidly. He had never known a woman like this. And she could not be left to fend for herself if this was how she spoke, how she acted and thought.

But that was for later consideration. If he dwelt on it, he might not take her a mile farther. For now, the goal was to enter Akka with impunity, an itinerant Bedouin tribesman traveling with his woman to rejoin his people.

"You'll do," he said finally. "And I do the talking."

She couldn't argue that. Although the queen, it seemed,

would argue anything with a gun in her hand. Still, it was always good to have a story; there were fewer questions that way.

And once he had her properly attired, it took but ten minutes more to transform himself, via the change of clothes in his bedroll, to an errant son of the desert. He was, after all, a man who moved easily between the two worlds, and was always prepared to function in both.

The *kachebia* turned him into a wholly different man, more commanding, more demanding.

More arrogant.

"Keep your head down," he ordered, in a tone she could not disobey, as they trekked slowly down the rise and toward Akka. "Never say a word. Follow my lead. Quell your instincts, they count for nothing on this journey."

"Yes, *master,*" she hissed through gritted teeth. "Whatever you say. Whatever you want . . ."

Oh damn. Everything she said had two interpretations. She had to stop, now, if she wanted to ensure his cooperation. Because there would be a point beyond which her weapon would be useless, and then she could call upon other weapons at her disposal. Once they were on their way, there would be time, there would be proximity, there would be needs and desires to be fulfilled, and other ways to repay him that only she knew.

Yes. He wouldn't abandon her, of that she was certain.

And so she kept her head down, and followed his path, and they made their way into Akka to the notes of a Bedouin flute playing eerily in the twilight.

It was hardly even a village. It was a traveler's rest, deep in an oasis of palms and hard by a pool of water, a place to decamp, to bathe, to rest and refresh oneself, and to barter with the Bedouins who camped there for necessities.

This was the first test. Sefra was two days' trip to the

west, the gateway to the Kalahari. They could make that on horseback. Buy the proper supplies. Connect up with a caravan or take the first leg alone, guided by the stars and the crude maps of the Sadi-Anram.

The village was in an oasis surrounded by houses of whitewashed *toub,* and winding walkways with blooming oleander, palm trees, and the scent of melon and basil.

The *souk* here, in the center of the village, provided everything from camels to cushions to coffee, all for a price. A steep price.

Water from the wellspring was free.

He chose carefully: fruit, flatbread, marinated hare for the first night out, another goatskin for the water, and a mule to transport their gear.

"I thought I had gotten all the money," she whispered as he paid the vendor.

"Not all of it, clever lady. Enough. Enough so you should watch your back with your weapons and your irresponsible ways. We can camp at the tall palms at the edge of the village. Come . . . ."

He led the way through a babbling crowd of travelers, beggars, traders, and merchants. Here and there, they were stopped as a vendor admired the horses, and offers were made in trade, in *baksheesh.*

"I hope we find this enthusiasm for the horses in Sefra," Charles muttered as they settled on a small dune just under a grove of palms not far from the wellspring. "Hunch over, *khanum,* you are sitting too imperiously for a mere woman."

She sent him a scathing look. "You enjoy this."

"It makes for less trouble. Subservience is the way of a woman in this land, *khanum,* and her consort is her master in all things."

"Not all," she muttered.

"Mind your tongue and keep your head down."

"And my weapons, as always, at the ready," she retorted, and could have bitten her tongue once again. Her weapons. That futile piece of cold steel in her hand was not her most potent weapon with this man. Only he had yet to know it.

He was tearing apart a piece of flatbread, which he then dipped into a little of the sauce he had purchased, and handed to her. "With your fingertips, *khanum*. No part of your body can be bared to public sight."

"I hate this."

"Eat. Bow your head and be grateful that the fates have allowed us to come this far."

"And how many hundreds of miles are there yet to go?" she asked waspishly.

"So many they cannot be reckoned. And so many one does not count the miles. They come as they come; we go as they go. And that is the plan."

"That doesn't sound like a plan; it sounds like fatalistic waffling."

"Sometimes all we can do is leave things to fate. Why else would we be here? How likely is it that you would have engineered that escape without something determining your need to break away from everything you've known your entire life? And how was it that those two things happened at the exact moment when one would coincide with the other? Go to sleep, *khanum*. These are weightier questions than can be answered even by the most gifted philosopher."

But she was determined not to go to sleep. There were questions yet to be resolved, and promises to be tested. He could sneak away in the dead of the night, taking everything with him, if she slept.

There was no kindness in him, no pity. He had meant to destroy his mother, and she had no conception of what he was capable of. The fury in him was banked now that they were away from the mountain. But that didn't mean it couldn't be roused.

How rash she had been, how unthinking of the consequences and ramifications of fleeing the Valley with him. He was still, would always be, a stranger. And she felt just cold-blooded enough to shoot him if he ever attempted to abandon her, and so she must always be on her guard.

And if he died . . . Well, at least she would have the money, the weapons, the rations and the ponies, and surely she could, somehow, make her way to England with those resources.

And one other thing she could trade . . .

She drew in her breath with a hiss. Always that. Always. How would she get on outside the Valley if all she could only think in terms of was her sexual value?

This was going to be enormously harder than she thought. And the first wall she had to breach was Charles Elliott. And by heaven, she swore, before this journey ended, she would make it fall.

They had done all they could. They'd sent men on horseback every which way, even up on the mountain, searching for Georgie and Charles Elliott.

"The man is clever." Moreton was addressing the Valley citizenry at a gathering at the Club the following evening. "And Georgie is with him. She knows some of the secret ways in and out of the Valley. And I shudder to think what that man has done to her to coerce that information from her. Olivia is distraught. And they've had a twelve-hour head start. They took two of the fastest ponies that Elliott brought in his stable, and enough dried staples and water to see them through the next few days.

"Now, they could have gone toward Capetown, but that seems too obvious a choice. So we won't waste time in consideration of that. They would not have gone east, because that would be the least likely way to get to England, which is where I think they will go.

"So all in all, west and then north is how I figure it. But that covers a lot of territory, making it virtually impossible to follow them. So we have a murderer on the loose who also has the wherewithal to destroy our paradise."

Moreton looked around. Everyone was horrified, as he meant them to be. "And who may well have kidnapped Olivia's daughter," he added for good measure. "And you can well imagine what atrocities he might commit in the name of vengeance on her. What line will he draw between her permission and his animal needs? Ladies and gentlemen, I don't know where to pursue this monster other than to cut him off at his port of entry, and so I am proposing that Olivia and I set off for England as soon as possible."

A murmur at that announcement, a little wave of palpable fear. He could almost hear them thinking: *But who will take over, who will run things, and plan things, and who will adjudicate and tell us what's right and what's wrong? And the children . . . what about the next ceremony of the peacock fan? What about . . . what about . . . what about?*

Who can do this? Who will do this? WHO *can be Moreton?*

A faint smile played across his lips. Indeed, who could be *him?* Well, someone would have to. The new life he planned with Olivia was far more riveting an idea than staying in this semen-soaked cesspool any longer.

He'd jank up a new cesspool at Aling, with pounds sterling floating in his spunk, and all the hot-tailed young tweenies he could handle to service his whip. God, he was hard just thinking about it.

All of that, the brothel, and Olivia, too.

He got himself under control.

"Well, admittedly, we're doing this on the turn of a tuppence, but think of what's at stake. Lydia's killer goes loose. And with all he knows about the colony, someone might come knocking on our door any day now and make trouble for you all."

He looked around the dining room. They were all properly terrorized now, if they hadn't been before, when they were just talking about bringing in the authorities to arrest Charles Elliott. Now the authorities might come in and arrest them.

It was the perfect pricking point.

"I'm thinking Mr. Smythe has the proper degree of amorousness and amorality to take over my stewardship of the Bliss River colony—"

Again, he looked around as everyone started nodding and concurring. Murmuring out loud, "Right on, Smythe, of course. Knows just how to run things and just what to do . . . He'll be Moreton . . . no difference—it'll be as if Moreton had never gone away . . ."

Moreton seized the moment. "We'll take a vote then. Unless anyone can think of someone else we can put in contention—"

Another pause. No response. He felt it though, that sweet pulse that meant they would give him anything he wanted, as long as nothing changed and they could keep doing all the things he'd given them permission to do.

"So, all in favor of Smythe—"

"Hear, hear—" It was one big loud roar.

"Mr. Smythe?"

Smythe stood up, waved, called out: "I'm honored to be the next Moreton of the colony."

Oh God, yes, Moreton thought, motioning for Smythe to join him on the dais where the Valley orchestra usually played. *The next Moreton—he's crowned me king and immortalized me forever . . .*

* * *

The morning broke over Akka, the sun rising like a huge ball of fire over the village square. Dogs barked, a rooster crowed, and a murmur of voices rent the air. Slowly, the village came to life. The women straggled to the wellspring for water for the morning coffee, and the merchants and traders began to set out their wares.

All of this Georgie watched with bleary-eyed fascination while Charles Elliott concocted a breakfast of coffee, rice, and dried fruit.

"You will learn to cook," he said, handing her a cup of strongly scented coffee.

"I have other talents," she mumbled, taking it in both hands like a child. It was searingly hot, and the warmth permeated her vitals and made her feel less fuzzy.

"So you tell me, but the thing that matters most in the desert is to be adaptable and resourceful. You won't survive five minutes otherwise."

"And I'm certain you're counting on that."

"No, *khanum,* you forget, in the desert we don't count—anything."

She made a sound and took the bowl of rice he handed her. It tasted like little wooden pellets. She could barely swallow a mouthful. She took a hasty swig of coffee and almost choked.

God, he was right, she needed sleep. She didn't know what she was doing right now. Didn't know what she was doing with a stranger bent on vengeance on the outskirts of the desert.

"What do you think is going on in the Valley?" she asked.

"Oh, I think Moreton made a nice scene, because he loves to dramatize things, and he sent riders hither and yon looking for us. If I had to guess, I'd say he's probably done with it and has given up the search."

"So there's no more threat."

"Unless he comes looking for you in England. But why would he do that?"

"He wouldn't like to lose someone from the Valley, especially someone like me, who wasn't fully—acclimated."

"You had me fooled," Charles muttered. "You looked completely acclimated to me."

And there it was again, the innuendo, the awareness. They could never talk about the Valley, then, without that shimmering knowledge between them: that she had caressed his penis, that he had had a full glorious view of her naked body.

And it didn't matter that she was shrouded like a corpse. He remembered. He remembered her hands, her nipples pressing against his back, his blowtorch of a response.

Her breath caught. She lowered her head. He remembered. He would not give in, but he remembered.

And as long as he remembered, and she could make him remember, the power was still in her hands.

Chapter Nine

Everything would come to a head in Sefra. He was just biding his time, Georgie thought, just waiting until they came to a large enough town where he would feel no qualms, no guilt about leaving her.

She was certain he meant to leave her, even if he were going on to England. Having her with him slowed him down. And now that there truly was no threat from Moreton, he had no reason to take her.

He did not need to keep one single promise he had made in the heat of the escape. No honor among thieves—she understood that perfectly. Even she would have promised the moon to anyone who would have helped her get out of the Valley.

But still, to England she would go, and she was determined that he would keep his promise to get her there. And so, she had just the two-day journey to Sefra to convince him. And words wouldn't do it. There was only one possible way. She had to seduce him, but she had to overcome the fact that tactic had not worked in the Valley.

But that was the Valley, she thought, trying to rationalize it. Something about the Valley was intrinsically off-putting. The lack of privacy, the blatant and public trolling for lovers, the air of decadence and debauchery . . .

Surely everything was cleaner and purer in the desert. *Even she?*

There wasn't much time. They packed everything up as the heat began to rise. He refilled the goatskins and loaded everything onto the mule, while she sat hunched up and unobtrusive in the shade of the palm trees.

She was a sight to see, Charles thought. All that sensual energy bundled into a couple of sheets and some native pragmatism he did not expect she possessed. She would do fine in Sefra. She would find someplace to operate a house of all nations and take in piles of *baksheesh* from curious travelers and wealthy pashas who paid well for foreign whores.

And eventually she would become a legend of the desert, the queen ruling over her conquests the only way she knew how.

Goddammit. He couldn't contemplate her without thinking about sex. Even when she was bent double and clothed like a sack. It boded trouble. He sensed it in the air around her as he helped her onto the pony. She was ready for a fight, determined to get her way the only way she knew how.

Well, he was immune. A woman's body was just an instrument for release, and the function was ever the same.

He hadn't ground his tool for months as he plotted this abortive course to Bliss River; two days more wouldn't make a difference.

And after that, they'd both find freedom.

They rode out of Akka at the same plodding pace.

"It will take a month to get to Sefra at this rate," Georgie grumbled.

"It requires a certain faith, *khanum*. Like everything else in the desert."

"Like promises?" she asked slyly.

He pretended he hadn't heard that.

Georgie ground her teeth in frustration. If she could have ridden naked out of town, she would have, just to prove the point that he was not as invulnerable to her as he thought.

But that was for later. She was better covered head to foot in the stifling heat and brutal sun. The road to Sefra was not easy; they had to ride single file, so any conversation was impossible. There were intermittent travelers on mule or horseback for whom they had to make way, and now and again, they came up behind a lumbering caravan and had to pull up slower still.

They stopped to take water at midday; then on again down the dusty rutted road that wound through the barren reddish plains toward Sefra.

Toward sunset, they finally made camp and set up the tent by a copse of bushes off to the side of the road. Charles went to gather palm leaves for the fire, and Georgie fed the animals and pondered how she might make her case on this first night of the precious two to go.

She eyed the tent. It wasn't all that large, which could be good or bad. He might choose to sleep outside on the ground as he had in Akka. But there, they'd been surrounded by the tents of other itinerant travelers and there was a sense of safety in numbers.

Here, they were all alone. And there were flies. And a kind of smoky scent in the air, as if a hundred other campfires were burning concurrently.

Charles put a match to the pile of *djerids* he'd collected and watched them flame up. "We will feast on rabbit tonight, *khanum*. The journey has made me ravenous."

Georgie was hungry, too, and tired and a little scared. But she'd never admit that to him. She put a pot of water on to boil, got out the plate and the utensils that were part of his kit, and threw a handful of figs into the steaming water.

Charles added the meat. When it was heated, he lifted it onto their one plate, cut some slices, speared one, and offered it to Georgie. And so they dined, one alternating with the other until all the meat was gone.

And now what? Charles wondered. It wasn't dark yet. Neither of them seemed tired. And the queen was restive. She'd pushed back her hood and loosened the ties around her neck; her body seemed to hum.

The last thing he wanted was to deal with the queen of tarts in that mood.

He leaned back on one elbow as they watched streaks of mauve, pink, and dark blue color the desert sky. He loved that best about the desert. The rich color. The eternal sand. The sense of infinite space.

But he had loved England more. "Tell me about the Valley," he said abruptly, and then caught himself. Damn and damn. Always the Valley. Always something to do with her carnal life.

But not his. Not his. *He* could be made of stone, for all he felt about her. He was asking just to pass the time.

"What is there to know that you did not see for yourself?"

"You lived there all your life?"

"All my life."

"It's unimaginable."

"Imagine it. We—I—grew up in a place where everything carnal was the way of life. Nothing was forbidden to adults. And you became an adult at age sixteen. There is a ceremony. A sacrifice of virginity for the greater good of the community. And then, you are penetrated, and you are free to go on your voyage of sexual dissipation. Everyone is available in the Valley. No one is excluded. Anyone who wants you can have you, and you can have anyone you want.

"Of course, we'd been educated that sex is the currency of life in our community. And we'd been watching this all these years, aroused by what was going on around us: the way people feel each other publicly and the promenade where all strut and display their wares. We know all about the potency of sex," she slanted a look at him as she said this. His face was impassive, his expression obdurate as if even this coarse narrative could not touch him.

But the line of his body said otherwise. He was aroused by her words, and she knew it. There was something awful and seductive about the Valley way of life. Hadn't Moreton truly understood that? And that was why and how the Valley could come into being?

She pulled at her makeshift covering, and it slid off her shoulders. The dress of course was a problem, but she could and would divest herself of that before too long.

She went on deliberately and precisely, "And you understand that we salivate with envy. We start to want so badly. We cannot wait until we're old enough to be fondled and fucked—just like that."

The words hung in the infinite air, resonating.

Just like—how? He'd never ask. He didn't say a word. And meantime, he was not unaware that she was slowly sliding the covering from her body.

After a while, she continued, "We are taught how to dress, how to approach someone, how to yield, how to pursue, how to incite desire in a man. And we learn all the wondrous ways of a man's penis . . . all the delicious ways a woman can make him erupt. All the ways that we can use every part of our body to stimulate, to please, to bring him to heel. And that, too, is life in the Valley."

The covering of sheets was now down to her waist. And she wasn't unaware of that or that her gauzy dress was soaked in sweat and clinging to her body, to her breasts—and neither, she knew, was he.

"There are no loyalties or commitments except to the next pleasurable encounter. And the men all want it. Every night they want it. Every day if they can get it. And in that way, the women accumulate power. They can say no. But then, there's always someone who will say yes to a good hard fuck, and no man is ever refused.

"And then, there are women in the Valley who just lie on their backs all day and get fucked by whoever decides to come by. And that, too, is life in the Valley.

"Some of the men keep at it all day long, just to see how many hours they can stay erect and pumping. There are competitions. And prizes. Women offer themselves to the winner with the most stamina. Who wouldn't want to ride the prize stallion?

"I won't even mention the triads and the orgies, other aspects of life in the Valley that perhaps you were not made aware of.

"But then, they introduce newcomers slowly." Georgie stood up, matching her motions to her words, and let the sheets fall to her feet. "They get you used to never-ending indiscriminate sex until you cannot go a day without fucking . . ."

She kicked off her boots.

"Or an hour . . ."

She pulled down her dress and it slid to the ground inches from where he lay, leaving just a fragile shift between some modesty and total nudity.

"And then," she added, "when you get bored with that—and that may take a year or two—they suggest some new forms of entertainment . . ."

The shift came off in one sweeping motion, and she was naked, standing over him, provoking him with her silky legs, her coaxing tone.

"Perhaps you should have kept your secret long enough so you could have explored all the prurient delights the Valley offers."

She stepped over him, straddling him, deliberately splaying her legs so he could not avoid staring straight up at her naked cleft, with the firelight playing over the intriguing hollows of her body.

A man would have to be stone not to look.

"Or perhaps your erotic tastes are more perversely refined than those in the Valley. You are rather a bull, as I have good cause to know . . ."

A man would have to be dead not to want to . . .

"Bloody God Almighty . . ." He jacked himself out from between her legs. "What the hell do you think you're doing?"

She froze, just for an instant, and then answered airily, "Getting comfortable. What the hell do you think *you're* doing?"

That bloody well was the question. Asking for trouble, it seemed, because she was ready to give it to him. And that hadn't been an innocent question about the Valley, even he was aware of that. He was utterly furious with himself for playing her game.

And because of that she was naked; her breasts full, with bulbous areolae and jutting nipples. His head was filled with images of faceless humping bodies, and there was nowhere to go to avoid her nakedness or the scent of sex in the air.

"Sit down and cover yourself." It was the best he could do, and it wasn't nearly enough. The queen wasn't prone to listening to anything he had to say or to taking orders from him. That was a daylight thing only, and only under duress.

"I'll sit, thank you," Georgie said sweetly, "but it's nice and cool without all those clothes and wraps."

Thank God, they were off the road. And the *djerids* had burned into crackly embers. And the moon was high. And there were no other travelers around because someone would offer a pasha's ransom to buy her naked as she sat and make her his sex slave.

She could be your sex slave . . . He pushed the thought violently out of his mind. She was too close for comfort. Too naked. Too willing.

"You can't keep doing this."

"Doing what? I was hot and took off my clothes. I certainly wouldn't disrobe when we're on the road. That would be stupid. I understand that. Although—"

Although he wanted her, he was hot, he was hard, he was ripe. She could feel it; she could almost taste it, that need, that pulse . . . that possessiveness. She knew it; she understood it more than he did.

"—perhaps it might be an impetus to some other gentleman to want to help me get to England . . ."

She let the words peter out. The air was explosive now, just the way she wanted it. He was determined not to give in to her nakedness and she was equally determined that he would.

"I might try that the closer we get to Sefra . . . getting naked, I mean. I'm sure there will be some man who would—"

"Who would *what?* Take you along for a cheap fuck? Go stand naked in the middle of that road tomorrow morning, *khanum*. They will grovel at your bare feet. They'll fuck you in the road; they'll be so grateful for a naked woman who's willing and Western—"

"Oh, I know they will," Georgie said furiously. "Just not you."

Oh, she knew they would, did she? She knew they would. The queen knew everything about men's randy desires, and nothing about her own, damn her to eternity. And sure as hell, not about his.

"Absolutely right, naked lady, just not *me.*"

He stomped off into the darkness, leaving her alone by the fire, her body both cold and swamped with a different kind of telling heat.

One more day. And he was not as unmoved by her nudity as he pretended. It was more than obvious that his penis was erect all the time now.

That was good. She could work with that.

And if she could get her hands on him, just burrow between his legs . . . anything was possible.

She got hot just thinking about it. Charles Elliott was not a saint. He wanted her, clearly. He was just better able to control his animal nature than most of the men she had known.

So she would have to push him a little more. Get him even more excited, even more inflamed. Make it worth his while to keep her with him.

Lord, she hadn't thought it would be this difficult.

She didn't know where he slept that night, but she slept alone in the tent. And in the morning, when she heard him moving around, she awakened, wound the sheets around her body until she was wholly covered, and emerged from the tent looking as proper and submissive as a *wife.*

He handed her an orange without a word. But nothing more needed to be said after yesterday. He knew what she was. He knew she was naked under her carefully concocted covering, and he knew she would walk naked through the marketplace at Sefra if that was what it took to get what she wanted.

He was almost of a mind to detour around Sefra. To keep her cloistered so that no other man could ever have the opportunity to feast on her nakedness.

The thought brought him up short. That was damned possessive thinking for a man who was resisting that very thing.

And there was still a long way to go. Bypassing Sefra would be folly when he could sell the ponies there for enough to buy provisions and the wherewithal to cross the Kalahari and make the port at Dar el Rabat. Two weeks at the most on camelback, and then by boat to Cameroon, Sierra Leone, and England.

The only question was, with her, or without her?

At this point, he would travel no faster either way. And she was almost obsessive about getting there with him or without him. And she would, too; he just didn't want to figure out how.

But the *how* would haunt him . . .

Damn it. Damn her. Damn the Fates. Damn her naked body under those shrouding sheets. It was all he could think about. She had done her work well, his rank lady. She had proven he was not a martyr, not a statue. That his will would never win the battle with his penis. And that he was no different from the men she knew in the Valley; he could be just as easily seduced by the thought of poling a willing naked woman.

Especially this woman, and those breasts. He was salivating over those nipples and areolae in the most covert way; he wanted them so badly he could taste them. He wanted to take them deep into his mouth and pull at them and lap at them one and then the other until she couldn't take the hot rhythm of his sucking anymore.

He wanted . . .

Almighty heaven, she had unleashed a storm of wanting and desires that had been too long suppressed.

But not yet, not yet. It wouldn't do to give in to her too quickly. That much he understood about her. It would be better to wait and see what else she had in store for him, if last night was any indication of the lengths to which she would go when thwarted.

He was a patient man. He had waited many years to exact revenge; he surely could wait another night, another two weeks.

And then and only then, the *khanum* could have everything she wanted. But only what he was willing to take, and only on his terms.

She would have to try harder. Sefra was barely a half day away. They would rest that night at the oasis at Ketsemet, and this would be her last chance to win him over. To make herself sensually indispensable so that he would take her anywhere.

Except that walking around naked didn't seem to accomplish that. Threatening to walk around naked in Sefra had brought much more of a response.

He did feel possessive about her, she thought. And somewhat responsible. She aroused *something* in him, even if he didn't wish to acknowledge it. Otherwise, he wouldn't have stormed off that way last night.

But he was the kind of man who wouldn't like to be ruled by his carnal needs. He would ruthlessly clamp down on any sign of weakness in that regard. And she aroused that weakness in him. The fact that she knew it made him resist her that much more.

Oh yes, that made sense. She had caught him terribly off-guard the first night she had gone to him in the Valley.

He hadn't expected her, or how experienced she was, how knowledgeable of a man's body, a man's needs.

And now, he was on the borderline of coveting her. Of feeling flaming jealousy at the thought of her naked with any other man.

She must feed that, she thought. And incite his lust for her in any way she could. That wasn't going to be easy if he didn't respond to her nudity. She would have to watch him carefully this night. Something about her had provoked his fury last night. Something had gotten him that worked up, that angry.

Maybe something as simple as his desire.

A man who was ruled by his penis could be molded like clay. But a man who fought his carnal instincts must be hammered and hewn into the fantastic lover he surely must be. And that was the challenge.

To find the weak point, and push it hard. To discover his secret need and make him want it beyond all reason.

And she had to accomplish all that in one night on the road to Sefra.

She must be crazy. She could do as she had threatened: find a half dozen others who would gladly volunteer to take her England.

At what cost? she wondered. How many nights on her back with men for whom she was nothing but a fast convenient fuck? That was a high price to pay. But that was what women in the Valley had always been: a convenient place to take pleasure in and then walk away from.

Why have scruples about that now?

She didn't need to ponder that question as she perched precariously on her pony, leading the mule and gazing at Charles Elliott's rigid back for the dozen or so miles to Ketsemet. The answer was simple: England was not the Valley. There were rules and morals and constraints she knew nothing about, or even whether she could conform. And she did not want to buy her trip to that new life in Valley currency.

It sounded excessively high-minded, and totally meaningless when she took into account her plan to seduce Charles Elliott.

She would always be a child of the Valley, she thought. And she knew only one way to get what she wanted.

Another purple-hued sunset drifted down toward the horizon through the palm fronds at Ketsemet, which was nothing more than a circle of palms surrounding a wellspring of fossil water and host this night to the lumbering caravan they had come across the previous day and one or two other travelers.

There wasn't much room for a carnal takeover here, Georgie thought, as Charles cooked some millet and dates and she hunkered down near the fire, contemplating her next move.

There was literally nothing she could do with so many people around, except crawl into the tent and undress. That would be a blessed relief after the heat of the day, even though the temperature would drop at night.

Tomorrow, everything would change, and there wasn't a thing she could do about it, or a weapon she could wield to force him to alter his plans.

Just for a moment, she thought of cold-bloodedly shooting him so he, at least, could not continue the journey. But to what point? She would be no better off than she was now, and her options would still be the same.

She had had no idea how hard life would be just this far outside the Valley, and how much planning and scheming was involved to get along. What would it be like in England?

She glanced up as Charles handed her the plate, heaped

with the cooked grain and some of the leftover rabbit. Nothing like the meals she was used to. She heaved a sigh and dug in with her fingers, while Charles ate from the pot.

"I'll get some water for tea," he said when they'd finished. "Maybe a bucket for a washup because I won't have you anywhere near that pool."

Ah? "Why is that?" she asked carefully.

"Because one doesn't know what you'll take it into your head to do," he answered grimly, "and who I'll have to kill in the aftermath."

A-ha! She ducked her head in a properly submissive manner. "Even if I promise to behave?"

"I don't believe you know the meaning of the word," Charles growled and set off in the darkness.

Yes! There it was, in that grudging distrust of her. Why else would he be so adamant about where she went and what she did?

These male signals she understood. He was weakening, which was saying a lot for a man like Charles Elliott. Something was causing him to shift his position. Something about her, something sexual.

Something he did not want to admit, even to himself.

It just remained to find out what it was. What about her was affecting the strong-willed Charles Elliott to the point where he would set aside his misgivings about her?

This was what she understood: that covert pricking up of a man's sexual interest. He probably hated himself for caving in. He probably hated her.

No matter. It was much easier to deal with him on that level. Charles Elliott was now the devil she knew.

She wondered what revelations the night would bring.

Chapter Ten

He brought water, hauling it back to their camp in one of their three goatskins.

"You can sit behind the tent, where you will be shielded by the bushes and no one will see you. But be careful of the thorns."

Yes, he most definitely did not want anyone to see her. Georgie rose up and stepped to the rear of the tent. He followed a moment later behind her, just as she began to disrobe.

Deliberately?

There was only the intense moonlight that flooded the landscape by which to bathe, and hazy drifts of smoke from the nearby campfires.

And there they stood, she utterly unabashed by her nudity, he in grim disapproval. And yet he'd suggested it. He'd wanted it, he needed it, for whatever reason.

These were the subtle signs of a man in heat.

"Am I to have no privacy?" she asked.

He raised an eyebrow. "A show of modesty at last?"

"If that were so, *you* would not be here. You may watch, if you wish."

He wanted to just walk away, to leave her wet and naked in the bushes, and if there were consequences, then there were consequences.

That was the way of the desert. Choices made; consequences accepted. That was the way of life.

But he couldn't do it, and he hated himself because he couldn't do it. Choice made, repercussions to come. He should have left her in Akka, and now it was too late. And way too late to save himself.

He poured the water into the cooking pot. "Get on with it."

She smiled faintly. "I did always like an audience."

He slammed the pot onto the ground, and it seemed to her that any reference to or behavior that reeked of the Valley set him off.

It was something interesting to contemplate. She knelt, took a fold of her sheets, dipped it in the water, and began to cleanse herself.

There wasn't much she could do with just water but wash away the dust and grime from this part of the journey. But even with Charles Elliott standing there like a statue, the bath was refreshing, the night air cooling her damp skin as she rubbed the cloth over her legs and belly and breasts—

And felt the air heating up between them, thick and dark with secrets. There was something he wanted; something he didn't want to want. Something about *her*, her body, her sex.

It was too shadowy to see his eyes, but she felt them grazing over her naked body, as tangible as a touch. Something he wanted to touch, to possess . . .

She felt a thrill course through her, and the familiar languid feeling of arousal attack her vitals. This she knew; this she wanted.

She made her movements slow, deliberate, caressing.

Anything to rouse his interest and make him reconsider his decision about her. Anything he wanted, anything.

He watched. Watched those slender knowing fingers sliding the coarse material of the sheets all over her naked body. Watched as she paid particular attention to the sweet spot between her legs, her thighs and belly, her arms, her breasts . . . squeezing the cool water over her nipples so that they tightened like buds, hardened, and protruded still farther.

He wanted to lick off the water; he wanted to rub her nipples with honey and eat them. He wanted . . .

Woman was ever a man's downfall. And never in his life did he think he would fall so hard for a tart's nipples that he would do anything to have them.

Even take her to England.

No audiences for the whore if she were with *him*. Just an audience of one with particular demands for a long, hard, hot trip in the desert. A man needed a diversion on such a journey, and playing with her nipples would provide him that. And he shared with no man that which was his.

She wouldn't say no. She'd been looking all this time for a way to get to him, to seduce him. Maybe this moment was inevitable. Maybe he had known even as she was helping him escape the Valley that he would keep his word about taking her to England.

Maybe he had secretly wanted what she had offered him. And perhaps the vast empty space of the desert was the place to capitulate to his lust for her breasts. There were no witnesses in the desert. No future beyond that day, and that moment.

That was his weapon, that was his price, and she would barter it for her safety; he was certain of it. And he was going to set the rules.

"No audiences," he said abruptly.

She felt a rill of excitement. "Excuse me?"

"You still want to go to England."

She blinked, picked up one of the sheets, and tied it around her hips. "You know I do."

"Then we'll continue on, under certain conditions."

Yes, yes, yes. He wanted it. Whatever it was, he wanted it badly enough to bargain with her. She could barely keep the excitement out of her voice, but she made her tone wary. "What conditions?"

"No flaunting yourself anytime anywhere. Modesty at all costs, at all times, except when you're alone with me."

"And then what?" Skepticism permeated her voice, deliberately to goad him, to make him come to the point. Except his penis was there already.

She flexed her hands; she wanted to grab it. She felt a tremor go through her body, her excitement escalating at the thought of him finally inside her.

"And then you have to give yourself over to me."

"Oh! And whatever can that mean?" she asked with a touch of coyness. Wondering why he had to play this little game in the first place.

"It means that I take what I want when I want it. And what I want is your nipples. I want to own your nipples. Not your body. I don't want to fuck you. I just want your nipples naked and available for me at the end of a long dreary day in the desert."

She was dumbfounded. "Just my nipples?"

"Just as naked and hard and pointed as they are now to do with as I wish."

She caught her breath. It was unimaginable that he didn't want to fuck her in exchange for taking her on the rest of the journey. "I don't understand."

"No, I don't think you do. But I will be just as demanding of your nipples as I would be of your body. Think about what that means and about whether you want to give your nipples over to me every day until the end of the journey."

"No fucking?" she asked faintly.

"No fucking."

Was it a relief, or was he a lunatic? What really would she be agreeing to if she said yes to his terms? And how unpleasant could it be to have a man fondling your breasts and nipples every day? How intolerable, really, to feel a man's fingers playing with those rigid tips every night?

She felt boneless and hot at the thought of it, her juices flowing like honey.

"What if I want to be fucked?" She had to ask, if only to annoy him.

"Then it's too bad. You are not free on this journey to do anything but service me with your nipples."

Her body tightened, her nipple tips got harder.

"Whenever I want them, *khanum*. However I want to use them. And I can be very demanding."

"I live to see that side of you," she murmured. Of all things—*her nipples—the easiest thing to give*. She was shaking with excitement. *How demanding?* She wanted him to make his demands now.

"Oh, you will, *khanum*. I will be the most greedy, the most ravenous lover of your nipples you have ever had."

She closed her eyes, trying to imagine all the things he would do, could do to her nipples, trills of arousal skeining all over her body.

"And I guarantee you will never desire another lover of your nipples after I have had them."

He let a moment pass, watching the moonlight play over her trembling breasts. "But that, of course, is only if you agree to those terms to come to England with me."

She swallowed hard. No fucking. And her nipples in his

hands, and untold pleasures guaranteed. Surely this wasn't
an onerous price.

She licked her lips. "I agree."

"Agree to?"

She swallowed again, her throat tight, her imagination
running riot. "I agree to give you my nipples to do with as
you will for the whole of our journey."

He closed his eyes for the barest moment. "And now
you will give over the gun and the knife."

That startled her out of her erotic reverie.

"I don't think so."

"My dear girl, believe me. I want those nipples more
than I want to abandon you. Trust me on that. The journey would take no longer without you, and it will be much
more pleasurable knowing that it will end every night with
my hands on your naked nipples. So let's just act like
adults, and give me the weapons. And I will give you what
I promised you in exchange."

"When?" she demanded breathlessly.

"Tomorrow, at the end of the day's journey. We will
procure a bigger tent in Sefra, and some rugs and pillows,
comforts to cushion our sensual explorations at the end of
our long day. Then, you will come to me naked, and give
me your nipples—and then . . . Well, you will see."

She felt like she was panting. "I can't wait for tomorrow. Look, my nipples are hard for you now."

"Tomorrow, *khanum,* when we are alone in the vast
spaces, and in our own tight little world in our tent, then
and only then will I take your nipples and show you what
a voracious lover of them I will be."

Her nipples were rock-hard under her makeshift robes
as they rode into the bustling walled city of Sefra early the
following morning. She hadn't slept. She couldn't get a

word he had said out of her mind, out of her body. He had aroused her hopelessly, made her hot with yearning, and suffused with that languid feeling that always preceded sex and left her deeply unsatisfied.

And he had disappeared soon after she had handed over the weapons, and she had no idea where he'd taken his ease. With another woman, for all she knew. With another woman's nipples, even. There were plenty of women drifting around and about the well.

She'd kill him. And now she was going a little crazy. It was her nipples he wanted; nothing could have been more plain from everything he said. He wasn't seeking out other women. He was keeping himself for her, for the moment at the end of the long first day of their journey when she would give him her nipples and let him take his pleasure.

She couldn't wait. And there was so much yet to do. First, the sale of the ponies and the mule. Charles waded right in to the heart of the *souk* to let everyone admire his expertise in horseflesh.

She followed behind, her head bowed and properly submissive, her eyes on the hem of Charles's robe as he strode boldly through the marketplace.

The tactic worked. Almost immediately they were surrounded, and he began negotiating most fluently, not missing a beat as they proceeded in between the stalls. She understood nothing, except they kept repeating one word, *cadi,* as they threw handfuls of *baksheesh* at him.

In the end, he had a sack full of banknotes and had given over his two prize ponies, and thrown in the mule and their meager traveling kit for good measure. He was enormously pleased with the bargaining.

"We're going to be very comfortable on this trip, *khanum.*"

"Really? As we walk?"

"No, no. We will be traveling on camel, with all the appropriate comforts a man of means can afford. It is time to bargain some more."

Cadi . . . cadi . . . The sound followed them as he made arrangements for three camels, a dragoman to guide them, enough hay to pack their possessions and to use to feed the animals, a trunk of food, two more water skins, a roomier tent, with a rug that fit the floor, and lush pillows and blankets, plates, cups, eating utensils, two nesting pots, a kettle, a low folding table, and appropriate clothing for her.

Appropriate?

Dressed in the dark, heavy cotton robe and veil, she felt invisible. And looked no different from any other of the women shuffling through the aisles of stalls in the market-place.

Cadi . . . cadi . . . They saw his money and they waved their wares in his face, demanding that he stop, that he look, that he buy.

"What does it mean, *cadi?*"

"It is the equivalent of *master.*"

He strode through the *souk,* pausing here and there to buy some more fruit, a ball of goat cheese, some wine, some sugar, and butter, a sack of millet and rice.

"And now, we go to meet our guide, and we will begin our journey."

His name was Rashmi, a portly unassuming middle-aged man in flowing robes, who awaited them by the north gate with the camels and all of the gear packed in straw and slung in panniers over the camels' humps.

"We walk for the first leg of the journey," Charles said, and motioned for Rashmi to lead. The keeper at the wall opened the gate, and slowly, in single file, they led their camels out of the west gate of the city and into the wall of heat and infinite sand and sky that was the edge of the desert.

They walked all the morning into the Kalahari, with the blazing sun behind them, into the vast swath of an emptiness underpinned only by the gritty yellow sand, the sun, and the sweltering heat.

There was not a tree, not a scrub of a bush to break the corrugated landscape. There was only the sun, the sand, the sky, and the plodding animals. At noon, they broke for water and food, and then they all mounted their camels and rode.

And all they could see was sand and more sand, unmarred, untrodden, vast, immeasurable, unconquerable.

Slowly, slowly, they rode into the boundless unknown, Rashmi navigating by the sun, by experience, and by instinct. They were to travel as far as possible the first day; the first day in the heat was the worst. After, the body became acclimated. After, everything was not as intense.

Georgie thought she would faint from the smell and the swaying of the camel, the scorching heat, and the closeness and warmth of her *abeya*. She wanted to stop desperately; she wanted to rescind every agreement and go back to stay in Sefra.

Anything but this suffocating endless torment of sweltering heat.

Eventually the sun began to sink down into the horizon, a golden ball in a sky painted with mauves and pinks that finally turned to twilight.

Then they stopped to camp.

Stopped in the middle of nowhere. That was the desert—nowhere, Georgie thought acrimoniously.

So they would make a somewhere. Immediately Rashmi and Charles began setting up the tents, Rashmi's near where the camels were staked, and her and Charles's a little farther away.

Between the two tents, Charles made a campfire from

straw and camel dung and set up the two pots, one with water, one with some meat and vegetables.

Georgie was ordered into their tent to prepare for the evening.

Surely he didn't—he couldn't. Oh, but Charles could, she thought, her heartbeat escalating. Perhaps it was all he had thought of the entire journey, what would happen when they broke for the night and he had her all alone, naked, in their tent.

She spread the rug over the floor, and arranged the blankets and pillows. She could see the shadows of Charles and Rashmi moving around the campfire, which threw a low muted light into the tent.

She could feel her heart pounding, her body quickening, her breathing becoming heavy with anticipation.

She felt the hunger to have him possess her and the contradictory need to goad him, to make him work for his reward.

Her breath caught; her body tightened and elongated with a furling need. Even this death trip couldn't kill desire, she thought raggedly. All she could think of now was his promise to be the most greedy lover of her nipples.

She didn't even want to eat. She wanted him, this minute, with her, his hands cupping her and his mouth feeding at her breasts.

Her body heated up, and she ripped the veil from her head, and the robe from her body.

Naked, he had said. At end of the day's journey, she was naked and ready for him to come for her nipples.

And yet he did not come. Her nipples grew tighter and harder with longing. She felt honey wet, her body strung taut with yearning.

They were eating, the men, excluding the lowly woman, the thought of possessing whose nipples had bent one man to her will.

She knew her power, and she didn't care. All she wanted was for him to keep the promise that had kept her going on this first part of the journey.

But now she was naked, she must confine herself to the tent.

What would he do? She could imagine ten things and a hundred. Every one aroused her still more. When would he come? When did men in the course of a day seek to sink themselves deep in a woman's body? When would this man come to claim her nipples?

Everything about her body was aroused, erect, aware. And yet, he did not come.

There was laughter outside the tent, and low conversation, and night sounds. The stillness was broken by the crackle of the fire, the cackle of a hyena, the mawing of the camels.

A swamping need coursed through her.

She knew so many things about sex, about men and their needs, and she was waiting on him?

She cupped her breasts, the curve of her palm and thumb surrounding the nipples. Her breasts were perfect, high, full and rounded, with dusky areolae and pointed tips that were aroused, protruding, and hard as stone.

Made for a man's hands, a man's mouth.

"Those are my nipples, *khanum.*"

His voice, low and commanding as it was, startled her.

"So I was told, *cadi,* and yet no one came to master them."

"Then you wait for me, and you wait on me, and you wait until I am ready for it. There are things men must do before they take their pleasure."

"And there are promises men must keep," she retorted, "when they bargain for that pleasure."

He smiled faintly. She wanted it already; she was desperate for it. Her nipples were tight and hot with it. She

couldn't hide a thing from him now. He'd deliberately pro-
longed the time until he came for her to intensify her
arousal and her need.

And now he would take her nipples. "You will have all
the pleasure you can handle, *khanum*. Give your nipples
to me."

She licked her lips and looked down at her aching
breasts. Her body was tight as a bow, waiting. And maybe
he knew that; maybe he did it deliberately to heighten this
moment. All she knew was, she was ready for it, ready for
his hands and the fulfillment of his promise.

She came to stand directly in front of him. He reached
out and his hands surrounded her breasts—she made a
sound as he touched her—his fingers over, his thumb
below. Then gently his fingers moved forward so they
grazed the hard points, and he squeezed each of them between one finger and his thumb.

A bolt of lightning shot between her legs, incandescent
and furious, and she gasped.

"Now, *khanum,* go about your business while I tend to
your nipples. You may have noticed I brought you some
food. You may sit and dine at your leisure, as long as I can
possess your nipples."

She couldn't breathe, the sensation of his fingers squeezing her nipples so subtly was so intense. She almost
wanted to get away from it. Her body bucked and shimmied seeking surcease, and as she tried to get away from
the pressure, he came at the hard pointed tips even more
relentlessly.

"Lie down then, *khanum,* and let me play with your
nipples."

"This is too much . . ." she moaned.

"This is not nearly enough. *I* can't get enough. I promised you I would be the most ravenous lover of your nipples, and here I've barely even begun and you think it's

enough?" He rubbed the nipple tips lightly between his fingers and then compressed them again, and she tried to pull away.

"It will never be enough. And this is but the first night of all the pleasure to come, *khanum*. I have wanted to fondle your luscious nipples from the moment I saw you naked in my bungalow. And now they are mine to do with as I want—as you want, *khanum*—even though you try to deny the fullness of your own pleasure as I rub and squeeze them . . ."

Her breath caught again. She had to get away from his inexorable fingers. She moved away and he was there with her, his only contact, his fingers surrounding her nipples.

"Remember, *khanum*, this was the price. This was all I asked of you, that you give me your nipples."

"I know," she whispered. "I didn't know."

"What could you not have known?"

"How insistent your fingers could be."

"And I could never have imagined how hard your nipples would be for me. You wanted this, *khanum*. You wanted me to take your nipples."

"I know, I know. But it's too much, it's too . . . much—"

"It's not too much. I'm going to hold on to these hard little tips all night. Whatever do you, even when you sleep, *khanum*, my fingers will be caressing your nipples."

"I didn't know," she moaned, shimmying her body away from his touch. "I didn't understand what you meant."

"You knew," he contradicted relentlessly. "You wanted this. You were furious before I came into the tent that I hadn't come to you immediately and begun the seduction of your nipples. No gentle Englishman here, *khanum*. I take what I want. And your nipples"—he compressed them again meaningfully—"are what I want. Every night after the journey, you will give me them, just like this, for whatever I want to do. Even if all I want is to hold them between my fingers like this for hours, or days, or months. If you're not willing to give them to me under those conditions, we'll kill the bargain now, and I'll take you back to Sefra."

He began thumbing her nipples, back and forth over the stiff protruding tips, back and forth, back and forth, in an erotic rhythm that sent liquid heat sliding through her veins. As she swooned, he began with his thumb, hard over the nipple, and then he compressed it, hard, compress, hard, compress until she sagged against him, and he guided her down onto a pillow.

"Well, *khanum*." He tucked the pillow under her so that her back was arched, and he took her nipples back between his fingers. "Do you want to take these incredible nipples back to Sefra, or do you want me to have them for my pleasure?"

She couldn't talk; the pleasure was so intense.

"Ah, *khanum* is overcome. Thank goodness you lay down; it's much easier to fondle your nipples this way."

She made a sound and arched her nipples up toward his caressing fingers. They closed around the hard points tightly this time, and she made a low growl in the back of her throat.

"Did you say enough pleasure, *khanum?* That you want to return to Sefra? That you've had enough of my voracious need to fondle your nipples?"

She writhed against his fingers, panting.

"I told you, I wanted to own your nipples." He held them so tightly now, so masterfully, just the very hard tip. "And now you must tell me, *khanum*. Telll me what you want."

She gasped, and arched at an even more acute angle against his fingers.

"*Khanum* appears not to like the way I fondle her nipples or surely she would have expressed her pleasure."

"No, no, no," she panted, her body pumping now in rhythm to his caresses. "More . . ."

"More what?"

"More . . . ohhhh . . . I want . . ."

"Sefra, since you are so displeased?"

"Nipples . . ." she moaned. "Don't stop—don't . . ."

"That is what I thought," he murmured in some satisfaction as he settled himself more comfortably for the night. The long pleasurable night. "That is absolutely *what* I thought."

Chapter Eleven

What had he done to her? In the cool light of morning, as she lay on her side in the curve of his body, and felt his hands still on her breasts, she felt the shimmering ache of unsatiated pleasure. He had made her swoon and yearn and beg for the release he would not give her.

She felt explosive still, and yet, there was pleasure. Incredible bone-melting pleasure just from the way he manipulated her breasts and her nipples. This was the promise and the passion to come from his preoccupation with her breasts.

The thought made her body heavy and languid with desire. She stretched and his fingers tightened around her nipples. A stream of molten heat spiraled between her legs, and she wriggled her hips against the cradle of his.

"Such erect nipples, even in the morning," he whispered against her ear. "I can't let them go." Gently he compressed them between his fingers. "I don't know how I will get through the day until I can fondle them again. So I must make the most of this morning that I have them in my hands." Three fingers now around each nipple, just *there*.

She went limp at the pressure and the lightning pleasure that bolted through her.

"Such responsive nipples," he murmured. "I can't let them go."

"Don't let them go," she sighed, rubbing her buttocks against his body. His rock-hard penis, rather, that he would not give to her. Not yet anyway. He was as stubborn as a rock. No fucking. God, she needed fucking.

No, she needed his fingers playing with her nipples. Holding them and squeezing them. She felt like she was swirling out of control. Every fiber of her being was centered on her nipples and the masterful pressure of his fingers.

She was wet with it, hot with it. She needed his penis. She needed something hard or she was going to erupt—

He felt her agitation, loved the wild twisting of her body against his, as she sought his root. Not this time. Much as he was bursting for her, much as fondling her nipples made him cream over and over, he would keep his word— no fucking. Her nipples were enough. At least for today. Tonight—well, a man had to be a martyr to contain himself in the face of such unbridled sexuality.

After a night like last night, any man would embed himself to the hilt in a body this responsive, this libidinous, and not move his penis for a week.

But he was not just any man. And this was not just any body. And those nipples were so tantalizing, so luscious, so voluptuous—he would make sure no one man possessed them the way he did, and that she wanted no other man to possess them after him.

"*Cadi, cadi . . .*" Rashmi, a shadowy figure scurrying around outside the tent.

Charles uttered a curse and then answered him. "We must break camp. I need to help him and you must get dressed. No, I will hold your nipples while you dress so I can have the pleasure of them to the very last moment possible."

It was impossible to dress while he was fondling and squeezing the tips like that. She kept backing away, and he kept pursuing her.

"How can I dress with your fingers in the way?"

"I don't want you to cover your breasts. I want you to ride with me this afternoon so I can fondle your nipples under your *abeya*. Tonight is too many hours away. Even five minutes is too much time away from them."

"It's too much."

"Too much? Too much—what, *khanum*? This morning, it wasn't too much. Last night, you begged me to take them and play with them. So what is too much when I promised I would be the most greedy lover of your nipples? I haven't yet begun to show you the depth of my hunger for them."

Her breath caught. That was his promise: that there was so much more to come. And she had agreed to give her nipples over to him. That was the bargain, and he was definitely keeping up his end of it.

So what indeed was too much? The pleasure? The time? They had all the time in the world in the desert. They could spend weeks hunkered down just here and he could do everything to her breasts he promised and more.

The thought made her shudder with excitement.

She bowed her head. "I misspoke. Nothing you desire is too much. And I will ride with you this afternoon even though it will be difficult to wait until then to feel your fingers on my nipples again."

He eased his fingers from her breasts and she shivered, suddenly cold, suddenly bereft.

Her reaction was not lost on him. She might be just a little raw with the way he handled her all night, but she understood who was her master, and she already wanted it.

His hands flexed. He didn't know how he was going to get through all the hours until he could have her breasts again. Even under the cover of her *abeya*.

He'd settle for that to have them sooner. To have her hot and swooning in his hands.

"Get dressed," he said briskly. "I have to help Rashmi load the camels. It's going to be a long, hot, dreary day . . ."

And it was—hot and dreary—starting from the moment they were ready to begin the day's trek, beginning with a restive camel that had to be pulled down and calmed with a plug of tobacco in its nostril. And then the inevitable walk out into that eternal nothingness. The interminable heat, the blazing sun, the infinite sky.

And Georgie's feeling that somehow she had reneged on the bargain just by that moment's hesitation.

Nevertheless, forward they went, with the camels lumbering after them. Mile after mile of yellow sand, rippled by the wind, baked by the sun. And now and again a ridge of sand dunes rising up in the distance, looking as impossible to traverse as mountains.

They had to be careful of desiccated animals that were prey for hyenas by night, and insects and scorpions, whose sting could paralyze a body for days.

They were aiming to travel twenty miles in a day, and on the fifth day, to arrive at a well deep in the Kalahari to refresh the animals and their water supply.

But meantime, there was the sun, the sand, and nothing much else.

No, there was a pool of memories of all he had done the night before. Memories to savor and arouse and incite desire.

She was too easily aroused even before she had come to this unholy bargain. And now, after a night with him, and all that unslaked need pent up in her, not even the desert heat could keep her from boiling over.

And how would she contain herself, seated with him on the plodding camel, and being fondled under her robes?

She felt her body spurt at the thought. Everything in her quickened, tensed, became erect.

No, no. It was too soon in the day to think about sex.

She glanced across to him, stolidly walking beside her. What was he thinking? It could be nothing more than how hot it was and how long this day's journey would be.

And then he looked at her, and she felt a deep tremor in her vitals. Her body gushed; her nipples tightened. He was thinking about her, her naked body, her breasts, her nipples. It was in his eyes and grimness of his expression. He was counting the minutes until he could possess them.

Perhaps he was sorry they'd begun this trip, perhaps he thought they should have stayed in Sefra where he would have had all the time in the world to explore his passion for her breasts.

And now they had to endure the heat, the discomfort, and the endless hours of this long trek to nowhere.

Their lunch break was quick: fruit and water and on their way again, this time mounted on camel.

It was awkward, being up with him; hard to find purchase to keep her seat and to make herself available to him.

"Lean back against me, *khanum,*" he whispered against her veil. "My fingers will find the way to you."

She sank back against his hard tight body. She felt his hands sliding up under her robe and sleek over her hips and belly and her breath caught.

"I keep my promises," he whispered, and his hands were on her breasts, and then he captured her nipples between his thumb and forefinger. "That is all I wanted, *khanum.* Just to have your nipples with me in the heat of the day. Just to be able to feel them hard against my fingers, to hold them like this, to fondle them like this, so you are aware that I alone possess them."

His words made her body weak. His hands were hot, his fingers gentle and dangerous as he held her nipples. He had only to pluck the tips gently to send her shimmering out of control.

She wanted him to. He wanted to. His body was taut as a bow, his penis a ridge of stone against her buttocks. He knew what he had the power to do with those fingers. If he would just tweak the nipple tip, she would erupt. She shimmied against him, goading him, but that only provoked him to cover both breasts with the palms of his hands.

She moaned in disappointment.

"*Khanum* doesn't understand the pleasures of her nipples. I must wait until the evening when she can be freely naked so I can show her."

"Show me now," she begged.

"And now she implores me; she who this morning thought my adoration of her nipples was *too much* now begs for me to service them at her need. No, *khanum,* even I, in my hunger for them, am finding that waiting thickens my desire for them and prolongs the pleasure of knowing they will be mine and mine alone tonight. And so, I will wait for the evening when you are naked and we are alone in our tent, and then, I will service your nipples as only I can."

She could barely breathe at the thought. *As only he could.* Her body was liquid with need, swamped with images of how he would service her nipples.

She could seduce him, surely, even high up on the hump of a camel. And he would do all those things and more, if she could just—

"And now, *khanum,* you must take your own camel. To have you near me is seduction in itself, and your body is hard to resist. For both our sakes, we must wait until there is privacy and time and you can be naked for me."

Anger flashed through her, and a sense of him playing with her on some other level. He reined in his camel, and helped her ease off into Rashmi's waiting hands, and it was Rashmi who got her mounted on hers.

And then more sand, more sun, more sky, and her simmering resentment that he would arouse her to this volcanic point, and not fuck her.

This was a bad bad bargain for her. She had no control, none. And her body felt ill-used. Well, not ill-*used.* Charles Elliott knew very well how to use a woman's body. He was toying with her, withholding his penis and letting her suffer for some reason. To pay for her sins in the Valley?

But the Valley seemed like another world now, and her whole life seemed centered on *him* and his pleasuring of her nipples.

Maybe that was the curse of the desert, the immediacy of it, the loneliness of it, the intimacy of it . . .

Maybe she had more power here than she thought. He was absolutely infatuated with her breasts, and that, she was certain, was real. And the only two times she had incurred his displeasure was when she had negated that. When she had said it was too much, when she had tried to take control.

Interesting. Then pure complete submission would confer power. Hers over him, acceding willingly to that which she had traded away already—his complete possession and domination of her nipples.

She had lost nothing in the bargain. Except that he refused to fuck her. But she got something in return: his obsession with her nipples and the pleasure he incited in them.

As only he could . . .
He owned them and he couldn't bear to think of an-
other man touching them, fondling them, stroking them.
As only he could . . .
That was power.
She shuddered. And there was more to come—tonight.

This was getting dangerous. He was besotted by her nipples, so intoxicated he hardly knew what he was doing or saying when he had his hands on them. And lord of all mercies, he meant half the things he'd said.

This was too dangerous. He was too out of his mind over them. He couldn't afford to fall in love with a woman's nipples. Not in the desert and not in the real world.

Except here in the infinite desert, he had all the time in the world to spend on her breasts. Much as she wanted to fuck. Much as he had to control himself with a mighty hand when he was with her.

It was hard. And he was achingly hard every minute of the day, and it was hard controlling himself, and even harder when he was fingering her nipples.

But that was the bargain, he owned her nipples. In the desert, there was no future, no tomorrow; there was only now, and his unholy desire to possess her nipples. And his ravenous need to make her beg for it, beg for his hands, his caresses, his touch.

And what would happen when they reached civilization? He didn't want to think about it. Didn't need to just yet because she was waiting for him now, naked, her nipples jutting and prominent even in shadow. And he went hot and hard with the knowledge that he was the one, the only one, who would fondle those nipples tonight, tomorrow night, and every ensuing night.

*   *   *

"Khanum..."

She wheeled around from the far corner of the tent to find him standing there, watching her, his penis hard and straining, looking as if it would burst out of his trousers.

He had removed his headdress, and his robe, and his shirt. He stood commandingly with his hands on his hips, and he was waiting for her.

...khanum...the power of a woman's body, a woman's breasts to make a man come to heel...

She felt it now as she sauntered across the brief space between them and pressed the hard points of her nipples against his bare chest. Just the nipple tips, nothing more, and he felt it so deep in his gut he creamed.

She felt his body shudder and felt pure triumphant pride that it was solely the touch of her hard nipples against his hot skin that had made him ejaculate.

"Show me the pleasures of my nipples, *cadi,*" she whispered. "It has been torture waiting for you to come for my breasts after all these hours."

He ruthlessly got himself under control. He couldn't afford to spew every time she touched him, and he couldn't take much more of the pressure of her nipples against him without coming again. He was already an iron bar of need just seeing her naked after all the hours she had been covered head to foot. And his penis apparently couldn't differentiate between an orgasm and arousal. It was poker hard all over again, and it wanted nothing but to embed itself in *her.*

Not now.

"It is more torture for a man, giving up the chance to fondle such luscious nipples for the greater pleasure of the freedom to play with them naked and for as long as he desires later. You don't know how much torture, *khanum,* because the imagination runs riot in the desert, and all the things that a man could have been and could have done remain only a possibility. But now, some things can become a reality. Give me your nipples."

She moaned at the back of her throat. "They are yours to take, *cadi.*" *As only you can . . .*

He lifted his hand and touched the tingling tips, and immediately her body spasmed.

He made a deep guttural sound of satisfaction and enclosed the stiff tips relentlessly in his fingers, pressing against them rhythmically as she swooned again him. "Now . . . *khanum* . . . now I will service your nipples." He plucked at them, first one and then the other, back and forth, once, twice, three times, and then together, pulling at the hard tips relentlessly, until she was moaning and convulsing and begging him to stop.

"I don't stop, *khanum.* I am the master of your nipples and I will pleasure them." And he pulled gently, implacably once again, and her body seized up and convulsed again and again, and she felt each pull deep between her legs.

Where his penis should be, she thought in a haze, but how much more pleasure could she stand? She could barely stand; her legs went soft as the gush of sensation eddied away.

And still he fingered her nipples. And she found herself arching her back to entice him to continue his delicious fondling.

"And so, *khanum,* I have pleasured you well. And see how you bend toward my fingers as if to beg for more. Yes, you want more. As much I will give you, you want. Your nipples will stay hard and even more erect, yearning for it. You will try to entice me to give you more. It is but the beginning of the many nights I will service your nipples. And only the nights, *khanum,* because that is the only time I have enough leisure to service your nipples properly."

She moaned, a desperate little sound. *"Cadi . . ."*

"Yes, I am your master. And your nipples are mine to pleasure as I will. I am not done yet. You are naked and we have the whole night . . . my reward for having waited—" He gently twisted one nipple and a stream of sensation gushed between her legs, and she gasped. And then he gently tweaked both nipples, and the skirling pleasure was so intense, her knees buckled and she sank onto the floor, pulling him down onto the pillows with her.

He was poised above her, supporting himself on his elbows, his fingers still surrounding her nipples. His hips rocked against hers, his penis a bulging rock between her legs. His face was inches from hers, and she licked her lips in anticipation that he would kiss her. Surely he would kiss her . . . after that unexpected flooding culmination. She was so ready for him, he could just slide himself between her legs. She was so wet, so ripe, so unaware of the potential of her breasts.

"All night, *khanum,* and you cannot seduce my penis, I promise you."

"I can try."

"I am determined."

"Your trousers are wet. I can feel it. You couldn't fondle my breasts and not lose control."

"Aren't you full of yourself, *khanum?* And yet here I am, fondling your breasts, and still in control."

"It will be my personal challenge to make you spew."'

"And it will be mine to prevent you."

"Why? *Why?* We can do whatever we want here. Anything we want. Everything we want."

"I am doing what I want, *khanum.* This is what you don't comprehend. I have what I want—your naked nipples in my hands every night." He squeezed them, and her body contracted. "You see?"

"I see," she whispered, but more than that, she saw that

she had him on his knees, cradled between her legs and nudging her tightly with the desire he was trying to deny.

There was a secret there, one that was wholly her own. And a journey still to be made that had nothing to do with her journey to England.

What was inevitable then? That she would be the one to give in? A woman always did. As hard and as desperate as she was to seduce him, she would give in, and she would submit to his pleasuring her breasts, breathlessly counting the days until he fell from his own grace into her arms and into her bed.

Chapter Twelve

The days thereafter fell into a pattern that were just a prelude to the intoxicating nights. Now that she was full of power and pleasure of submitting to him, she spent the long tedious hours of the journey in a haze of anticipation.

Everything was heightened, even more so because of the heat, the long scorching hours wading through the sand, the fact that they both were shrouded head to foot. They each spent the travel time deep in remembrance of the previous night's pleasuring, impatient for the night to come.

And what did that do but arouse them both still more. Because the more nights he spent with her naked, the more he played with her breasts, the more he knew it was coming, the moment he couldn't deny, the moment when he couldn't refuse her his penis.

But he meant to hold out until then—and beyond. It was a test of will, to be able to hold this woman's breasts in thrall and still not capitulate to her. It was a test of his resolve not to give in to her.

But it was coming, he felt it in his soul. He needed to own *her* through the pleasure of her breasts. There was nothing she wouldn't give him now, nothing more he wanted than her response to his hands.

It was all he thought about all day long. And he knew it was all she was thinking about too. And he hated it that he couldn't have her naked and to himself all day long. The night was never long enough for all he wanted do to her. Inevitably they fell asleep, invariably he awakened with his hands cupping her breasts from behind, and her bare curvy bottom wedged against his rampaging penis, and there was very little time to think about pleasure then.

But they couldn't take the time to stop for a day's sensual play, so he was prone to let his imagination run riot until that breath-catching moment he entered the tent, closed out the world, and took her breasts in his hands.

Her nipples were always hot, hard, and erect for him, her body ripe and immediately responsive. He had only to flick his thumb across one rigid tip to make her churn.

The first time he took that nipple into the wet heat of his mouth, she almost fainted, the sensation was so intense. After that, he couldn't keep his mouth off of them, and she couldn't wait until darkness fell so he could suckle her.

All of this was outside her experience, even in the Valley. There was never a man who took this kind of time in play before he got down to business. It all revolved around a man's *business,* and every woman was available for the asking.

But this—this was luscious, the attention he paid to her breasts. Sometimes he covered her nipples with honey or wine and spent hours licking and sucking them all through the night as they lay together languidly among the pillows.

And now, he could not stop himself. Sucking her nipples was too much, even for his iron control. He was starting to want more. He wanted to spew his essence all over her breasts. He wanted to rub it into her nipples.

He wanted . . .

He wanted too much.

But that was how it was in the desert. There was no sense of reality, only the desire of the moment to be fulfilled. And that was his most secret desire: to cover her rigid tips with his cream and watch her rub it into her nipples.

So he came to her that night, laid her down on the pillows, undressed himself, straddled her, and began the torturous pleasure of rubbing his penis back and forth over her nipples as she lay under him.

She could but watch. He wouldn't let her touch him. He wanted to come solely from the sensation of sliding his shaft between her breasts and all over her nipples.

It didn't take long. His penis was so stiff, his body so tight with all that pentup need. And then *she,* with her knowing eyes and her magic fingers, put out her hand and grasped him right *there,* and he shot like a geyser.

All over her breasts, her nipples, trickling down toward her belly. Some on her chest and neck, her cheek. Her one hand still tight around the base of his penis, her fingers massaging his essence into her skin, into the curve of her right breast, her areola, her nipple.

He felt himself coming again just watching her fingers rubbing his fluid all over her nipple. He jammed himself against her hand once, twice, three times. He felt himself gathering, spewing, and drowning as a huge spurt pooled on the tip of her breast, and she held him still, and rubbed his thick cream into her skin with her free hand.

They slept, as they always did, back to front, with his hands on her breasts and her buttocks tucked against his hips. But this night was different—he was naked, his erection ferocious, his penis there for the taking, wedged, sometime during the night, between her legs, so that her naked cleft sat against his shaft.

This was delicate. It was as if they both realized it at the same time and awakened simultaneously. It was still dark. Their world was still theirs, with no intrusions. The intimacy was there, heightened by his nakedness, by the memory of him stroking himself on her breasts.

He felt himself elongating at the thought. His fingers tightened around her erect nipples. She wriggled to settle herself more decisively on his shaft, spreading her lips to enfold his hardness.

Her body shuddered as she felt the length of his rigid shaft jammed against her. She could ride him now, even if he wouldn't fuck her. She could still have the hardness of him right where she wanted it, right and tight against that pleasure point between her legs.

Now if he would just . . .

He would. He knew, from the undulation of her hips, from the thickening scent of sex, just what she wanted, and he rounded his fingers over her nipples and pulled and plucked them.

Her body melted. She ground her hips down onto the stone-hard ledge and rode his shaft, caressing and fondling him, and shimmying and writhing as if she were desperate to get away from his fingers.

And yet she wanted more; she pushed her breasts against his fingers, demanding he do more, more, more, and he did, pulling and tweaking the rigid points until she almost couldn't stand it, until the sweet-hot moment he squeezed them, hard, and they both spiraled into a hot bone-crackling orgasm.

No words after that. What could express what she had felt, what he had done? She shifted her body so that she was not enveloping his shaft. He cupped her breasts; she slipped her fingers all over the semen on his penis.

"Don't ever waste your cream again," she whispered. "It would be better still if you filled me with it."

"No fucking. Those were my terms."

"What do you call what we are doing?"

"Exactly what I said, pleasuring your nipples. Anything else is incidental."

"Tell yourself that, *cadi*," she murmured. "That is *your* truth."

"And what is yours?" he wanted to know. "What is your truth after all these days?"

She smiled, a smile he couldn't see but he could sense, the smile of a woman well pleased. "My truth is that you have done as you promised. You have been the most greedy, the most voracious lover of my breasts, and in that, you are the master of all things."

And then, as dawn broke and filtered through the tent, as she awakened, and her body unfurled like a flower, she shifted herself so that he was lying below her and she was propped on the pillows, with her breasts just within reach of his mouth and tongue, as she tempted him to feed on her.

This was the most intimate moment, one she loved to watch closely, when he took her into his mouth and played with one nipple, one breast, licking it and pressing it, and curling his tongue around it until he took it wholly into his mouth to suck on it.

It was as if he were pulling a molten thread of pleasure from her vulva to her nipple, and it was so keen, so fierce, she almost couldn't bear it.

And in this position, she could do nothing with her hands, nothing to touch his shaft, nothing to incite him. He was an iron man, hardened like stone, thriving on the heat of her responsiveness, withholding that one thing.

How much more could he do to her and not fuck her? It was but a passing thought as he tugged and pulled at her nipple with his lips. And then everything came to an explosive point, her body bucked as waves of pleasure rocketed through her. And then she just didn't care.

He laid her down on the pillows, his own body as ready to blow as it ever had been. She had only to touch him; he had only to slide between her legs and she would take him willingly, wantonly, and ride him home.

But he didn't want her to touch him. That was the Valley way. This was his. For the next five days in this hot, circular little world, her breasts and her body belonged to him, any way he wished to use them.

Today, they would make the well; perhaps they would rest a day before continuing on. He could have her then, day and night. He could imprint her with his lust for her breasts.

Even as she lay there, spent, he wanted them. They were so round, so full, the nipples so erect and prominent, made for a man's mouth, a man's touch.

But thinking like that was dangerous. His obsession with her breasts was far too dangerous. And when they reached the real world, what then?

He didn't want to think about it.

In their world, there was no one but themselves, no one to see, no one to hear, no one to know, and he could do with her as he wished, everything he had promised. He could indulge his most voluptuous greed morning and night.

Nothing else mattered except that. And they had at least five more days of hedonistic mornings and nights to come.

Only five days—?

Her breasts beckoned. She turned and looked at him, a sultry heat simmering in her gaze. It was still early, so early. There was so little time. And she wanted it. And he just could not leave her nipples alone.

*   *   *

She had too much time, as the journey progressed that day, to think. It seemed to her the more he played with her breasts, the more she needed him to play with them.

It was the strangest equation, intensified by the fact she was under her *abeya* and her nipples were constantly erect. And wanting. This was a new sensation for her. She couldn't get enough of his handling them and sucking them. She wanted days and days of just that—the two of them alone as they were nights and mornings only now, and his unbridled possession of her breasts.

She was breathless most of the day and sunk in a swamp of remembering all they had done during the night and the early morning. He was utterly enslaved by them, and she was totally enthralled by the pleasure he gave her. Waiting for this evening when they would make the well seemed an impossible task. She wanted to strip off her robes and have him take her nipples *now.*

The heat was getting to her, the desert heat and her own libidinous heat, stoked by his covert glances, and her body's traitorous need to feel his hands on her breasts.

Five more days to go . . .

Only five? It seemed as if they would go on forever, as if there were no end whatsoever to the sun, sand, and sky, as if they were in their own glorious little world where no one else could intrude.

Only five more days . . .

It seemed like five days before they would even stop for the night. She felt an escalating urgency that there would never be enough time for all she wanted him to do to her.

Five days . . .

She sat hunched over her camel's neck as she scanned the horizon for anything that looked like a place they could camp. But there was only sand and sun for as far as she could see.

And yet Rashmi led them with the confidence of a guide

who knew all the secrets of the desert. He had to know theirs, but he was being paid enough to camp far away from their tent and ignore them. It was almost like having a ghost in camp.

And that was well and good. Her pleasure was too private for anything else, and she wanted it now. And there was only the sun and sand to comfort her.

As they proceeded farther west and north, ridges of dunes rose up like waves before them.

"Never go alone on the dunes," Charles cautioned. "You will lose sight of everything, get turned around, get lost, and possibly die."

"I never want to be alone," she murmured, and he sent her a sharp, telling look. He wanted it more than she: their private time could not come soon enough.

Three hours later there was a speck on the horizon.

"*Cadi, cadi*—we are here, we are here—" Rashmi was almost dancing for joy.

And it wasn't even dusk.

"We'll make camp here for a day," Charles decreed.

"Too much time, *cadi.*"

"I am weary. The camels are weary. We need rest, we need water, we need time."

Rashmi bowed. "As you say, *cadi.*"

But as they came closer, they could see that there was barely any shade. There were three or four scraggly palm trees overlooking a wellspring that wasn't more than ten feet across.

"It is enough," Rashmi said. "We will rest."

He helped Charles raise their tent as close to the trees as possible, helped him off-load the camels, and then, she and Charles retreated to the privacy of the tent, while he fed the animals and started coaxing a little fire for cooking.

"Tell him to go away," she moaned, ripping off her robes and veil.

He reached for her nipples, pressing them firmly between his fingers. "I couldn't wait another minute to take you like this."

She felt breathless, as if the sensation of his fingers squeezing her was as new as the dawn. "We have all afternoon and night and all tomorrow to ourselves . . . it's not enough—"

"I don't want to move."

She contracted her body slightly, so that he was forced to come to her. "Don't move then. Don't stop—just keep doing that to my nipples."

He tugged at them. "We should have something to eat or drink."

"Are you hungry?" she whispered.

"Only for your nipples . . ." He bent over and took one hard tip into his mouth. Just the tip. Between his lips, compressing it, and pulling at it while he still held her other nipple between his fingers.

The familiar darts of pleasure assaulted her vitals.

"Don't stop . . ." she begged.

He made sound around his sucking of her nipple and then covered it tightly with his tongue, and fed even more avidly on it.

The whole afternoon, the whole evening, without coming out of the tent for something to eat, something to drink, he feasted on her breasts until she lay weak and sated on her throne of pillows, her body bursting for still more.

Then they ate and drank just to take a small respite from the intensity of his devouring possession of her. But he positioned her against the pillows so that her breasts were thrust forward, her nipples erect and protuberant, and it was his visual feast while he ate.

Then he disrobed, his eyes never leaving her naked body, and she saw that his penis was hard as an iron bar, and that he had wasted some cream.

"Don't speak of it," he warned her. "My semen is mine to waste."

"It could be mine."

"I will only give you my cream for your nipples."

She eased herself up from the pillows and reached for his penis. "Then give it to me now."

"Don't touch me. Lay down . . ." He moved to straddle her, positioning himself just above her hips so that the head of his penis was even with her nipples.

She couldn't help it; he was so huge and luscious and ripe that she had to take him in her hand. The moment she moved the undershaft across one blooming nipple, he shot all over her chest.

She was dripping with his essence. It was thick, creamy, clinging to the tips of her nipples, oozing down to her neck, her shoulders, and still she held him, she pumped him and she made him ooze and spew some more.

And then with her other hand, she swiped some of his cream from her nipple and licked it from her finger.

"Fuck me now," she begged. "I'm so wet for you, and you—you've barely shot all the cream boiling inside you. You want to . . . I want you to . . ."

She was too tempting, with her stiff nipples and bulging areolae clotted with his cum, and her legs spread, and her coaxing words. But this was not about his taking his pleasure.

It never had been about that. It was about their bargain, about what he wanted and what she agreed to. Nothing more. Nothing less.

In spite of the seduction of her nipples and her body, and his uncontrollable lust for her breasts.

He shifted himself so that he wouldn't be tempted to just slide his penis between her legs.

"No fucking."

She rolled up to a sitting position. "Then let me ride your shaft again while you play with my nipples. At least I'll have the feel of you between my legs, and I know I'll have your cream."

She was Eve, the way she coaxed and tempted him. She climbed up onto his thighs, nestled her buttocks into his hips, and positioned his penis between her legs. Then she shimmied and wriggled to spread herself as widely as possible onto his shaft, while pulling and nudging his penis into submission.

"That feels good," she whispered. "That's perfect. Now . . ." She arched back against him and he slid his hands over her breasts and downward to her belly and hips and back up again to catch her cream-coated nipples between his thumb and forefinger.

Her breath caught. There was something inexorable in his touch, something indomitable in the way he held her nipples. It was like the first time, when he wouldn't let her go. He was not going to let her nipples go no matter how hard she rode him, how many times she climaxed.

He had her where he wanted her now, and he would hold her there, just by her nipples, all day, all night, forever.

A different kind of excitement coursed through her. She ground down more firmly against his shaft.

And then she waited. And waited.

And he held her, and held her, not moving, not caressing her, not squeezing or pulling. Just there, surrounding her nipples with his fingers and holding her so she felt the very nakedness of her body.

Her breath went short. She couldn't sit still. She wanted

to coerce him to move his fingers, to stroke and caress her. She shimmied her breasts, she bounced on his shaft, she undulated her hips, she contracted her belly—and still he held her.

And he held her, like his fingers were some kind of ornament just encircling her nipples, and there was nothing she could do to dislodge them.

He held her. Not too hard, just firmly enough so he possessed her nipples. Just like that.

Through the afternoon. Into early evening. She sat mounted on his thighs, her cunt lips spread on his penis, his fingers compressing her nipples gently, firmly, possessively.

And he whispered in her ear. About her incredible nipples. About how hot and hard and responsive they were. How much he lusted after them. About how he spent every day's journey planning how he would fondle and feel them to pleasure her. How he couldn't get enough of them. How he needed them naked day and night.

And this was the one night he wouldn't let them go.

And she whispered to him that no one had ever fondled her nipples as he did. That only he could make her nipples so hot, so stiff, and so responsive and that no man had ever made her feel such voluptuous pleasure in them. He was the master of her nipples, and she didn't want him to move his fingers from them—ever.

And so they sat, with her body arched against his and her straddling his penis, and him holding her just by her nipples.

The pleasure was incandescent, fierce, of the mind and the body.

Now and again, he spurted. Now and again she rubbed it into his penis and licked it from her finger.

She rocked gently against his shaft as the sun slowly

sank and the light in the tent waned. Her body spasmed, suddenly, without warning, a blast of orgasmic heat taking her unaware.

And still he held her nipples.

Pleasure, pleasure, pleasure—there ought to be another word for it, she thought hazily. It wasn't nearly strong enough for what she felt, for what he made her feel just by manipulating her nipples.

Five more days . . .

They had this whole night, and the next whole day. They wouldn't move. It was their world, centered wholly and completely on his worship of her nipples.

She was a goddess, in thrall to his fingers and his mouth and what he made her feel.

As only he could . . .

The most voracious lover of your nipples . . .

There could be no one more insatiable than he. Every promise kept—

As only he could . . .

Five more days . . .

No no no. She would be his harem of one, and they could stay in the desert forever. Wasn't he the son of a Bedouin prince? They could travel and he could root in her day and night. The only responsibility they would have would be to their sex because he was accustomed to the heat and all things of the desert.

"*Khanum?*" His voice was rough, ragged, his fingers spasming on her nipples. It was finally too much, too long, too hard. She was too exciting, too provoking, too naked, too everything a queen and a temptress should be, and all his will and strength could not stem the flood rising within his penis.

"*Cadi?*" she whispered, grasping his throbbing shaft.

And he came—against everything he wanted, everything

he promised, and his obdurate will—like a geyser; all his pentup emotion, every creamy drop from all the times he never fucked her . . . an endless spume of fruitless denial.

And she pulled his penis tight against her belly so all his creamy semen coated her, chest to crotch, slathers of it, luscious, thick, and sticky, and still she pumped him for more.

Deep in the desert with only five more days to be naked with her, to have those nipples and that body and to do everything he wanted to do with her, involuntarily and unforgivably, he lost control.

"Ah, *cadi*—" she whispered, pushing him backward, onto the pillows. "Even in this, you are the master of me."

Chapter Thirteen

Now there was firelight sending an orange glow into the tent as Rashmi cooked the evening meal.

They lay side by side on the blankets, neither speaking. He was too shaken by the depth of his orgasm; she was simmering at his willful waste of it.

"This could have been for us both," she said finally.

"You aren't comprehending, *khanum*. This is not about me and my needs, and since you have had enough pleasure to fill a well, I can't understand your irritation."

"My irritation is in the fact that there is so much pleasure to be had."

"But those were not my terms, *khanum*. I want what I want, irrespective of what my body thinks it wants."

"You are not stronger-willed than your penis."

"Trust me, I am."

"Not today."

"No. Not today." But that didn't negate his desire to keep their bargain, or his rising need to possess her again. To mark her breasts as his own. "But I will keep trying; a man's will should be able to override his penis."

Rashmi's voice sang out.

"The food is cooked," Charles translated. "You needn't dress. I'll bring the plate to you."

He was a desert brigand, she thought as she watched him duck out of the tent. Tall, dark, brooding, bare-chested, bold. And this, no matter what might happen after, was the adventure of her life.

And dear heaven, *after* was not that far off; her adventure would be over, soon.

Not to think about that. There was still the delights of the night to come. And tomorrow, and five days beyond that.

Forever, it seemed, now.

The evening meal of overcooked lamb, lentils, and tea did not enhance the mood. "Well, he is a guide, not a cook," Charles pointed out. "And we will feast on so much more before the night is out."

She felt that little trill of anticipation. "And we need not break camp in the morning?"

"No," Charles said slowly, "just this once, we need not break camp in the morning."

They spent the night in a gluttonous haze, exploring how much sensation she could feel through her nipples, until she was wrung out and aching and just a little raw.

In the morning, there was coffee, dried bread, fruit, served early, and then a whole morning and early afternoon of nuzzling and nibbling as orgiastically voluptuous as anything he'd done yet.

He had never known a woman like her. Never known a body like hers, so ripe and so willing, to try, to feel, to explore. She was a true child of the Valley, because no other woman anywhere would have welcomed his attentions like that, and given herself over so completely, so fully, so wantonly.

It begged the question of what it would be like if he

were to fuck her. If there were any kind of full-blown liaison between them.

But that was impossible. There was no fantasy involving her that ever culminated with her by his side. She was a born courtesan, not a consort, not a mate, not a wife. And once he had that clear in his mind, it would be easy to let her go.

Would it?

He stared down at the cup of water in his hand. He had told her that his father's people marked their women, that he wanted to mark her breasts as his own. He felt adamant about it, more possessive than ever about it. In spite of his feelings about her and what would ultimately become of her.

And that was because their desert sojourn was another world where all things were possible, and everything he said, everything he wanted was true, and nothing was a lie.

And he owned her breasts.

He'd purchased two items in the *souk* at Sefra she knew nothing about: a little pot of henna powder and a brush, and a tiny glittery diamond suspended from a silver filament.

These he brought to the tent the evening of their overnight stay in this wellspring oasis and he settled himself on his haunches in the tent, and began mixing the water with the henna until it attained the consistency of ink.

She watched avidly, wondering what he was going to do with the thin brush and little pot of ink.

"Now, *khanum,* according to our agreement: to do with as I wish . . . give me your left breast."

Her heart thumped. "As you will, *cadi,*" she whispered coming to stand next to him. He rose up with his little pot of liquid henna, dipped the brush into it and began painting her breast, around the nipple and areola, making elongated half ovals that looked like the petals of a flower. Eight petals, with her nipple at the center, to be fed on by his hummingbird tongue.

It was the most erotic thing he'd done yet. Her body liquefied as she looked down at him painting her breast; it aroused her intensely that he had claimed her in this way, and the thin feathery feeling of the brush at the edge of her nipple made it stand out even more prominently.

More erotically.

He laid her down so the henna would dry without a smear. And even that innocent gesture sent his imagination careening, and made him breathless with desire.

Heaven help him, he wanted her right now, and again after. The feeling roared deep inside him, almost out of control. To see her lying there like that . . .

Almost he wanted to fuck her. Almost he wanted to spill his seed inside her body, outside, on the breasts, in her mouth, and all over the tent.

Almost . . .

Too, too dangerous. And yet, he would go one step further in his growing obsession with her breasts: the silver filament.

And if he adorned her with that, then what? All his life he would imagine her wearing it, wearing it not for him either, but for whatever men she would take into her life once they left their tight isolated world in the desert.

The desert was her life, and his will and desire, for these ensuing five days, and he felt almost irrational about it, that he must mark her any way he could to make her his.

"Take me," she entreated him, as he stood looking at her, at the petals that framed her nipple, at her naked body so restive and needy.

He ignored that. "I have something for you."

"How can this be? Is this adornment not enough?"

"Apparently not. Do you want to see? Come to me now."

She rose up in a fluid motion, her flower breast tempting him almost beyond endurance to touch and feed. Endurance, yes, a man must have the endurance, the stamina of an elephant with a wanton like her.

And none of that diminished his rampaging desire for her breasts. Nothing he knew about her destroyed his ever-raging need for them.

Dangerous, so dangerous. And now he was walking an even thinner line—a boundary between sanity and enslavement—and he didn't care.

He held out his hand. At the end of one finger, the filament dangled, the speck of diamond glimmering in the dimming light.

She licked her lips. "Where is it worn?"

He lifted her right breast and slipped it over her nipple. She could barely feel it, and yet it was there, the diamond dangling from a circlet of silver appended to it. It was so there, her nipple tightened still more.

"Wear this under your robes for me. Let me imagine, as we travel the whole day long, this filament of silver surrounding your nipple in place of my fingers and my desire."

His words made her shudder, made her juices flow. "I will wear it for you, *cadi,* but it will never replace the feeling of your fingers fondling me."

"Nor should it. It is meant only to remind you and keep you ready for the delights to come."

Her body quickened. It was barely late afternoon, and there surely were more delights to come this day. "In that spirit, I will wear the gift."

He nearly came in his trousers just looking at her. So dangerous. It was one thing to use her breasts to ease the boredom of a desert journey. It was quite another to raise her expectations by putting his mark on her, by giving her a gift that was a sensual enhancement.

He was in deep trouble with her, and the only saving grace was the fact he hadn't fucked her.

He had five more days to plan how things would go once they were on their way to England.

Things would be different once they reached Dar el Rabat. Their desert world would be as if it had never existed. The nipple petals would fade. She would put aside the filament, and she would never be naked and free like this again, because she would never have this kind of privacy and isolation from society ever again.

Five more days—and everything would change.

Only five more days of those naked nipples and breasts . . . how would he go on without them? Of course he would. It was just a woman, a particularly enticing, intoxicating woman, but a woman nonetheless and the same as dozens of women and their breasts whom he had known.

Five more days. Then there would be many changes. *She* would change. She would understand there were things she could do, and things she could not do. And one of those things was, she could not offer her breasts to strange men. And another was, she had to conduct herself properly, modestly in her father's house.

She *would* understand that every man was not fair game, and that every man would not want to fuck her. And that every man was not infatuated with her breasts.

Would she?

She would figure it out, once they were away from this fantasy desert world.

But until then—oh, until then, her breasts belonged to him and he intended to feed on them until the very last minute.

*   *   *

Four more days . . .

They'd left the wellspring oasis after that night, having bathed, rested the camels, let them drink, taken on more water, and buried whatever food had spoiled.

They'd walked the first ten or so miles, and rode the remainder, while she tried to keep the filament balanced on her nipple and maintain the proper submissive posture.

It was impossible.

They'd spent the succeeding night in the middle of nowhere, aware that time was growing short. That their world was suddenly subject to time, and that he had no time at all to play with her.

And that they were tired, all of them, from the tedious journey.

Three more days . . .

Slow the journey down; make the time last. Pretend they weren't heading for Dar el Rabat and England. Tell Rashmi to take them to some other place where they could continue to experience endless nights of delights she would never speak of, never tell . . .

Two more days . . .

Not enough time, not—even he wanted to prolong the nights, the mornings, the mere hours that were left. They were awake all night, the pleasure of him at her nipples utterly indescribable and edged with the terrible knowledge that within the next day and a half, there would be no more.

So because of that, there must be as much as possible. And more.

She was wrung out in the morning, coated with him, sinking into it, wrapping herself in it as she got ready to forge through the desert sand.

Everything would change in not even a day . . .

He just couldn't help himself; all he'd wanted to do the

previous night was spew all over her until he was bone dry. And he was—dry as the desert, and still hard as a bone, and in hours it would make no difference whatsoever.

It was over. Everything was over.

Dar el Rabat, the coast, and the end of their desert idyll, was just beyond the horizon.

Dar el Rabat sat perched at the end of the ocean, with fleets of ships bobbing in the curve of the harbor, and mud houses rising up on tiers and ridges from the waterfront.

It was a city of tradesmen and merchants, fishermen and sea captains. There wasn't an hour that a ship wasn't steaming in or out of the harbor to fish or to trade.

It was the gate to the Gold Coast of West Africa, the golden door through which came the curious, the idle, the greedy, the rich.

And when you came to it from the desert, it was the gateway to freedom, afloat in the sea of a grassy plain, bordered by palms and camel-thorn bush, and rising up suddenly on the horizon as if it were a mirage.

They came to Dar el Rabat early the next morning and into streets already bustling with mules, camels, and the babble of a dozen languages and travelers of all nationalities.

Even in the morning. Time did not stand still in Dar el Rabat. Of that Charles was keenly aware. And that to further his purpose was now the order of the day: he would take care of Rashmi first, and everything else after.

Rashmi's services cost fifty *krans,* and he took charge of the camels, which he would take back to Sefra within the week.

Charles then spent the morning selling off everything they'd bought for the trip for another five hundred *krans* to a half dozen different merchants in the city's several *souks,* which gave them enough money to book passage to Cameroon, scheduled the following afternoon.

Georgiana followed several paces behind, utterly dumb-struck by the sights, by the sounds and the scents, by the vast expanse of water as limitless as the desert. This was only a part of the world beyond the Valley.

So now she was truly in his hands, waiting, watching, dizzy with the kaleidoscope of all she was absorbing that she had never seen before.

After he finished conducting business, he took her arm forcefully and they prowled the crowded streets, seeking inexpensive accommodations for the night.

The dream journey was over. There was a certain grim-ness in him now, laced with the knowledge that England was the goal, and deliverance to her father, whatever that might mean, the means to the end, and anything else was out of the question.

He must treat her like a fragile virgin.

Dear God, was there anyone ever less a virgin than she?

Although, shrouded in her *abeya,* she looked like the most chaste of the chaste, her eyes down, her head cov-ered, her stance properly restrained.

"I hate this place," she muttered, as they traipsed down side street after side street, sloughing off the curses of those who got in their way. "It is too crowded, too noisy, too dirty, too busy . . ."

It struck Charles all at once that this conceivably was the first city she had ever been in, and that it was the first time she would have even seen a body of water like the ocean. Or even this many people in one place. Or had been to a market. Or gone on a boat.

Dear heaven, Georgiana Maitland *was* a virgin. It al-most knocked the breath out of him as he comprehended that things of common experience to anyone who traveled were wholly foreign to her.

And she had wanted so badly to escape the Valley.

How on earth would she cope with what was to come?

Sympathy. Damn. The devil's tool. He ought not to have any sympathy for her; she could very well take care of herself. She'd gotten this far by wit, guile, a certain hardheaded pragmatism, and the seductiveness of her breasts.

And she still had his money.

She was not an innocent in a den of wolves. And his obligation to her only went so far. Some might even say he'd already amply repaid her for helping him escape the Valley.

By the terms of their bargain, he had only to take her to England and to her father's house. The rest . . . well, the rest was none of his business.

Like hell . . .

This trip through the Kalahari was just the beginning. They would have a week on the steamer to Cameroon, possibly two or three days there, another week on the ocean to Sierra Leone, and two more weeks on a steamship to England.

And that was the best timetable, if the connections were made. So this end of the journey could take as much as a month—or more.

And then, she couldn't possibly go ashore in Greybourne dressed in her desert garb. And there would be arrangements to be made from there to get her to Aling, wherever that was.

And none of this took into account where Moreton was.

God, Moreton. He hadn't thought of the bastard in the past two weeks, not once. Sick, slick, sanctimonious Moreton. What if he were on his way to England as well?

Could he be? With all he had to lose? He'd be better paid staying where he was. Georgiana would never betray him, and for himself, he just didn't care.

Just the beginning . . .

He shook off the thought. "You're hungry," he said. "We'll get some fresh fish. We'll dine in style."

"I don't want to eat. I want *you* to eat."

He left that remark floating in the air for a long moment. The thing was, he couldn't turn off the need either, but he sure as hell was going to try.

"That part of the journey is over," he said finally, tightly. "It's not possible to be that way in civilization. It's just not possible to go on that way anymore."

"Why not?"

She would ask that. And she would not understand. In her world, all things sexual were the norm. Naturally, she wouldn't comprehend the constraints, especially since, to all intents and purposes, they were still in the desert.

"We need to ready ourselves for the next part of the journey," he said brusquely. "No distractions now. It will be arduous enough without that."

"You don't want my nipples anymore?"

"Look around you, *khanum*. There are hundreds of things of interest besides your breasts."

"You didn't think that last night. Last night, they were the only thing in the world."

"The only thing in *that* world, absolutely. That world is gone now."

She looked around them at the busy street, at the mud-daubed buildings, at the mules and drays inching along the narrow way. "Well, I don't like this one. I want to go back into the desert with you, and I want to stay there forever. And then maybe you'll fuck me, too."

He shook his head. "I told you, no fucking."

"You came so very close, *cadi*. I wear your essence all over my nipples and my naked body, you came that close. So why can't you—?"

"We made a bargain: You held up your end. And now I

am taking you to your father. And I could not face him if I had fucked you across all of South Africa and beyond."

"I see. But you can face him having spent yourself all over my nipples for two weeks."

"That was the price for taking you, *khanum*. And I spent you well."

"Yes, you did. You deliberately did. You spent me so well, I want nothing more than to be awash in your cream all day. And I can't because you won't, and I don't understand why."

"The price of taking you to England was my owning your breasts for two weeks. Nothing more, nothing less. I made no other promise to you. I did not fuck you. I did not swear undying love to you. So now you make your choice. If you will continue, we get something to eat, and we find some rooms for the night. If not, Rashmi might take you back to Sefra for another fifty *krans,* and you can set up there and cater to the trade. You will have no end of men clamoring to fuck you and pay you well for the privilege of doing you. And in that way, you might, in time, get to England anyway."

"Bastard," she spat. "You son of a bitch . . . You put your mark on me. You gave me that gift."

"Women will believe anything," he said heartlessly. "It was all a lie. The ink will fade. The diamond is virtually worthless. All of it was a ploy to keep us both interested. I couldn't let things get boring, could I? You understand, there are only so many ways to fuck a woman's breasts."

She screamed—in the middle of the narrow street, she howled. And people turned around and looked, and one or two men actually started toward Charles, as if they would defend her, God help him. But of course they would— she was that kind of woman.

And then she got very quiet.

And Charles got very wary.

"I see," she said. "I begin to see clearly for the first time in *weeks*. I see that I was blinded by excess. I see that I should have kept my weapons, all of them, to myself. And I see that I am in fact the victim of my own need and my own greed. And for that, as usual, a woman must pay."

She went silent again. And even he knew she had very little choice. And that she was probably scared and leery of what would come next. And she wouldn't trust him worth a damn now.

Not that it mattered.

Didn't it?

He suddenly caught the glimmer of something silvery in the street reflecting the sun. He knew what it was instantly; he knew what it meant and he did not want to examine what he felt about it, but before he could make a move to pick it up, she ground it into the dirt with her heavy desert boot, and slanted a simmering look at him.

"Very well, *cadi*. It shall be as you say. But isn't it always? You will take me to England, to my father, and then your debt will be paid."

Chapter Fourteen

There was so much she didn't know, so much about men, so much about life outside the Valley. And life in England at this point was an utterly foreign concept, she thought, as she tossed and turned on the narrow cot in the inexpensive lodgings he'd found for the night. It was little more than a two-story mud-walled building with barely furnished rooms, and no amenities, that were to let for the night to itinerant travelers who were moving fast.

There was only one cot in their room, and a ledge on which he slept, wrapping himself in his robes and using his headdress rolled around his personal things, for a pillow.

So she couldn't root around for the gun, the knife, or the money he'd gotten for their desert gear. He'd probably kill her if she tried. And she'd probably kill him before the journey was over.

She was a fool. She knew better than to trust men, better than to take what a man said in the heat of passion with anything but a grain of salt.

She should have known from the way Charles Elliott resisted fucking her that she was nothing more than a diversion.

But he'd said that all along; this was the way of his father's people. Women had one use. She'd knowingly played on that and bartered the one thing she had for the price of an escort across the Kalahari and beyond.

Why was she so annoyed?

Because he had taken it a step further by painting her breasts? Because he seemed so enthralled by her?

Because she was so naive?

Oh, never again. She was a quick study, and if a man could use a woman that way, then certainly a woman could turn the tables. She'd threatened it often enough, perhaps it was time to grab the bull by its balls and see what happened.

Somewhere in this vast new world she'd journeyed to, there had to be a trustworthy man who would take her on and take her home.

Meantime, Charles Elliott would do. She still had the money she'd stolen from him. He still had a shred of honor, in that he'd brought her this far and he still meant to continue on the journey.

So presumably he wanted or needed to get to England, too. He would be useful, until she found a more interesting one with whom to replace him.

Yes, Charles Elliott was infinitely replaceable.

Thank the fates he hadn't fucked her. So much easier to remain removed from the situation without the messy emotions attendant to that.

She'd seen enough of it in the Valley. She'd had enough of it in the desert.

The thing now was to get to England, to get to Aling and her father, and to a new life that didn't involve men or expectations or sex.

*   *   *

This wasn't going to be easy, Charles thought. He hadn't slept the entire night, and he knew she hadn't either. He was just better at keeping his restiveness under control.

But his mind reeled like a ship on a storm-tossed sea. What the hell was he going to do with her now? He'd made a huge mistake, letting his fascination with her breasts get in the way of a hard-headed bargain.

Damn, he should have left her in Sefra or Akka. She could have gotten back to the Valley from Akka, and she'd be a damned sight happier there than she was going to be in her father's house.

He had a vision of her padding down a massive carpeted staircase in a huge formal country house and into a crush of party guests stark naked, with her petal-painted breast on display.

By all that was holy, surely she knew better than to do something like that.

He wouldn't have bet on it. But it wasn't his problem. *No?* Fine, he'd just keep her shrouded and subservient until they reached Greybourne.

Really?

Probably not.

But then, she was angry enough not to roil the waters right now. And she was smart enough to know that she was way out of her depth, that she knew virtually nothing about life outside the Valley, that things were very different in the real world.

And that, for the time being, she needed him.

And what do you need?

That's not a consideration. Getting her off my hands is. Finding that piece of shit Moreton and making him pay for my mother's death is.

Period.

Hell, you're not thinking about going back to the Valley?

He didn't know what he was thinking; he was in the twilight world of dozing before dawn, and all these thoughts were rushing over him like a waterfall.

And crowns to *krans,* Olivia would turn up in England. She wouldn't like the idea of Georgiana returning to Aling on her own, would she? Or the possibility she might reveal all the secrets of the Valley?

Moreton surely wouldn't.

It was conceivable that Moreton could well be by Olivia's side. Those two were unholy as hell.

God, he was going off cocked and stuffed here. The heat was making him delusional. Moreton Estabrook was not that Machiavellian—

And they were probably just as happy to get rid of Georgiana. She could do them no harm in England. And she'd done irreparable enough damage to *him.*

It was time to move, to start the day. They had perhaps two hours before they had to board their ship. They could bathe, have some breakfast, buy some food for the boat trip. All things he knew to do that Georgiana did not. How would she ever have made such a journey without him?

She wouldn't have, he thought suddenly. She'd still be in the Valley if he hadn't been bent on avenging his family's deaths. She'd be waking up naked in some horny man's bed this morning after a thorough Valley fucking the previous night. And she'd probably be ready and willing this morning to have him pole her again . . .

Nothing to stop him either, this phantom lover . . .

He vaulted upright abruptly.

Goddamn her . . . Not this bloody early in the morning . . .

He reached for the little stone pitcher of water they had

been given, poured some into his palm, and slapped it on his face.

Warm, brackish, just enough to get a man's mind off of things pouring into and filling up a woman's body . . .

He reached up and shook her and she came awake immediately.

"What? Is it time to go?"

It's time to cum . . . Shit. Everything about her reeks of sex. And I'm too susceptible . . .

"It's time," he said brusquely. "We need to go in search of a bath, coffee, and some food."

"I'm ready." She stood up, adjusted her *abeya,* and pulled up her veil. The very picture of modesty, containment, obedience.

. . . and a wanton . . . And that anomaly was ever the downfall of man . . .

And thinking about the water sluicing off her naked body, off her naked petal-painted nipple in the public baths of the *hammam.*

This was the first stop, before breakfast even. He needed to wash the desert off his body, the scent of her off his body, the imprint of her nipples off his body, the thought of her breasts out of his mind.

And she would be scrubbing away at the henna paint, at every trace of the essence of him . . . every drop would swirl around the stone floor of the baths and mix with water, diluted, impotent, gone forever—that was what he wanted, a clean fresh start to this part of the journey. *Wasn't it?*

And then there was the ship—a creaky, barely seaworthy steamer that provided passenger service twice a week up the coast to Sierra Leone.

It scared Georgiana to death.

For one thing, it was crowded, and for another, animals traveled as well as families, and merchants and traders with boxes and cases of their various wares. Sleeping quarters were little more than benches belowdecks, and there wasn't much more room above.

And the boat pitched alarmingly as it took on its bi-weekly load. Charles didn't give her much time to think or protest. "There is no choice, *khanum*. This is the most efficient way to get us where we need to go."

"Or kill us in the process," she retorted, as he once again took her arm and marched her up the gangplank.

They were underway within the hour, Georgiana huddled on a bench up against the cabin wall. This was worse than anything she could have imagined. She was going to die, absolutely; this rattlebones of a contraption couldn't possibly navigate and still stay afloat.

And yet it did, rolling in water that was green as a serpent and that frothed and boiled against the shore. Slowly, painstakingly, under an ocean blue sky that merged eerily with the far horizon, the ship plied its way up the green-fringed coastline that was broken now and again in the distance by purple-hazed mountains and the odd old stone fort standing like a sentinel deep in the forest.

They could just see everything, and almost everyone hung over the railing to catch glimpses of fishing villages and natives as the steamer chugged by.

Georgiana was hard put to comprehend the charm of it. She was miserable, faintly nauseated, scared, and a dozen other things she couldn't put a name to.

There were too many people. And braying animals. And braying men, for that matter, not one of whom looked even remotely approachable.

As if a woman dressed as she was would ever do such a thing. She felt as if she were in prison and only Charles Elliott had the key.

She had to stop this. She couldn't let herself be daunted by every new experience on this journey. And besides, what could scare her now, coming from the Valley? A stranger was a stranger anywhere in the world. She had given over the most intimate part of herself to men she knew nothing about for the sole purpose of their pleasure, and she had done it willingly, and for years.

If she could do that, she could take on anything.

It was a matter of perspective. And not letting Charles Elliott get to her. He was still her best chance of getting to England right now.

It was just—the queasy feeling in her stomach. And the late afternoon cup of tea did nothing to quell it. And the slipping and sliding of the ship's hull in water. And the confinement of the *abeya,* close and hot against her naked body.

And smug Charles Elliott, leaning over the railing, enjoying every minute, every sight.

A week of this?

Dear God . . .

A week . . .

Sierra Leone was civilization, all wooded hills, and a low peninsula forming three bays with inviting beaches surrounded by cottonwood and palms, and a waterfront built for business with wharves and warehouses situated hard by the harbor adjacent to the town.

"This is Liberty Town," Charles told her, as they watched the ship drop anchor. "It has been called the Liverpool of West Africa."

"It looks like everything is made of stone."

Stone hard . . . "No. Wood. You'll see as we get into town. There are not only houses, but a variety of shops and a church, all along one main avenue, not unlike . . ." *The Valley,* he'd been about to say, and caught himself. "Anyway, we can buy anything we need here. This is the jumping-off point for the next part of the journey. If we're lucky, within the next couple of days, the *Malabar* will put in to shore, and we'll be on our way to Greybourne."

"How long on board the *Malabar?*"

He squinted at the sun. "Two weeks, maybe."

They had no gear to speak of. They trekked into the flower-scented air on shore, down the long main street, around sheep and goats, and hawkers touting their wares, and the international babble of visitors on their way in, on their way out. There were men at prayers, and men squatting around a square, playing *warry,* and soldiers and villagers on parade. There were jackdaws everywhere, and the incessant heat and no relief anywhere but farther inland toward the mountains.

This was a place where no questions were asked. You showed your money and every consideration was given you. In this way, they found similar accommodations to those in Cameroon—a bare mud-walled room with two cots and a washstand—at a guest house for itinerant travelers.

They spent any number of hours in the open-front shops, the only respite from the heat, where they found everything for sale from china to leather goods, and nothing they could really use.

One or two days here, if they were lucky.

She could buy some bolts of cloth and make herself a dress, she thought. Just to get out of the heavy *abeya.* Just to feel like a woman again; Charles was treating her like a piece of furniture. One he had decorated to suit him, and then decided didn't fit his taste.

Ah, blast him. Yet there wasn't anyone more likely among travelers with whom she might strike a bargain. And Charles seemed to be watching her all the time, as if that were exactly what he thought she might do.

Well, she had to be prepared, didn't she? Who knew what Charles might take it into his head to do? No honor among thieves. Especially when they had no more use for each other.

Once they boarded ship, just two weeks until they would reach Greybourne, wherever that was . . .

Dear God, all the things she did *not* know . . .

How dependent she must be on him . . .

But maybe, by the time they got to Greybourne, things would change. Maybe she would have the luxury of being able to abandon *him*.

Charles could almost see the wheels spinning in Georgiana's mind. She was too restless, too calm; a quiet fury simmered just below the surface. This trip for her was too stringent, compounded of her rebellion against her needing him and her fear and anger about all she did not know, and about what was to come.

How could he even let her out of his sight for one minute?

How could he keep watching her without wanting her?

This was insane. He had given in to every base impulse and he was paying for it now. And there were still many weeks yet until they reached England. He wasn't sure he would be able to stand it: either his screaming penis or watching her trolling for someone to seduce to take his place.

By the heavens, *that* wouldn't happen. He'd fuck her first. He might fuck her anyway just to keep her in line. Obviously it was the thing to do, and so who had he punished all through their desert trek by not doing it?

She was still playing his submissive companion, and hating every minute of it. But Liberty Town was not a place she could disrobe and display herself and invite bids from all comers.

No. She might do that on board the *Malabar*. She might do that when they arrived in Greybourne. He could see it

in her eyes; one penis was as good as any other. And what did it matter who kept the bargain to take her to England?
Damn it all to hell.
She knew nothing about life outside the Valley, nothing about the ugly nature of men.
Not true. You showed her quite convincingly . . .
And he'd done it to himself, creating such an erotic vision of her breast that his penis was in constant turmoil and he was endlessly aroused by just the thought of it. And then he'd just pushed it away.
A man would do anything to get what he wanted.
So what would a woman do, especially a woman like Georgiana?
Even now, beneath the confining robes of the *abeya,* there was something about the way she moved that made men look at her—and wonder. It was part of her allure; it was her feminine secret. Every man she passed would have paid a king's fortune to have her reveal everything beneath those robes, and would have died happy in the process.
Or was he just deluding himself?
Or regretting his foolish move of marking her body for himself?
All of that and more, he thought. And if they were going to be together in close quarters for the next two weeks, by damn, he would get his hands on her naked body again.
And maybe that was all the reason there needed to be.

There was only one way to get a man to do what you wanted him to do, and Georgiana was not averse to resorting to it.
There was no help for it. She had to ensure she got to England. The more she thought about it, the more scared she became that, in the ensuing day or two until the *Malabar* arrived, Charles Elliott would find no good reason to continue on the journey with her.

And there was no one else who would do. It wasn't that she hadn't looked. No. It was just that no *man* seemed even remotely likely or to her taste.

And perhaps that was the real problem, that in spite of the fact she was experienced at this, she did not want to hand herself over to some stranger.

Better the devil she knew . . . And Charles Elliott was a devil, but at least, somewhere in his black heart, he had some scruples.

So, if she offered to pay him—the only way she knew how—he couldn't refuse her. It was all a matter of presentation. Without a doubt, he was enthralled with her breasts. So that was the point of approach.

This time, though, all the pleasure must center on him and his needs. And no fucking. Fucking was the root of all problems, and he'd been absolutely right to deny them that.

But there were other ways, other things. She would focus wholly and completely on his penis. Draw petals around its head, if necessary. Draw on *him* until he was bone dry.

Two weeks on board ship instead of on board a camel. Payment for his time and expertise.

Oh yes, especially his expertise—compensation the only way she knew how. Keep him satiated the whole voyage long so that he wouldn't have time to think about anything else.

That she could do. With *him*.

That should work.

She broached it that evening as they sat on a curb outside of a vegetable market and ate some fish for dinner.

"It seems to me that you've been amply paid for the first part of this journey, but we have yet to discuss the terms to continue on."

He felt a moment of shock. Now what? Or now, who?

"There were no further terms," he said stiffly "We agreed at Dar el Rabat that was payment enough."

"I'm thinking it wasn't, *cadi*. We have so many more miles, so many more weeks to travel. And I will not be beholden to you in any way. If we continue on, then I must give you more."

He felt a rill of arousal. "More—what?"

"More pleasure, *cadi*. For these two weeks on board this boat, I will own your penis, to do with as I will. No fucking though. We cannot have fucking. But otherwise, I will give you all the pleasure you can handle as payment for your taking me this far and on the next leg of this journey."

"No fucking?" he said faintly.

"By your own terms, *cadi*."

"That was then, *khanum*."

"That's as may be, but that is my proposal. Or we may do nothing. Or you may well determine to leave me here. It seems to me those are the choices. And that is what I have to barter."

"And no fucking."

"Too many problems involved with that. You might find you like it too much, and then where would I be?"

Oh, the pure carnal certainty of the courtesan that *he* would be the one to become enslaved. He must consider. This was what she knew best: taking a man in hand and manipulating him. It was all of a piece to her. No matter where she was in the world, she could always play this card and win.

It was working with him. Just the thought of her handling him for two weeks, just the thought of touching and fondling her sent a bolt of erotic need through his vitals.

How hard had he tried for the last couple of weeks to train himself to live without it? Lying to himself that he could live without it—

And now this.

Ever a whore, using everything physical to lure her prey.

He had never been immune from the first time she had pressed her nipples against his bare back that first night in the valley.

"Where would you be?" he said, in answer to her question. "On your back, with my penis between your legs, instead of in your hands. But I know from experience that can be almost as good. You're right, *khanum,* it is a long journey and I am but a man. And I am hot for a woman"— her faint smile of triumph did not escape him—"so I'll take those terms, and put my penis willingly in your hands."

Chapter Fifteen

The *Malabar* put into harbor two days later, a blasting horn heralding its arrival. Passengers, luggage, sundries, and cargo were efficiently ferried ashore on surfboats in the ensuing hours until dusk, and those embarking on the return trip weren't allowed on board until early the next morning.

Space was limited, but Charles had managed to secure a cabin on the lower deck. They bought a trunk and filled it with food, fresh and tinned; bottles of water; tea and coffee; a small portable cooker; soap and a bucket for washing; some bedding; candles; matches; a teakettle; and a frying pan.

And they waited, to be among the first on line for the surfboat the following morning. Even then, after they'd settled everything in their tiny cabin, they still had to wait. They spent several hours abovedeck watching the crew load in cargo for the return trip.

Charles watched Georgiana eyeing the men who were climbing up the ladder onto the deck. How did a man ever know what a woman was thinking? Especially *her*. Particularly after her brazen offer of two nights ago.

And she was still looking for fairer game?

Or were they looking at her, now that she had leave to bare her head, wondering who she was and whether she was free and if they could somehow effect an introduction.

That was easy enough on a voyage like this. The quarters were small, the gathering spaces even closer quarters; there would be no avoiding conversation or questions. Travelers would share experiences, meals, entertainment, a beer.

He'd done that. He'd had any number of women throw themselves at him, hoping for a night in his bed. Being sequestered on a voyage was much like a trip into the desert: a world of its own, with its own little closed-in society, and the same unspoken rules. No one would know, no one would tell.

Georgiana prowled the deck for possibilities.

Let her.

Only two weeks more, given decent weather, to England.

Two weeks more and he would be home again. *Home.*

Had there ever been a home? Certainly not in the tents of Jalal Bakhtoum, the uncle who had raised him. There, his thirst for vengeance was fomented. There, he had learned the hard lessons of the life of a Bedouin prince who must uphold his family's honor.

But there, too, had been fostered his love of horses; his uncle bred them. Horses brought prestige; they were a symbol of power.

He had grown up with them, lived with them, and trained them alongside his uncle. The horse had been his release, his companion that slept in his tent like a brother.

No wonder he had chosen the horse as his pathway to the road of revenge, the currency by which he had planned to avenge his father's death. And on top of failing to do that, he'd abandoned a damnable amount of money in horseflesh in the Valley.

Someday he'd start over again in England.

Another lesson learned at his uncle's knee. All you needed was a plan.

His uncle had simmered his plan for years, seasoning it and testing it, testing him.

You must always have a plan . . .

And here he was, afloat on the ocean in West Africa, redeemed, in the company of the courtesan of courtesans, with no plan at all except to let her get her hands on his penis that night.

How far he had fallen from grace.

You must always have a plan . . . the enemy is cunning, always moving, ever-changing . . .

And so it had been: the wheel had turned and his mother had died anyway, just not by his hand. And in the end, who would know, who would tell, that he had not dealt Lydia the final blow? And that all the money spent, all the years he'd spent in England had yielded nothing but this one result: he never wished to return to Syria and his father's family again.

Argentina had seemed a good compromise. Close enough to be reached, far enough away that he wasn't accountable to anyone, *and* a climate perfect for raising the ponies.

But not England.

And now England was close enough to touch, to taste. In the traitorous body of the wanton Georgiana, he would feed on memories of England, and the part of his soul he'd never wanted to face.

Now Olivia remembered why she hated London. It was cold and foggy and inhospitable. Everything was behind closed doors, no matter what you wanted. Everything was contained, controlled, and restrained, from where you slept to the traffic on the streets.

She hated London. She'd hated the whole trip, fast as it had been. Moreton had been a whirlwind, lifting them up and transporting them almost to another time and place. To memories she'd never wanted to revisit.

And yet here she was, on the wings of Moreton's desires once again, wondering if there was ever a time she hadn't done exactly what he wanted.

"Come, come, old girl," he chided her as they took dinner at their hotel. "We've had the best and fastest ship coming over, the best accommodations, the best food, the best fucking really."

"You've had the best," Olivia retorted.

"My dear, you're just not seeing the larger picture. Look around this dining room. All those young things with their proper dresses, and hidden bosoms, and dainty mannerisms—can't you see how they are aching to burst out of all constraints? These are your doves, my dear. These little beauties just screaming to be sexual under their excellent good manners. Trust me. I've had many like them, and they are just waiting for the invitation."

"Ummph," Olivia grunted. "I grant you . . ."

"How many bedrooms at Aling?"

"Oh, I've forgotten after all these years. Ten? Fifteen? Something obscene like that."

"Exactly," Moreton said. "Something obscene. A golden egg. Don't think these nobs would pay a pretty ha'pence to fuck them? Because you know, my dear, they are going home drunk and dry. Those tits won't give a morsel without some payment in kind. So our pickled prickles will be regular cunt hounds tonight. Watch."

It was their first night in town after the arduous journey from the coast. They were in the hotel restaurant, and

Olivia was fiddling with her food, and wanting desperately to bathe and recreate.

And instead Moreton wanted her to play the voyeur. Not that that didn't have its charms. There just wasn't much to see when people couldn't be free to be naked and sexual.

Still, there was some fascination in watching the subtle mating dance going on among the idle and beautiful who had nothing better to do.

They ate and drank with abandon. They touched, they flirted, they stared deep into each others' eyes. He brushed her breast. She squeezed his knee. He dared to kiss her. Her hand disappeared under the tablecloth.

Oh yes, oh yes, those mantraps would give only so much away. Then their lip lovers would get tired and retire to some nearby cake house and get it all off on a stale piece of pie.

Not at my house . . . things won't go like that at my house . . .

Moreton's eyes lit up watching her. If there was one thing about Olivia, it was her immediate grasp of all things sexual. Only a suggestion needed, and the thing came to her full-blown, already a plan.

She hated those women, and she loved those strutting cocks and all the possibilities they represented.

"They are very wealthy and very bored," he added insinuatingly just to reinforce her ideas further. "And looking for novelty and safety—and discretion. What would they pay for that, I wonder?"

"While we get the pick of the pit. Yes, I see it now. All that lovely money melting into our pockets. My dear Moreton, you were right all along. This is our next step, exactly."

She was licking her lips already. Nothing could be better. He wanted to implement their plans that very moment.

But with Olivia, it paid not to rush her. To let her believe she was in control.

He pushed down his excitement. "Well, my darling, it's up to you."

She took a deep breath. He was right. There were things to be settled. Henry. Aling. She couldn't get there fast enough now. "A sling is close enough, my darling. In fact, just within our reach. We'll leave first thing in the morning. Won't Henry be surprised?"

The *Malabar* had shoved off at noon, and set a rigorous course northward. The crew provided tea and biscuits at four. After that, the travelers were on their own until tomorrow when the ship would break for native vendors farther up the coast.

You always had to travel prepared.

He wasn't prepared, Charles thought. Not since he first stepped foot into the Valley had he been prepared. And everything about Georgiana and this misbegotten adventure had knocked him upside down.

And there she was, already in their cabin, already naked, waiting for him, her breasts so full and proud, the petal paint ever so slightly faded, which made his penis immediately come to attention.

Just as she'd planned.

"So. It's time." She was as businesslike as a madam. He had the feeling he had only to hand over his crown and she'd crown him.

No. Yes. This was something he could not deny.

No fucking . . . That remained to be seen.

"You can just lie down. I'll do everything else."

Practiced words. Words she had said to a dozen men dozens of times. Nothing personal here. Did he want there to be? A penis is a penis. Once you knew how to handle it, a man is clay in your hands.

Who knew that better than she? This was just payment for passage; nothing more, nothing less.

And he would take it that way. He deserved it. No complications. No emotions. Just pure jack-off pleasure at the hands of a well-schooled tart.

He removed his clothes slowly, watching her face, and then stretched out on the bed, his expression impassive, his body speaking eloquently for him.

She climbed over him and straddled his legs so that his penis poked up between her thighs, reaching for that delicious hollow between her breasts.

He'd been there. He remembered, so did she. She grasped him with both hands, and his body jolted as if he'd been shocked.

In a sense he had been. Her hands were electric, golden. Firm, gentle, purposeful, slipping and sliding her fingers, massaging the whole of his shaft and pulling up meaningfully against the head.

A man had to be stone not to spurt his guts. He felt it coming, a rill of pleasure sneaking up on him when he most wanted, most *needed* to control himself.

But these things were beyond control, beyond sanity, especially with *her* and that body, and those breasts, and the petal-rimmed nipple he had sucked and fondled. He couldn't fight it; he couldn't contain it.

His whole body gathered. He reached upward to try to hold her breasts. Her magic hands pulled him up and up and up, and he exploded into her hands.

Somewhere in the dizzying spiral of pleasure, he heard her low growl of triumph. But all he felt were her hands, and his body reaching for them, reaching upward, outward until he exploded all over her.

She let him down gently. How easily she had taken him. But then, he was only a man, and she was as naked and enticing as Eve, as she coated her nipples with his ejaculate, watching him watching her with that knowing feminine gaze.

Was there ever such a woman?

"How was that, *cadi?*"

"It went very well, for starters." No need to let her get too full of herself when he was desperate to fill her.

"I'm thinking so myself." She squeezed a drop more from him. "Only, I think—no breasts."

"What?"

"*Umm.* No breasts. How can you enjoy the benefits of my experience if you are constantly trying to upend me and hold my breasts. And if you do that, what won't you do next? So, *cadi,* no breasts. No nipples. No sucking. Well, that doesn't include me. I must make certain I owe you nothing at the end of this voyage."

"I would keep our bargain in any event," Charles growled.

"But this way is so much more enjoyable, don't you think?"

Enjoyable? He didn't know what to call it. Prisoner of those hands maybe. Besotted over those breasts, absolutely. He would have kept the bargain, no matter what she thought, and taken less than this, because she was so green, he could not let her stumble around by herself in the real world.

When had he started feeling responsible for her? No. He wasn't. It was just those breasts . . . and her hands which were idly exploring his scrotum and between his legs.

He drew in a sharp breath as she insinuated her fingers deep under his scrotum and began to stroke him there.

"Ah, *cadi* likes that . . ." she murmured. She shifted her body so that he could spread his legs and she could delve deeper. "*Umm.* I like that . . ."

His body went soft, fluid, stiff as a pole. Who had made the rule about *no fucking?* He felt her pushing his legs apart still farther, and then suddenly her head was buried between his legs, lapping and sucking at his scrotum and the flesh below.

He bucked; he writhed. He sank into the wet hot draw of her voracious mouth.

Courtesan's tricks . . . as she worked her way from between his legs back to his scrotum, and then up along the underside of his shaft with her practiced tongue, and up still higher until she engulfed his penis head in her mouth.

Molten gold. Ribbons of hot gold undulating, flowing, faster and faster, erupting hot and hard and deep into her mouth.

And she kept pulling, endless, deep, pulling him until he came crashing down, and violently, pushed her hot greedy mouth away.

"I can do more," she whispered.

"No more." He could barely get the words out. He felt as though every pore in his body had been sucked dry. She was too good at what she did, at what she knew. And if he even imagined how much of his seed she had swallowed, he just might go again, except he didn't think he could squeeze out another drop.

"There's always more."

"Fine, there will be more. Just not now."

"Ah, so even *cadi* can have an excess of sex."

"Talk to me in an hour."

"As long as an hour?"

He looked at her. She lay propped up beside him, her free hand threaded through his pubic hair at the very root of his penis. She looked unutterably complacent, certain of her talents and her ability.

And he had played right into her hands. Still, he couldn't move one languid muscle just for looking at her mouth and imagining it closed around his penis and sucking. Just imagining the taste of his essence on her tongue.

Imagining too much in this situation that was solely a completion of their bargain. She would do fine, no matter what happened. With just that one bedroom trick, she would have men salivating after her, willing to give her anything she wanted.

It could be her specialty. She could sell tickets, take on— oh, how many men a night? Five? Ten? Fifty?

He went rigid just thinking of it. Imagining her, the queen of cocks, sitting on her satin and gilt throne, naked, and men lining up, dropping their pants, and handing her hundreds of pounds in payment.

Ten, fifteen minutes at the most—and gone. God, she'd be wealthier than the monarchy at that rate.

Yes, the queen would do just fine . . .

"Maybe sooner," he murmured. "I seem to be at full staff suddenly. But no fucking."

"No fucking, *cadi*. You said it yourself as a condition of taking me into the desert. You will not want for pleasure, I promise you."

"I want your breasts then."

"No breasts. My condition for *this* trip, and I thought that had been agreed to."

"I'm not so sure I can keep my hands off your nipples."

"I will keep my breasts out of reach then, and my hands and mouth on your penis, and in that way, we will spend the time on this part of the trip."

Spend the time? Spend him, she meant.

No, he couldn't eke out another drop right now, hard as he was.

"How many men have you had?" he asked abruptly, perhaps deliberately to get both of their minds off of blowing him again.

She scurried to a sitting position. "Well, talking about that will spoil things nicely. You don't need to know. I don't even know."

He made a sound.

"How many women have you had, *cadi?*"

"Only you."

"That's the right answer, but the wrong lover. Why should it matter?"

"Just curiosity. It doesn't matter." He didn't think it did, anyway, but deep in his craw, he felt something else—that she was too young to have been touched that way by however many men who had done so, that she treated it too cavalierly, that she should care a great deal more than she did.

And yet he sat here fantasizing about all the men who might come after him, all the men in the world who might fuck her. So there was no altruism here; it was prurient curiosity, meant to arouse him to the boiling point.

Well, he was there, what with her tight luscious petal-ringed nipple just within reach, and the thought of plunging his shaft deep between her legs.

She ran her hand over his erection. "Not yet an hour, *cadi.* Perhaps you'd like to have something to eat before I service you agin."

"I will have your nipples for dinner, *khanum.*"

"Not on the menu."

"Then perhaps they shouldn't be displayed as if they were."

"This is how I dress for dinner."

Yes, someday, for the man she would love, she would be naked in his house all day and all night because how could he bear to make her wear clothes?

"I need your nipples." His voice was rougher than he intended, the need almost painful in its intensity. How could he not need them, after those two weeks of constant attention to them, the incessant pleasure of fondling and sucking at them?

After marking them as your own?

"Let me pleasure your penis, *cadi*. I will make you forget all about my nipples. You know I can make you forget everything." She smoothed her hand all over his penis, and his body vibrated against her expert fingers.

She took him in both hands and began a long swooping motion up and down, with alternating hands, drawing him still harder and tighter, pulling him toward her as if she could make him thicker, stiffer in her hands. Tugging him, and pumping him finally, up and down with just the right pressure in the circle of her incredible magic fingers.

This time, his body went liquid, his orgasm sweetly flooding every molecule of his body and then slowly, deliciously, softly, effusing what was left all over her hand.

He slept. He didn't want to. He fought it, but she had prodded him beyond exhaustion. And so he finally slept, not comprehending how much she knew about the functioning of a man's body, and the lengths to which it could be pushed.

She, however, was hungry, and she wrapped herself in her robe, and crawled around the tiny cabin, fishing out a piece of bread and a bottle of water.

It would do. *He* would do. He was a most responsive man, and now that she controlled his penis, everything would go smoothly until the end of the trip.

She couldn't envision having taken on a stranger to accomplish it.

Nevertheless, her body was tight with longing. No fucking was not necessarily a good thing, when she had spent hours playing with a man's penis only to give him a full measure of culmination and remained unfulfilled herself.

No. Restraint was the order of the day. This way everything was neatly pigeonholed and the rules were understood. He had delineated them himself, and she was adamant they wouldn't change just because it was her hand juicing *him*.

But he would try, she was pretty certain of that. He was a man, after all, and her naked body was just within reach all the time. She understood perfectly that it was hard to deny a man what he had already tried and tasted.

Her body grew hot at the thought. She hadn't forgotten one minute of their time in the desert, and even she wanted to put it out of her mind. But every time she looked at her petal-rimmed nipple, she was reminded of it, and both nipples would tighten and her body would twinge. She could almost feel his fingers . . .

She felt like pouring the water over her heated body. But that would be a waste, and she would be no less steeped in sex two hours from now.

The thing was to keep his hands away from her body and to give him as much juicing as his penis could take . . .

Maybe she could tie him up?

No bedposts here, but still—imagine him spread-eagled on a four-poster bed. Lovely, she could just nibble on him and he couldn't do a thing about it.

She let out a long panting breath. She could just munch on him right now, come to that. There was nothing more enticing than a sleeping penis, all latent power, and deliciously quiescent to do with whatever she wished.

She took a long drink of water, set it aside, threw off her robe, knelt beside him, and took him in her mouth.

He awoke slowly, gradually to the sensation of someone's lips moving up and down his shaft in a compressing motion, as if he were being slowly devoured inch by inch.

He held his breath. He didn't want to move. He just wanted to lie there, reveling in the feeling of her mouth squeezing, and nibbling, and nipping.

She was just at the edge of the bedding, leaning over

him so that her breasts brushed his hip, her nipples hard against his thigh.

His body jolted. His shaft jutted out like a poker; his breath caught, his chest tightened, as she shook him between her teeth like a bone.

All he had to do was overpower her. Just roll right over her, pin her to the floor, and pound her into the ocean.

And instead, primed and pumped, he spewed an ocean of semen into her waiting expert hands.

Chapter Sixteen

They continued on that way for a week, barely ever leaving the cabin except for necessities: cooking a scant meal of tinned vegetables and rice, or making tea, or buying some fresh fruit and fish from the natives who came out on surfboats when the *Malabar* made anchor close to shore.

His mandate was to "stay still," while she fed on him every bit as avidly as he had on her. It felt like his penis was a machine, juicing up two or three times a day for her delectation. She couldn't seem to hold it, stroke it, suck it, or pump it enough. She always wanted more. Penetration was not necessary for gratification.

She liked it when he was standing, and he could angle himself into her mouth. She liked it when he was prone, and she had full control of him in her hands. She liked burrowing between his legs and using her tongue and lips to make him swoon. And she especially liked that suspended moment of pure unalloyed pleasure when he surrendered.

But—no fucking, no breasts. He felt as though he would explode if he didn't touch her breasts, if he didn't penetrate her soon, but he was in a constant combustible state anyway.

And she warned him. "I will take drastic measures if you insist on my breasts."

Drastic measures? In a five-foot-square cabin, with nothing but some thin bedding on the floor and some shelves anchored to the wall?

Her threat made him smile. "I insist."

She smiled. He knew that smile, that smile said she'd thought about it, and she had a plan. Always have a plan. The wiliest of temptresses always had a plan, and he should have known that by now.

And this wily temptress knew just how to drain him dry. He fell off to sleep swearing he would fuck her in spite of her ridiculous rules. No fucking only counted when *he* made the rules.

He awakened to find his arms above his head, securely tied.

"What's this?"

"Drastic measures, *cadi.*" She was smiling again, that smug triumphant smile he was growing to dislike intensely. "And now, perhaps, I will give you my breasts."

This was torture, as she straddled his chest and her breasts swung that close to his mouth. Torture, with her legs spread so widely that she had to cant her mound with its thick pubic hair tightly against his rib cage.

He considered for thirty seconds swinging his bound arms over his head and around her neck, but that would take a fair amount of flexibility, and he was melting like wax just looking at her, just salivating over her nipples, and the tight pressure of her cleft against his body.

She leaned forward, cupping the breast with the petal-rimmed nipple.

"Mine—"

She smiled, and shifted her body. "Mine." She moved,

sinuous as a snake down his body, pausing to rub that nipple against one of his protruding nipples.

His body bucked; the sensation was so indescribable, so naked.

She shifted herself over his towering erection to straddle his thighs. To lift that breast and settle his penis against it and wipe off a smear onto that nipple.

He heaved again, consumed by the vision of his essence coating her nipple, and she grasped his penis and began rubbing it against both her nipples, one and then the other, back and forth back and forth. He could hardly stand it, back and forth; his body went hot, thick, volcanic. It was more than any man could stand, and yet he was still standing and begging for more.

Molasses—his body had turned to molasses, thick, sweet, sticky. It oozed out slowly, lusciously onto her nipples, dripping onto her breasts, onto his belly, one long continual orgiastic note of pleasure, his body pitched to play it forever, resonating, following its flight.

He came down slowly, like a cloud, and she covered his penis with her body and laid her head against his chest.

He listened for a moment to the throbbing of his body, of the engine that powered the boat, of the engine of life.

He felt sane suddenly, unfogged, clear-sighted, and he couldn't for a moment define what had thrown everything into sharp focus.

Maybe it was his bound hands and the fact his coy mistress had caught him unaware. Maybe it was that his cunning courtesan had played him like a cardsharp.

She was a wonder, this wanton, with her hands, her mouth, her nipples. She made a man forget exactly what she was and where she came from. He didn't doubt for a moment that the price for these services came high.

Not to say he wouldn't pay it. But now the stakes had changed. Now that he comprehended the depth of her power, he had to teach her that she was not in charge, that he was not a man to be led around by his penis.

Had he not already told her so?

She could be forgiven for not believing him. He had acted like a man whose mind was governed solely by what his penis desired. A man who could be distracted by a naked woman, her hard succulent nipples, and her volatile foraging tongue.

He still could be, but now with that keen edge of insight, he could enjoy it even more. He could play with her to the point of perversity and never count the cost.

And now, there would be penetration, deep hot and wet, and there would be fucking. A week of hot, hard, pound-her-to-the-ground fucking.

He went stiff envisioning it. There was nothing about her that didn't heat him to a white-hot frenzy to possess her. Well, it was time to stoke the furnace. Time to light the fire and let it skyrocket until it exploded into ashes.

She wouldn't untie him yet either. "We're not done yet today."

"Oh, I'm done, *khanum*. To a turn. There's nothing else you could do to squeeze another drop out of me."

"Well, maybe I just like having you at my mercy."

"Enjoy it while you can," he murmured.

She crawled over to the trunk, which was situated by the door, and pulled out a handful of dates and a bottle of water. "Oh, I'm enjoying it, *cadi,* more than you can imagine." She took a gulp of water and bit into a date while settling herself back against the wall.

"Tell me something."

"Is there *anything* I can tell you?"

She leaned forward, so that her breasts brushed his chest again, and tipped the bottle of water against his lips.

"Tell me what happens when we come to the end of this part of the journey."

He sipped, bringing his hands over his head so he could grasp the bottle with the limited motion of his bound hands. "What happens? Simply, we go to London and find your father. The complications: we need to transform ourselves into civilized human beings; at a minimum, we'll need clothes, transportation, and some idea where to even find your father . . ."

"Oh, that I know. Mother always said Aling was within a hour's traveling distance of London. And still it was too far away for her."

Doubtless, he thought. Olivia would never like to be far away from the society of *men*. He couldn't imagine what manner of man she had married, or what kind of man he was that he could abandon his child to the licentious lifestyle of the Valley.

He didn't sound like a man who'd be willing to pay a reward for her return to civilization. But that was thinking too far ahead. He had other rewards to think about . . . a week of rewards with Georgiana in his bed and at the mercy of his penis.

"An hour? An hour . . . that's definitely a clue."

"Someone will know. Mother said that Aling was famous."

"Then indeed, someone will know." He had no doubt of it, either. They were all in tight, these hard-line country squires. They all knew each other from the cradle, knew each other's secrets and scandals, and they protected each other to a fault.

She was such an innocent about things like this. Such a child.

She took the water bottle from him and took another swallow. "Talking about Aling isn't very sensual, is it? I now regret I even asked. What will be, will be. I'd much rather focus on your pleasure in the coming hours, *cadi.*"

"So would I."

"Good." She set aside her water and lifted his arms above his head again, which immediately sparked a spurt of life in him. She smiled and she climbed onto his chest, buried her head in his pubic hair and took his elongating penis into the heat and wet of her mouth.

She was facing away from him, and as she started devouring him, she lifted onto her knees to take him deeper into her mouth, which gave him an unobstructed view between her legs of her long, enticing cleft framed by a lush bush of hair.

He hardened up like iron as her bottom undulated erotically before his eyes. He could just hear the sensual little sounds she made, and he heated up like a blast furnace.

So close he could almost taste her. If his hands were free, he could penetrate her—

Not free, but not useless. He lifted his arms and pulled them into his chest, just barely missing her buttocks. Now . . . the excitement was unbearable . . . now she was his for the taking.

He cupped her buttocks with one hand and she started, but she never stopped eating him. Good. But it was hell concentrating when she was lapping at him like that.

He rubbed the soft curve of her bottom, cursing that his one hand was useless. No, not useless, as he began softly massaging her between her legs.

He felt the heat and wet of her against the palm of his hand. He felt her writhing against his touch as he began stroking her cleft. Just like that, her sucking in concert with his stroking, feeling his way into her heat.

Parting her labia and stroking her there. Feeling her urgency as she bore down on him, hard. Deliberately wrig-

gling and twisting and pushing to make certain she felt
him inserting his fingers. Feeling her body swoon at his
sensual invasion, and clamp down even harder on his
penis.

And then deep in the searing wet heat of her, thrusting
his fingers in rhythm with her sucking, and the surge of his
hips meeting every pull and draw of her mouth, his fingers
tight and hard inside her.

They rocketed off together; he erupted in her mouth;
she came, swiveling and shaking her hips furiously to get
away from his incessant fingers thrusting and twisting inside her.

She could barely talk after. She was full of him, all over
her body, all inside her. And she was not happy because
she was sprawled out over his legs, her legs spread wide;
she couldn't see him, and his fingers still held her prisoner.

"No fucking, *cadi.*"

"I changed the rule. You were right there, how could I
help it?"

"How could you not? That was the bargain. Let me
go."

"Untie me then."

"Oh no, you are twice as dangerous with your hands
free as without now that you've turned everything inside
out."

"Only you, *khanum,* and don't pretend you didn't
adore that."

"I don't adore being sneaked up on."

"Hardly. You knew I was here."

"I thought you were disarmed, which proves I cannot
trust any man to keep his word. Let me *go.*"

"It was *my* word, *khanum:* I determined that there
would be no fucking so that I could concentrate on your
nipples. And now I want to concentrate on what is be-

tween your legs." He wriggled his fingers and she wriggled her hips. "And your nipples. And if I could have both right now, I might die happy."

"You might die altogether, *cadi*. There is a gun somewhere in this cabin, and enough money to see me to England. I can do without you now that we are well on our way."

"Can you?" he murmured. "Do without me, I mean? Or perhaps I should say, do without my penis? I'm just incidental to all this. Can you do without my penis?"

Men were so smug, she thought; of course she could do without it, even though it was lusciously long and deliciously thick. And hard. He hardened up like concrete, malleable one minute and rock solid the next. But "do" without him, without *it*—

Her body rocked as his fingers took her again, twisting and thrusting into her suddenly, erotically so that she felt wide open, and wholly naked to him.

She could . . . do without—

Maybe . . .

She hated this obverse position. There was no control, and he could do almost anything he wanted with her even with his hands tied togther.

Damn him. She felt nearly breathless as his fingers pumped her and she felt her body liquefy. She seized up. She rocked her bottom hard and tight against his twisting intruding fingers, and she came, the creamy sensation spiraling up from his fingers and spreading outward, not tight, not hard, but just radiating heat in a long coil of pleasure deep between her legs.

She dropped her hips hard, making it impossible for him to maintain his erotic hold on her at that angle. He sniffed the air. It was full of her erotic scent, and his own, commingling like the lovers they were going to be.

"Not only can't you do without it," he said, his voice

laced with certainty, "you want it, you want everything, *khanum*, and if you can't admit it, your body gives you away. You are too naked, too wet, too willing all the time. And you know you have met your match in me. I am the only one who can give you all the fucking you need. Do you doubt it? You know I can service you like no one else. So, you will untie me, and you will spread your legs, and I will demonstrate just how hard and relentless a man's penis can be."

It was a thrilling promise. He had amazing endurance, and stamina beyond belief. And incomparable length and heft and rigidity.

Like no man she had ever known in the Valley.

And now that he had penetrated her . . .

As long as she had kept him from doing that, she could have gone on just as they were. She could have kept eating him until they reached London. She would have let him feast on her breasts.

But the reality of penetration aroused her every suppressed need to have him deep inside her. She couldn't imagine anyone else between her legs. He was every bit as hard and thick as man could be, and he filled her to the hilt, bracing his whole upper body on his arms so that they could both watch as he nudged her nether lips and slowly, inch by inch, pushed his penis into her.

And then they lay hip to hip, his body rocking against hers as he fit himself tightly and inexorably into her.

It was as if no man had ever stretched her this deeply, this intensively. No man had ever been thick enough to fill her so completely. Or long and strong enough to plumb her so fully.

No man but him.

Orgasmic thoughts that rendered him breathless.

He got himself under control with just a little spillage.

Nothing that counted. Nothing compared to what would come.

Her hands grasped his arms, almost as if she wanted to keep him high above her and only feel him between her legs.

Fine with him. At that angle, he could mount her even harder, even higher. Make her scream.

He undulated his hips, testing her, teasing her, pushing incrementally tighter and harder. Then he contracted his belly and forcibly thrust himself into her and began his rhythmic ride.

She met him: every thrust, every drive, every move. Her body was slick with her own wet and the heat of the cabin and the smell of their sex. She danced her own dance of invitation, pushing him harder, further, higher, the way only she knew.

Her whole body shimmied and writhed, sinuous and uncontainable; the sensations were so overpowering, so inescapable. He wouldn't let her go. He came at her and came at her with the same pounding rhythm over and over, unyielding, implacable in the way he possessed her.

She had never had a man like this. He was relentless, but he had said he would be, relentless and hard, and he was all of that and she couldn't get away from him . . . couldn't get away from his driving relentless penis . . . didn't want to . . . wanted to keep him going . . . more and more and more. A piston, banging away at her, taking her, plunging her suddenly, unexpectedly into a long slow molten slide to spiraling culmination.

And silence. Except for the creak of the boat, the low growling chug of the engine. The sound of voices far away. The heat, the scent. His expressionless face. Her shimmering body. All these impressions she gathered to her as she lay there with him tensely, tightly wedged between her legs.

"Finish," she whispered.

"I am not done yet. Did I not say I would give you all the fucking you need? You're not nearly finished. Not while I'm still mounted on you. Not while you're still naked. So I'd guess you'll never leave *this* bed, *khanum*. You love your nakedness too much."

He could say that now, and watch her eyes widen and her lips part and her whole body shiver with anticipation. But what about later?

What about—not thinking about later?

"You love my nakedness too, *cadi*. Else why would you still be embedded between my legs?"

"I love this—" He drove himself into her. "Every man loves *this,* and the wanton body that welcomes him. A man loves that and nothing more, *khanum*. And a hard hot fuck is all I am willing to give you, and what you most desire. So, when you need it, when you want it . . ."

"And my nipples? Are they mine?"

His eyes darkened. "I own your nipples."

"By that measure, *cadi*, your penis is mine."

"Take it, *khanum*. Ride it hard."

"Oh, I will. You won't know where you end. And you're not there yet, *cadi*. I want it deeper, harder, *harder* . . ."

He took her then, primed, and pointed, an iron bar between her legs, driving her hard and high, at her core, her center, making her body shudder and shiver with each potent thrust.

She couldn't believe she wanted more, but she did. Just him, just there. Just like that.

Nothing slow, this time. This time it was explosive and intense, centering wholly and completely *there,* shooting off like a firecracker hot into the air, and then mushrooming out in sparks and spangles between her legs. On and on. One after the other, booming little orgasms from that one long shooting star.

She rode it down, wallowing in every nuance of it, every shiver, every drop of heat filleting through her body.

There had never been anything like this, ever. No one had ever told her there could be anything like this, anyone like him. And her worst nightmare was now a reality. She loved it too much already, and they were but a week away and a week closer to her destination and her destiny.

Who had decided there would be fucking?

Oh yes, *he* had. Making the decisions, taking her when she didn't want him to, making her need his fingers and now his penis, and now what was she going to do?

There was nothing else *to* do but let him service her. Why not? He was better than anyone she'd ever had, maybe than anyone she *would* ever have, and it was the perfect way to pass the time.

She'd think about what was to come later. *That would be him . . . no, no wordplay. It was beneath her. No. She was beneath him. Oh damn . . .*

It wasn't even midday yet, and she was so suffused with the scent and need for sex, she couldn't think of anything else.

And he hadn't taken his pleasure yet. He just rolled his hips against hers, watching her, waiting for her.

She didn't think her body could stand another orgasm. She felt tender, well used, a little overwhelmed even. But there he was, still rock-hard and waiting for her.

He waited. He rose above her like a god, on his haunches, still in possession of her. And waiting, his fathomless eyes glittering with something unnamed.

She comprehended what it was, suddenly. He knew too much about her. He knew everything, just from the way she fucked, from the way he made her convulse.

She closed her eyes, unable to bear looking at him. After all this, all the taunting, teasing, and sex play, after all her experience and his knowledge of it, there was only one truth, and he was too aware of it now: that she knew the mechanics, the words, what to do and how to do it, but little more.

She was unschooled in all things; she felt untethered, unfinished somehow, even immersed in this miasma of goading sex. It was all him, all his need, his want, his doing. She performed, nothing else. And she'd hardly been doing even that, judging by her explosive response to him.

Still he waited.

How much he knew that she did not. For all her bravado, how unseasoned she was. Life in the Valley provided no sustenance. Everything was tainted. Everything was wrong.

He waited, pushing and nudging himself deeper, and deeper still. She never imagined this depth, this insatiable greed for any man's penis. Give and go, that was her assignment in the Valley. Provide the willing body, the vessel, the relief, and the freedom from recriminations.

He wanted all give and give and give. And no recriminations.

He still waited, pumping his hips.

All the fucking you need . . . the most greedy lover of your nipples . . .

Her body contracted, the memory of his mouth pulling at her nipples coursing through every pore. She felt him keenly now, his heft, his heat, the hard invasiveness of him.

Now there was another truth: her knowledge of what her body was capable of. And that he was the man to push her to the limit.

She angled her legs against his buttocks and lifted her hips, drawing him into her still deeper.

"I'm ready, *cadi*. Ride me *hard*."

She wanted it now. She needed it in a way she had not the first two times. He saw it in her face, he felt it in her body, and he saw the knowledge of Eve lurking in her eyes.

Chapter Seventeen

He lay awake deep in the sultry night, with her cradled against his body, and let his mind roll with the movement of the ship.

They were a week away from landfall. A week away from the culmination of this strange erotic journey. He didn't want to think about how it would end or what would happen to her afterward.

In a sense, it was inevitable. He had brought her this far on the strength of his promise to take her to her father, and once that was done, that would be the end.

It *would* be the end.

They would take two or three days to get to London, and from there an hour to Aling. Then he would hand her over to the mysterious and aloof father who had had no compunction about abandoning his child to the mercies of the Valley.

What kind of man could do that? What kind of man could he be? Full of vinegar and rectitude, no doubt. Not able to rein in his lascivious wife all those years ago, or to convince her to remain in England, for certain.

So he let *her* go, and cut his losses. But his daughter?

She had been so young. And he'd just left her there. To be given over to *them,* to be nurtured by *them* and their supreme arrogance.

And here was the end result: this child of the Valley, schooled in sex, wicked as sin, innocent as a baby, trading her body for her desire to escape *them.*

So how far had she come, after all? Thousands of miles on her back and willingly so. And he didn't see how that was going to change in her father's house. If her father would even welcome her there.

Well, there were other things to consider before that was even a consideration. Like propriety and manners and dress.

No. He wasn't going to dress her until the last minute. Keep her tight in this self-contained little world they had created until the end, until it no longer could exist. And then, and only then, because he must, corset and contain that voluptuous body.

How would she feel about it, she who had been raised without constraints of any kind? Or did it come to a time when one yearned for boundaries and parameters?

Anyone?

Even him?

He shoved the thought away. He wasn't without sin either. But a man could atone in a woman's bed and be lauded for it, whereas a wanton only brought a man down.

But that was yet a week away, not to be thought about now. The end would be swift and sharp, like the swipe of a knife. Cut her loose and into the hands of the father who had denied her for so long. Let him take responsibility for teaching her the ways of properly raised women, and fitting her into his life.

She fit too well against him right now, as she stirred restlessly against him, all soft, naked, hot. He came instantly to attention, and all thoughts of what might hap-

pen a week hence shot out of his mind as she sleepily
rubbed her cleft against his thigh.

That rough graze of her pubic hair against his taut thigh
muscle. The innocent undulation of her hips. That low
sensual sigh as she settled more comfortably beside him.

Those amorous little movements aroused him deeply.
But these intimacies meant nothing to her. For her, it was
all part of the theater of sex, part of the scene that she
played out with any man in her mind.

He had a sudden vision of Georgiana at Aling, encircled
by an army of virile young men, graciously agreeing to service them all. A feast of fornication for her carnal side-
show.

They had taught her well.

Who would tell her these things just weren't done? Who
would ever refuse her? Not even he, and he would have
wagered he was the strongest-willed of any man she would
ever know.

He too had been felled by Eve, and the taste of the apple
was so sweet.

Well, reality would set in too soon in any event, and he
could prevent none of it. Whatever her fate at Aling, it was
not his concern. And he would have no second thoughts
about taking everything she offered in the meantime.

His body was so hot all the time. He was such a curious
combination of hard and soft and need and heat. She was
in a constant state of arousal just being near him. And in
this wicked little world, she was never more than three feet
away from him at any given time in those close quarters,
and barely an inch away from him now.

Her petal breast lay tight against his chest, the nipple
tight and hard like the center of a flower, demanding to be
fed upon. Beneath her, between her legs, the rock-hard
ledge of his thigh, perfect to rest upon. Before her, in the

dim light of dawn, the long thick shadow of his jutting penis, delicious to feast her eyes upon.

Her arousal was instant and complete. She wanted nothing more than to embed him between her legs. But not too soon. Too soon, he reaped the rewards of her accommodation. Too soon and it would be over almost before she could savor it.

And she must savor it because everything else would be over too soon.

His fingers brushed her enticing nipple and a thin thread of ecstasy rippled through her. It was like gold, hot, glowing, swirling, skirling pleasure, indefinable, delicious, different every time.

Amazing when she thought about it.

She hated to think. She wanted to feel, and what he was doing to her nipple sent corkscrews of molten feeling skeining down between her legs.

Nothing explosive. Just soft twisting sensations that made her want to climb all over him and sink onto him and keep him there, deep in the dark unfathomable part of her, forever.

And of course, if she were on her knees and straddling him, he could pleasure both nipples, and she could enjoy his penis just nudging and rubbing her, begging for its place.

She eased up on her elbow, and onto his thighs, taking his penis in her hand and positioning it against her midriff so that its thick length grazed the underside of her petal breast. And then she leaned forward and rubbed the back of his penis head against the nipple, back and forth tightly the way he liked it, so he could feel the hard point against the softness of her bulbous areola. So he could pour his creamy essence all over the flower of her breast.

Watching as she rubbed it and stroked it into her skin.

She would wear him forever. Every drop she squeezed from him, she caressed into her skin, her breasts, her body.

And then she held him, massaging him lightly with both hands, pulling at him gently higher, harder, inciting him to lust for her still more.

When his body was a frenzy of nerve endings waiting to explode, she lifted herself onto her knees and bent forward to offer him her breasts.

He wanted so much more. He was bursting with it, aching with it. He didn't want her nipples. He wanted full instant penetration, as deep and hot as he could go.

She canted her lower torso away from him, so that his penis head could only push between her legs. Not that fast. Not too soon. She wasn't denying him, exactly. She was prolonging him. Giving him her much desired nipples to suck and play with. Easing his penis to the heated slit of her cleft to just push its way in.

But only just so far. An inch, perhaps, so she could envelop him in her heat and wet. That was enough until he sucked her nipples. She had a craving to have him suck long and hard just on those hot hard tips before she let him penetrate her fully.

He kept pushing, and she kept retreating, keeping an inch inside her and tempting him with her breasts.

"*Khanum . . .*"

"*Ummm?*" It was very hard to balance her body to keep his penis at bay. And his hands. He stroked her everywhere he could reach, everywhere she wanted to feel him touch her. He knew somehow; he knew well. But she needed him to suck her nipples.

"Let me in."

"Soon." She undulated her hips away from the persistent pressure of his penis.

"What do I have to do to fuck you?"

"Suck my nipples, *cadi,* and I will let you in a little far-ther." Immediately she felt the hot lick of his tongue against one nipple, and a thick hot lick of desire curlicue downward. "Yes . . ." She let him push farther into her heat. "Yes . . ." as he sucked avidly at her breast.

Not too fast. Not too soon.

She held him like that, two inches enfolded in her labia, her hips shimmying, her body a glaze of pleasure, as he nuzzled and tugged at her nipple.

"Now . . ."

"The other nipple . . ."

"Torture, *khanum . . .*"

"Only for me," she whispered as his mouth closed over the other breast and her body jolted from the pure naked feel of it. She pushed farther forward, to give all of her breast, and still to hold that two bold hot inches of his penis inside her.

She could feel him throbbing, feel him fighting to main-tain some control. He filled her and yet she was empty. He was thick and hard there, just between her legs, com-manding, as he tried again and again to penetrate her far-ther.

She knew his tricks. His greedy sucking sent streams of heat and pleasure slithering through her body that soon would spill all over his brazen penis head and drown him. She wanted to engulf him, immerse him in her sex. She wanted to tease him and taunt him and push him to the edge of his endurance.

She had never felt like doing that with anyone else she'd ever been with.

Keep him at bay. Make him beg. Make him lust for her like no other woman he had ever known.

He grasped her hips, pushing downward, hard. "I have to—"

She shimmied away from his pulsating penis. "Not yet."

He pushed again, urgently. "There is no not yet, *khanum* . . . there is only"—he canted his hips up like a cannon and drove his penis hard and deep into her as she gasped for breath—*"now . . ."*

Now she was not empty. Now she sat back on his hips, filled so deeply, so thickly that her pubic hair rubbed against his. Her breasts were swollen from his voracious sucking, her nipples tight hard points, constricted from the hot wet pulling of his mouth.

This was now, the moment perfect. She had him between her legs. She could see his face clearly, in the filtering light, the emotion there even with his eyes closed, his mouth in a straight line, wrestling for control.

She rested her hands just on his breast, just at his nipples. And she waited, not wanting to move.

He didn't want to move either. If he moved, he would blast her and never stop.

He had to stop. It was enough to be embedded so deeply within her. Just for the moment, it was enough. Of all the moments that were left, it was enough. How many moments? He had a strong urge to calculate them, all the moments that were left. Then he would know how many more times he could fuck her before it all ended.

But just for now . . . it was enough, because everything about her and her sex sent him into a frenzy of lust. She was a queen, sitting there, straddling him, mounted on his throbbing penis.

And he was within a breath of blowing everything he had into her.

She rocked against him, teasing him, writhing her hips and sliding herself down the long pole of his shaft, up and down, testing his endurance, his stamina, his will.

Oh no, no teasing, not now. He drove upward into her, hard and meaningfully, pumping her like a piston, ignoring her rhythm, her guile.

He had waited too long for this release; morning was already nigh and she had been playing with him all these hours. There wasn't a man alive who could have endured such torture.

And now, he heaved upward one more time, one more great driving thrust, twisting into her, and he exploded, erupting like a volcano, hot and thick and pouring his seed into her as deep as he could go.

She came in the backwash of his orgasm, a flooding, rich, thick, languid mushroom of pleasure, blooming up and out and over.

She didn't want to acknowledge it. She wedged herself against his hot, sweaty body and took his sopping penis in her hand.

It's almost over . . .

There was an urgency between them, suddenly, as if they had to cram all the sex possible between that moment and when they would make landfall.

They didn't come out of the cabin. She was always on her back, her legs spread, inviting him in. He fucked her every way he could think of: standing, sitting, on her back, and from behind.

She especially liked from behind, where all she could feel was his thick rutting penis penetrating her obversely, and his merciless fingers tugging at her nipples.

"Who said no fucking?" she murmured once, only once during a break in their coupling when they were actually eating.

"Never mention it again, *khanum,* or there will be consequences."

There was a glint in her eye that he didn't like. "Truly?"

"You can count on it."

"I hope so."

A little brazen of her, he thought. "Take the consequences then . . ."

And he burrowed his fingers between her legs.
"Whenever we aren't fucking, I will penetrate you with my
fingers, so you will never get away from my possession of
you."

Whoever said I wished to? But she never spoke the
words. He made her breathless with his ferocity, but time
was growing short. He was always reaching for her. Or
when he was utterly spent, he took her with his mouth,
furrowing tightly between her legs and licking at her trea-
sure. And she took him in her mouth, and lapped up his
cream.

He fucked her standing, sitting, on her back and from
behind. She took him by hand, and she topped him and
mounted him and rode him hard and high.

He memorized her body with his hands. Her long legs,
her curvy bottom, the contours of her wet and welcoming
cunt. He knew her breasts by heart now, every nuance of
her response to his sucking and playing with them and he
fucked them often with his fingers shoved up between her
legs.

She loved that too; she loved it a lot. She adored all of
their steamy sweaty sex and everything he devised to do to
her as the hours ticked by and day wore into night into
dawn into day.

How much time? Suddenly, as in the desert, there wasn't
much time.

They never talked about time. They only felt and fondled and fucked each other and never looked at the time.

And they never said a word about what would happen
when they reached Greybourne. Journey's end. Two,
maybe three hours from London, and from civilization.

A scary new world—civilization. A place where there

were mores and rules, and things she would have to learn. A place where she would no longer be able to inhabit a tent in just her naked body.

In civilization, she would become Georgiana again. And he would no longer be her *cadi*.

Two more nights . . .

If she could have, she would have chopped through the ship's hull so it would sink and she could live in this perfect little world forever. They lay still after another savage coupling.

I don't want to go . . . She couldn't even form the words on her tongue. He had fulfilled his promise, and there was nothing to keep him once they reached the safety of her father's house.

This was a diversion merely, predicated on attraction, need, desire, and on the fact that she was well used to servicing men and men were used to taking whatever a woman offered freely.

That was all. Really all.

I don't want to go—

It was how she would acclimate to her father's house and her father's rules that was worrying her, she decided. That was the sticking point. What would happen once she crossed the threshold of Aling.

If he lets me in . . .

No! She couldn't think about that yet. That was wasting time. And there was hardly any more time.

It was terrifying how close they were to Greybourne. A night and a day perhaps. They could hear, all the time, conversation outside the cabins, snippets of discussion about the weather and transportation once they reached England. Where to stay, and how to go post or hire a carriage. The best routes to travel. The best places in London.

It was horrible, knowing your future was hours away.

And he was no help, with his impassive expression and his ever-wandering hands, and the way his body and his need blotted out everything else in sight.

But her desire matched his on every level. And she was perfectly willing to obliterate every thought of the future with sex. It was all she knew how to do anyway, and that ought to have frightened her more.

Instead, she threw herself into every last moment with him, knowing the moment the *Malabar* dropped anchor, everything would change. Wishing fruitlessly that if they just kept themselves isolated enough, everything would stay the same.

The weather got colder, the sky darker. The dampness invaded the cabin, the dusky light overlaid everything as the ship chugged inexorably through the calm waters of the channel toward Greybourne.

They separated slowly each time, dreading to hear the inevitable ring of the bell, the shout and rush of passengers on deck, the first view of land, of home, of England.

She sat hunched on the bedding, wrapped in her robes against the chill morning air. The ship's bell tolled as they passed Penzance and Plymouth and Torbay. Soon . . . soon, the song of the bells. Home to Aling, to her father, to a life of civility and sanity.

She knew how to walk away; she'd never done anything else. And anyway, a man never stayed. And that would be the end of it. He'd redeemed himself, salved his conscience, resurrected her life. His father's and Lydia's murders would go unavenged.

The will and desires of Moreton had prevailed once again.

She had not thought of him in weeks. The beginning of their flight and the reasons for it seemed like something she'd dreamed now. The Valley was the stuff of fiction, and Moreton was its evil emperor, reigning supreme, his harem by his side.

Of whom she might have been one.

She *was* one. Charles Elliott's *one,* passage paid, and soon to be expunged from his life as well.

So be it. She wrapped the robes more tightly around her naked body. Already she did not like the seeping dampness, the clammy air. It made her feel dank; it suppressed every hot feeling.

Or was that to the good?

He was making tea. In the cold light of the morning, there was nothing else to do but make tea. The warmth would be as comforting as his body was not. There were barely hours to go before they docked at Greybourne.

He handed her the cup and she wrapped her icy hands around it. He settled himself next to her and sipped his own cup thoughtfully.

There was nothing to say. The bargain was the bargain, fairly met on both sides. But now, the reality of cutting her loose loomed. Before the week was out, Georgiana would be at her father's house, in her father's hands, and he would be free to roam the world again.

The musky taste of the tea was like fog in the mouth, like fog on the moors. Places he'd roamed and loved—forbidden love, love at odds with everything he'd been taught and raised to believe.

And yet, he loved.

The smells, the sights, the sounds, the whole tenor of English life, he loved. It had been the biggest conflict of his existence, that divide between his two worlds.

Nor would it ever be easily resolved. He was still his father's son. And his mother's. Moreton Estabrook had murdered them both, and he was aching to exact revenge.

But he needed to return to the moors to finally and properly mourn Lydia. And he would never return to the desert, nor live among his father's people again.

Vengeance would come later; the need was there, and he was a master at plotting and patience. That part of his desert heritage he would never deny. He could wait, as long as he had waited to confront Lydia, if necessary. And he would see.

And meantime, there was Georgiana, with her tumbled hair, her insatiable body, her wild impetuous nature, her innocence—all damned.

He had no idea what awaited them at Aling.

He set aside his cup and began rummaging in the bedding and tossing things at her: the gun, the knife, money. All those nights, with those articles knotted into his head-dress, used as a pillow in the rare hours he got to sleep. He'd protected it all against her, who had the resourcefulness of a dragoman and the guile of Eve, and was scared to death now of what lay ahead.

He eased himself back by her side and picked up his cup. "There are all the *krans* we have left. Useless here. We need the money you took from me."

She stared at him over the rim of the cup. "For what?"

"We need to dress you properly before we engage to go to London. And we need to book a coach and at least one night at a cheap inn. And that might just about cover it."

"There are shops in Greybourne?"

"I should think, it's a fairly large port town, a lot of ships in and out from all over."

The bell clanged; a bullhorn of a voice rang out, "Weymouth . . ."

"Give over the money, Georgiana." He said it softly, he said her name. For the first time in weeks, maybe ever, he said her name.

It was almost like a spell, that word, breaking the intimacy between them, cleaving through the connection, the heat, the sex. Everything.

She felt her body grow colder as she reached for the edge of her *abeya* and untied a knot at the hem. Banknotes fluttered onto the bedding.

Many, many banknotes. He'd forgotten how much money he'd had in that pouch. He'd forgotten everything but endlessly inserting himself into her pouch.

He picked up it up and counted it meticulously.

Everything intact. His papers. His money. The gun. He watched as she eyed it speculatively, and then he took it, the knife, and all the money and packed it up again.

"And now?" Georgiana asked, her voice brittle.

"We can do no more."

The words had a double edge. On any level, they could do no more, together or apart.

They sat in silence over a second cup of tea.

An hour later, the bell tolled again. And that deep bull-horn voice of doom: "Greybourne . . ."

The end was here.

Chapter Eighteen

The thing she noticed first was the church spire looming over the thicket of masts in the harbor at Greybourne. It was nearly noon, the sky was overcast, as the *Malabar* chugged into the harbor and into the chaos of ships along the quay.

Warehouses, gray as the sky, lined the wharves, which were alive with activity. At any given slip, a ship was loading up to leave, or off-loading barrels and crates onto drays and lorries.

In the midst of this, there were rowboats ferrying out to ships anchored offshore, and swans following them in graceful punctuation.

The noise of a port town was audible even on the deck of the *Malabar* with its noisy rusty engine straining to make the last few fathoms to the dock.

Close in, the harbor was not a particularly pretty sight, and the smell of rotting fish and the dank air overshadowed everything.

So many people. So many ships. So much noise.

She started to shiver. This was worse than Dar el Rabat. And it was so cold. And there were so many wagons and the drivers kept shouting at each other, and cursing at each other—

This was an awful place, horrible. She didn't know why she ever thought she wanted to come here. She could never live in such a place. She wanted to go back.

Charles could arrange it. She would just go back and everything would be the way it was before he ever invaded the Valley.

Except, no Lydia. Oh God, no Lydia, and she'd forgotten all about that—and her mother, and Moreton. All of that, in the swamping undertow of fucking him endlessly in payment for his bringing her here.

What would she trade for a return trip?

And a return to what?

Moreton's Valley, Moreton's way . . .

No. No. She forced herself to consider the quayside scene once more.

It's not that bad. It's just cold. And this thing between Charles and me is over, and he'll become nothing more to me than one of any of the dozen faceless men who were serviced in that old life. And now my new life starts. And I don't know what to expect. That's why I feel so panicky. I just don't know what to expect.

Better. Maybe. But she still felt shaky and unsure. And cold. God, she was cold. In this weather, the enshrouding robes of the *abeya* did not protect her against the cold or the future.

And she looked exotic and foreign next to the plain-dressed Englishmen and women who populated the ship. The difference was stunning standing next to them on deck here; it had been inconsequential in Sierra Leone.

So long ago, their sojourn in Liberty Town. Two or three weeks? That long ago? She felt as if her mind were babbling. She just could not encompass the breadth of the scene before her, or even comprehend what came next.

All she could do was try to concentrate on one thing at a time. And not think about herself and her fears.

She wrapped her arms more tightly around her body and leaned over the deck rail. Far away, over the view of the bobbing ships, there was a prettier side to the harbor. One she could see in the distance: buildings that were better kept, tall trees, winding streets, the church spire thrusting up into the gray clouded day.

Greybourne was aptly named.

People lived here, worked here, had families here. The business here was not fornication and gratification. This was the real world. So could it be that the Valley was Eden after all?

She shook off that notion. It would do her no good to romanticize what in effect had been business transactions in the valley. The difference was the currency: sex.

She could not present herself at Aling like this. Charles was right. She needed the proper clothes, the proper attitude. She had to show her father that she could be a proper daughter in a proper setting and make him proud.

It was just—it was so crowded on the wharves. And the people were so rustic, and raw. And loud. And they crowded you, even on deck, they shoved and nudged and pushed you out of the way.

And where was Charles, who had gone off to see about debarkation? Why had he left her in this awful place, naked and alone?

"Do you see, my dear, do you? Was I not right?"

They were in the offices of the Trans-African Shipping Company, pretending to be wealthy importers looking for a new venue to ship their goods, having found out that Greybourne, rather than Brighton, was the port of entry for England-bound passengers from West Africa.

The clerk had just gone to fetch the company head, and

they were standing at the window overlooking the bustling wharves, and they'd caught sight of the very thing they'd hoped to see: the *Malabar* chugging up the inlet into the harbor, newly arrived from West Africa.

"Well then, Lord Estabrook." A portly gentleman entered the room, rubbing his hands together. "Goods and services, hey? Well, we all need those, don't we? What are we talking about specifically?"

"We have to get out of here soon," Olivia whispered. "If we want to catch them . . ."

"Leave it to me," Moreton murmured, and turned to the gentleman who was now seated at a desk shuffling papers and preparing for a long afternoon of haggling.

Moreton disabused him of that idea quickly. "Mr. Cable. So pleased. Here's the story: we have a source of native decorative items, iron and ivory out of the Agonjo region that we are seeking to import here. So I won't take very much of your time right now. What I need from you is a schedule of shipping and the pricing to study the feasibility and cost of doing business with you."

"But I—"

Moreton cut him off. "No, no. Here's my card. Send me the information and I'll make an appointment after I've gone over your routes and pricing. There you go. Come, my dear." He took Olivia's arm and steered her to the door. "I'll look forward to hearing from you," he added over his shoulder as they exited the office and flew down the stairs.

"Quickly now . . ."

"You're a genius, Moreton . . ."

"Too easy," Moreton murmured as they came out of the building onto the wharves. "This way . . ."

"But what if they're off already?" Olivia fretted. "What if they're gone?"

"They'll still be in Greybourne," Moreton said confidently. "They still have arrangements to make. And she can't have the appropriate clothing. Or he, for that matter. Nor can they have much money. They're still here, my dear. Ripe for the plucking. We fixed it just right. They won't be hard to find. And remember, our sole purpose here is to hasten them home."

There were dozens of inexpensive sailors' rests in Greybourne. It wasn't hard to choose one that was reasonably clean and where the proprietors included a meal and asked no questions.

It was a soggy little room under the eaves of a four-story inn hard by the warehouses on the quay, and not much different from where they had slept in Dar el Rabat. It was furnished in almost the same way: one bed, a dresser, a worn carpet, a pair of kerosene lamps, a table, and two chairs. Hot water, a shilling extra. A window that looked out onto a scraggly rear garden.

This was the end of the journey.

A farewell coupling didn't seem quite the thing to do. Georgiana didn't know what to do. And he was so businesslike, and so aloof, she wanted to scream.

At least it was warm in the room, but that was only because of the residual heat from the chimney flue that ran up the far wall.

It was enough. She sat curled up on the bed, staring at the walls.

Soup, biscuits, and tea were sent up for dinner. They ate in silence, and after, Charles began plotting out what next they needed to do.

"Clothes, for one. There are several dressmakers in town who might have something to buy ready-made. You'll need shoes, stockings, a corset, undergarments. A nightgown. A hat, a coat, a suitcase, a purse . . ."

He was talking a foreign language. Stockings? Undergarments? A *nightgown?* She, who had slept naked since the ceremony of the peacock fan?

He hadn't stopped, hadn't even noticed the appalled expression on her face. " . . . a brush, a comb, gloves, handkerchiefs, soap . . ."

But he did notice after a while the deadly silence, and then he looked at her. She looked overwhelmed and angry and unhappy. But what had he expected? He was hurling all this at her, all the things she needed to give her the appearance of respectability, and they were things she'd never worn, never used, never cared about.

Well, then, that was her father's part. His part was just to get her there, and there was nothing that said he had to dress her like a queen.

Except, for some perverse reason, he wanted to.

"Georgiana—"

She wanted to rip off her *abeya* and turn back the clock. Wanted to be naked and hot and coupled with him, her legs propped on his chest, his penis plunging deeply, wildly into her.

This is as dressed as I get when I'm in male company . . .

Was he remembering that too?

"You can't arrive at your father's house dressed as you are."

Yes, I can, she thought rebelliously. *I can do anything I damned want.*

No, she couldn't. If she wanted at all ever to convince her father that she wanted to be with him and to stay in England, she couldn't, and that was her grim reality right now. That, and saying good-bye to him.

"And it's too cold anyway."

You could warm me . . .

She turned her head away. Useless thinking that. That was over. Maybe she could kill him instead.

Time to act the part of an Honorable's daughter and just bury the rest away.

The words stuck in her throat. "You're right, of course. I should never want to call such attention to myself."

No way to avoid it, Charles thought, but he didn't say it out loud. She was wary enough, the queen, and on very shaky ground in her quest to go to her father. Nevertheless, after a month travel, and all that sex, she still bore herself like a queen, and nothing in the world, not even that god-awful shroud, could disguise either her beauty or that proud posture.

She was made to be in England, and England was made for her.

And on the morrow, when she was properly clothed, then she'd see.

She slept later than she'd intended, even on that uncomfortable excuse for a bed in that cold and damp room. Maybe it was because she was feeling so distraught and just needed to shut everything out. Maybe it was because she didn't want to face everything that came next.

There was no help for that; the sun would infiltrate even through the dusty windows, and tomorrow would always come, no matter where in the world she was.

But when she awakened, she found that she was alone, and there was a tray on the table with a pot of tea—surely cold by now—and a plate of hard scones. And the water in the pitcher on the dresser was lukewarm, which suggested that Charles was long gone, and had chosen to let her sleep.

She didn't know if she felt the better for it. Everything was still too strange, and she was still too cold.

She poured some of the tea, for want of something to do, and settled back on the bed with the blanket wrapped around her.

In the Valley, she thought, the sun would be shining, the weather heated, breakfast consumed, and the residents going about the pursuits of the day. Sex. Cards. Horseback riding. Sex. Eating. Sex. Gossip. Polo, now, even with Charles's minimal instruction. Gluttony. Sex.

She felt a certain nostalgia for the regimentation. Everyone knew what was available, what to do, and when to do it. Sex anytime anywhere; everything else fixed around that.

And then the next day, the cycle began again.

Was there something comforting about that? Really?

Where was Charles?

She felt edgy, uncertain. There were no more threats; there was nothing to keep Charles here. They were done with sex. Done with the Valley. Done with everything except taking her to Aling.

He wasn't gone; she was fairly certain of that. He was probably out finding something *proper* for her to wear. He was just the kind of man to know about things like that. No more shifts and gauze and paper-thin slippers that could be divested at a moment's notice.

No more sex . . .

Her choice. But why had she seen it so clearly in the Valley, and it suddenly seemed so blurred and distorted here?

Him. The unknown, unobtainable him, that was why.

No. No. No. He had been the means to an end, and she had been a convenience. That was the end of that story.

But still . . . after him—who?

She had to stop this, had to stop thinking about sex, thinking about him, thinking about them, coupled, together.

There was a knock on the door.

"Yes?" Her voice quavered a little. Who in the inn knew she was alone in the room?

A woman's voice answered. "Your bath, missus. The mister arranged it before he went out this morning."

He hadn't left her, hadn't forgotten her.

Georgiana jumped off the bed and unlocked the door. Two hefty men bore in a copper tub, followed by two servants and the landlady, all carrying large ewers of hot water.

"Put it by the chimney breast there," the landlady directed, "so she'll get a bit of the heat. And careful with the water now, there's precious little of it. I've got some soap here, and some clean toweling for you, missus. The water cools off fast in this weather, so you want to make best use of it now."

She couldn't wait for them to leave, the landlady not wanting to, obviously unable to hide her curiosity. Finally, she locked the door emphatically behind them, stripped off her *abeya* in one motion, and, grabbing the sliver of soap, she climbed into the tub.

Ahhhh—hot. Blessed blessed heat, seeping into her bones. *That* was what she missed: the heat. She slid down as deeply into the water as she could, wet her hair, and started rubbing her body with the fragrant spit of soap.

What had it cost him, this, the most basic of needs, in this charnel house of an inn? She would never ask. It was enough it was done, and she soaked in the heat and the wet and the scent until time ran out and the water turned cold.

Oh, yes, he knew about all things feminine. She was shocked at just what that entailed, here. A hideous one-piece undergarment topped by a corset, a chemise, petticoats . . .

And the corset! An instrument of torture, surely, but he knew just how to squeeze her into it, just how every piece should fit and and everything should go. And the god-awful stockings. And the stiff light lady boots.

The litany of requisites he had recited to her yesterday all now constricting her body, her sex, and her life.

"This is what it will take to become my father's daughter?" she demanded, her voice a huff of breath as he pulled one last time at the corset.

Even he thought it was a damned shame to truss that body into it, but he wouldn't have told her that for a fortune in gold.

"A lady properly dressed wears all of this," he said noncommittally.

"If this is how I must dress from this day forward, coming here was a very bad idea."

"Cheer up, my *lady*. At least you will be not be cold. And you will go to your father in a recognizable fashion."

And as someone too beautiful to behold. Even in the constraining undergarments, she radiated sensuality. And he didn't know how he was managing to keep his hands off of her.

Corsets helped. Normally. But on her, the undergarments only engendered a raging urge in him to strip them off.

His need gnawed at him. He had forgotten how arousing undergarments could be. On the right woman.

On her.

Whose right woman would she become now?

He couldn't allow his thoughts to take that track. She was distracting enough as it was.

And she hated everything she had to wear, and everything about this last leg of the journey. "What further brutality must I endure in the name of dressing *properly?*" she asked imperiously.

He waved his hand at the clothes he had purchased and already laid on the bed: a clay-colored skirt to be worn with a blouse the color of amber and a short matching cape jacket.

She put them on grudgingly. Pretty. Plain. Heavy against her skin, pulling her down, down. Stockings on her legs— she felt rooted to the ground. She hated them; she hated him.

She wanted to go back to the Valley, now, instantly.

There was a comb, and a hat. A small valise. He'd thought of everything, including for himself.

It was the only thing that kept her from bolting, that he had to constrict and stuff his body into these god-awful clothes too.

No longer was he the desert brigand. The flowing robes were gone, and there was nothing to mark him as anything but a gentleman except his sun-dark skin, which contrasted starkly with the white shirt, dark suit, and long frock coat he now wore.

"You have become Charles Elliott," she murmured, as she combed her tangled hair.

"And you are the daughter of the Honorable Henry Maitland, my lady. And so our roles have changed."

They had changed, she thought, everything carnal about them both obliterated by the constraints imposed in this society. She hadn't expected that, the tightness, the rigidity of conformation.

And yet, he seemed comfortable with it, as if he understood it, as if he even embraced it. Oh, but how, after all their unfettered weeks together? If she could comprehend that, she thought, she could do this. She could slough off everything about the Valley and she could be her father's daughter instead of Charles's desert whore.

She wanted desperately just to be his desert whore.

She knew how to do that. And she loved it, she especially loved it with him. And she didn't need much more than that—the pleasure was almost secondary to his obsessed possession of her.

All of that, she wanted. Where would she ever find such

an intense, devouring sensuality ever again? What man could equal his sexual appetite, his stamina and prowess?

What could her father give her that would equal that?

And yet, by his own hand, he had restricted and inhibited her, contained, confined, and hemmed her in with these repressive clothes. What were they meant to do but obliterate every sensual feeling and utterly suppress her desire for sex?

Well, he had underestimated her. Nothing could blot out the driving need for sex. It throbbed like the drums of Ngano, night and day, just beneath her skin.

Standing this close to him, as she combed her hair and twisted it away from her face, she felt it. *He* felt it. It simmered in the air between them, flaring like sunspots.

She took a pin and jabbed into the topknot.

"There's a train to London in the next hour," he said coolly, ignoring the heat between them. "I suggest we get ready to go."

"I don't want to go."

Everything in him tightened up. It would be so easy to capitulate to her now. Another day would make no difference. Another year would make no difference for that matter. And he could feed on her breasts, on her body forever.

Except for one thing. And even now he wasn't certain his imagination wasn't playing tricks on him. But still it was something about which he could not take the chance.

This morning he thought he'd seen Moreton.

Logically it wasn't possible. Moreton was stuck in the Valley, sticking himself into some willing hole.

And he'd only caught the merest glimpse of the man's face, of the way he held himself, the way he walked. Nothing conclusive.

Nothing he would tell her. But suddenly time was of the

essence, and every other consideration went out the window, except getting her to Aling.

"You wanted very badly to come to England, my lady. I think we should go."

There was no arguing with that tone of voice. She tucked the comb and the sliver of soap and her *abeya* and boots into the valise, closing it up. Packing away another life. There was nothing else left.

Had there ever been anything except the pure proprietary animal need of two people on an isolating journey? Any woman would have done in that scenario, and she needed to remember that and get on with it.

She took the flat-crowned piece of felt adorned with two feathers that he called a hat and tied it onto her head.

Ridiculous thing. The cape next. The valise. Down the steps. Pay the landlady. Charles with his hand at her elbow guiding her out onto the street.

Dazzling sunlight today, beaming through the clouds. The same misery: too many people, too cold, too much noise.

For her, a horrible gray day . . .

"We go this way."

This way was a long winding street that curved up above the harbor. It was a brisk walk too, difficult in her more feminine boots that were not broken in.

Not even the rows of shops along each side of the street could distract her. The upward climb was onerous, tiring. The sun hurt her eyes.

Fifteen minutes later, they reached the summit where the view of the harbor was spectacular. From here, the channel looked like an ocean sparkling in the sun, the ships riding the swells like toys and the tall masts like matchsticks scraping the sky.

Here, at the top of the hill, the road flattened out and fed into a broad boulevard lined with homes and office buildings and stores in one direction, and, just at the inter-section, the train station, already crowded with carriages and taxis and travelers.

He had their tickets in hand, purchased from an agent on the wharf earlier that morning. So it was just a matter of elbowing through the crowd, until they found their car. Scanning each face. Helping her up into the crowded car-riage. Settling her on the nearest bench, making sure he had the window seat.

Looking out over the crowd with minutes to go before departure. A sea of anonymous faces. Nothing there.

And then, he saw him—Moreton back beyond the crowd, looking directly at him, smiling his evil smile.

Chapter Nineteen

And then, the man was everywhere. Was that him nudging his way through the crowded carriage? Or on the platform at Malverne? On that bucking horse chasing after the engine past Stratton Church?

His brain had to be sun-damaged. Moreton Estabrook was still in the Valley, fucking and scheming his way to infamy.

Georgiana was preternaturally quiet. But then all of this was new to her. There were no wide open spaces on the train ride to London. In the south, they passed vast swaths of farmland dotted with small village homes that gave way to smaller villages, the houses set closer together, and narrow streets and market squares. Everywhere, a glimpse of the bustle of daily living as the train flew by. Everything growing crowded and more congested as the train steamed closer and closer to the suburbs of London.

Almost over. Almost there, whatever *there* meant. Georgiana had no sense of *there*. Just noise. And people. And a babble of voices that all seemed to be speaking some foreign language.

And everything hurt: her ribs, her feet, her head. The

price to escape the Valley was beginning to seem too steep if it meant she had to acclimate to all this.

And then the endless vista of land and encroaching houses and roads and cold blue sky and the endless towns: Featherstone, Milford, Haystoke, Smythe.

She'd wanted this. Yearned for this. Sold her body for this. And her soul, too. But how could she have known where it would lead, when a man like Charles Elliott was so completely beyond her experience?

Well, there it was. The lessons of the Valley had not included a primer on this. In not too many hours, she would be on her own. In her father's house, stepping into another world, another way of life.

The house of her childhood fairy tales. The one Olivia couldn't wait to escape. Was it not fated that her daughter had escaped to return to it?

Aling. All she knew of it was what Olivia had told her. Olivia had brought no pictures, no momentos. She had thrown off the shackles of genteel society and everything it stood for, everything that went with it, to come to South Africa, to wallow in Moreton's debauched Eden.

And yet she spoke of Aling to her daughter, enough so that Georgiana had felt as if she had a place, as if she belonged somewhere.

But now, this close to London, she wasn't so sure. She felt *out* of place, out of her element. She felt, now that the fog of sensual heat had cleared, that she'd made a big mistake thinking she could just walk in on her father and expect he would welcome her with open arms.

And an even bigger mistake letting Charles Elliott fuck her. And thinking more about that than anything else.

More stops coming closer to London: Westchester, Spawn Hill, Haverford. Almost there, almost there.

The tension in her escalated. Now she avidly watched

for the signs. Heymouth, Windsor, Wandsworth . . . too fast, too fast. Buildings everywhere, and crowded roads leading into the city, the train tracking right alongside, and then, with a slow long easing down the track and with a great smoky heave, the train steamed into Victoria Station.

The journey was over.

Charles knew London, which was another thing she didn't know about him. He knew it like someone who had lived there. Had no hesitation where to go, or what to do. Just took her arm and propelled her onto the platform toward the exit and the nearest hansom cab.

Outside there was gloomy misty twilight as he bundled her into the cab and gave an address for someplace called Wexley. Nor did he explain. There was something grim in his expression, something she didn't wish to question, she was too tired to question.

It took a little time to get there; traffic was a tangle of carriages, cabs, and pedestrians. Impressions bombarded her. The same crowdedness, the same noise. Streets like valleys with buildings rising up on either side. Gas lights. Drivers yelling curses. Carriages swerving. Whistles and church bells. Clattering across a bridge over a narrow expanse of water. Quieter but no less crowded on the other side.

Everything so different. She would never get used to it.

The cab pulled up alongside a row of brick houses with wide stoops not far from the bridge.

Charles thrust some notes into the driver's hand and hustled Georgiana onto the sidewalk, covertly scanning the surroundings. There was nothing else in sight, just the muted gas glow of the streetlights marching in a row down the street and around the corner. A hovering fog. And the familiarity of returning to a place he knew.

It was a welcome feeling after all these weeks and after the last few hours of feeling as if they were being stalked by an enemy.

God, for all he knew, Moreton was around the corner.

He took Georgiana's elbow and mounted the steps of the nearest house. Number thirty-six Wampton Road. Everything about it was the same as he remembered, even the worn brass door knocker.

"Oh, oh mind your horses, I'm comin', I'm comin'." And a minute later, the door was opened by a rotund old woman dressed in purple, carrying a parlor lamp, which she held up to Charles's face, stared at him uncertainly for a moment, and then, "Bless my stars. Mr. Charles."

"Miss Elmina . . ." He took her hands. "We need a room for tonight."

"Come in, come in." She threw open the door and they entered a narrow hallway. To the left, there was a staircase with walnut banisters; to the right, an archway leading into an overstuffed parlor. There was furniture everywhere, grouped around an ornate marble fireplace, three or four chairs, two sofas, a parlor table, two chairs by the front window and another table between them, covered in lace. Heavy curtains draped from elaborate cornices. Étagères in the two corners, crowded with ornaments and bric-a-brac.

It was stuffy as cotton wool, and claustrophobic besides.

"A room you shall have," Miss Elmina was saying, consulting a large book that was propped up on a lectern just by the entrance to the parlor. "Will your old room do? It has that little alcove, you remember? Dear me, you are the last person I ever expected to see. Again. I thought you'd gone to South America."

"So I did," Charles said. "And here I am again. This is Miss Georgiana. I'm escorting her to her father's house."

Miss Elmina was silent for a moment, and Georgiana saw she was tussling with the idea of them sharing a room on the basis of that minimal information. Then she said, "I see. Well, that's your business, Charles. So go on with you. You and the lady. Dinner as usual, in about a half hour, or Dora can bring you a tray. We'll settle everything else tomorrow."

"That's satisfactory. I'd appreciate your sending up a tray. Georgiana?"

She climbed the steep staircase to the third floor like a zombie. "His" room was the front room, the one with the not-so-subtle suggestion that its alcove could serve as a separate sleeping area for her.

And indeed, there was a sofa in the alcove, as well as a table and lamp. And the bed that took up most of the space in the room proper. There was a fireplace, fronted by a chair and table. And a wash sink, and a built-in cupboard and drawers backed the closet where this room would have connected with the back bedroom.

Charles walked around the room, lighting the lamps, brusquely checking everything out. "There is a bathroom down the hallway. And a little sink over there. You'll want to wash up."

Georgiana stared at him. He had no idea how tired she was, and how much that corset hurt. Or how scared she was, of what was to come, and this new permutation—a room in a strange house among people he apparently knew.

"I don't want to do anything but get out of these clothes. And hear your explanation as to what we are doing here."

"Oh, that's coming, my lady." He was at the window, drawing curtains. "I just thought we both needed a few minutes' respite." He waved her to the couch. "Sit down."

She sat, her posture stiff. "I just had no idea this journey would be like this. And this damned corset *hurts.*"

"I'm sorry to tell you, my lady, the corset goes on forever," Charles said, amusement lacing his voice. "Listen. I lived here, after I finished university, and before I went to South America, as you heard Miss Elmina say. It was safest place I could think to come."

Safest place? Those were two words she never expected to hear, and the words that made the most impact. Safe from what?

From whom?

"Anywhere else," Charles went on coolly as she said nothing, "someone could track us down. Anywhere in London proper, in any event."

Georgiana swallowed. "And who would be looking for us, *in any event?*"

He didn't want to tell her. He was hoping she wouldn't insist he tell her. "It's just better not to take the chance."

"*Who?*"

Bloody hell. "Moreton. I think Moreton's in England. But by God, I can't figure out why."

As promised, Dora delivered dinner some forty-five minutes later: some barley broth, lamb chops, mashed potatoes, stewed celery, blancmange and apple pudding for dessert—a boardinghouse dinner, and extremely welcome at that point.

Georgiana was ravenously hungry, having gotten out of the undergarments and shrouded herself in her *abeya.* She sat curled up on the couch, ruminating on the ramifications of Moreton's being in England.

He'd gotten tired of the Valley? How could he? He was king of the world there.

Tired of sex, perhaps? Moreton? *Never.*

Or maybe he was ready to conquer new worlds. Perhaps he had a master plan to convert the whole of England to his philosophy.

That she could see. And it would definitely be a long-term plan, so obviously Moreton had to start now.

She said as much to Charles as she devoured the lamb chops.

"You have to have imagined it. There's no earthly reason for Moreton to come back to England."

"I know." But he didn't know, and that was what made it so impossible. A mind like Moreton's was unfathomable. On the surface, there was nothing for him to gain. And life in England had to be too constricting for a man with that depth of depravity in his soul.

Moreton had everything he'd ever dreamed of in the Valley. Why would he ever think of coming back to England?

The thing was, talking about him brought back everything about Bliss River. Every heated moment. Every feeling. Everything that had happened between them they were both trying to suppress.

It was always there, bubbling away, waiting for the moment of implosion.

She was but hours away from being returned to her father. He was not going to throw her on the floor and fuck her. Not tonight, and especially not in Miss Elmina's house.

That part was over.

Tomorrow she would disappear behind the doors of Aling to be cloistered in her father's house. That was the bargain, the barter, the payment for services rendered.

The end of that chapter.

And Moreton be damned. The man was too much in everyone's consciousness, the world he created too easily theirs on demand.

Such an evil genius. So charismatically amoral, you could only fall under his spell or get out of his way. And if you didn't—

The thought arrested him.
You died . . .

Where was Aling? Georgiana thought it was in Kent. Or Essex.

By all that was holy—

Charles was in and out of the room all morning, first with tea and toast, and then back downstairs to confer with Miss Elmina, which gave her the opportunity to dress, and to hide the misbegotten corset deep in the closet where some unfortunate boarder might find it months from now.

It was so much better without it. She felt more like herself; she felt as though she could finally breathe, without all that whalebone compressing the life out of her.

But she couldn't understand Charles's sudden urgency to be on their way so early this morning. If anything, she wanted to prolong the moment when she would see her father.

But this was the inevitable end. The second ending. The first was after they'd debarked from the *Malabar,* and it became clear that she had paid her debt to him in full, nothing more wanted, nothing more owed.

She didn't like that kind of ending. And she wasn't so sure about a new beginning either; all of it felt like she was on a runaway train, and hanging on for dear life.

And Charles now thundering up the stairs. "Pack your bag, my lady. We're leaving in ten minutes. I've hired a cab."

Perhaps an hour outside of London, wasn't that what Olivia had said? And here they were, rolling at a brisk clip down a turnpike east of Wexley, on their way to Aling.

"I should send a message," Georgiana said fretfully. "I was but two when he left; he won't know me. He'll require some proof, which I don't have, which I never even thought about bringing with me."

"He won't refuse to see you."

Georgiana stared out the cab window. Her hands were cold. And her body. The morning air was as damp and clammy as the day before. And it seemed as if the sun never rose in this place.

"How can you know that?"

"He'll be curious at the very least. And there can't have been any other one claiming to be his daughter turning up on his doorstep. I daresay it's not common knowledge that Olivia and he had had a child."

She thought about that. Her father had willingly gone to Bliss River Valley with Olivia. Stayed because Olivia was pregnant? And gotten out as fast he could, once the baby was delivered?

If he felt that strongly about leaving her there, as evidence did show, he certainly would never have made it known he had family at all.

What stories had he told then to account for it? Or had he just taken mistresses by the dozen and told some fantastic lie about his wife—that she was insane, that he never could marry until she died.

In her youth, she'd never given him a thought. Moreton acted the father in her life until she got old enough to comprehend what his role was in the Valley.

Dear Moreton, the gardener of Eden, planting his seed and spawning no child . . .

Why hadn't her own father come for her? Why hadn't he even tried?

Or had Olivia prevented him with her own set of lies?

There would never be normalcy for her, a child of wickedness, schooled in the Valley. And this dream of reuniting with her father was about to turn into a nightmare.

* * *

In the rolling landscape of Kent, south of Maidstone and east of Tunbridge Wells, just outside the little village of Medwyn, stood Aling, the country house of Henry Maitland.

They came to it straight out of the village off the turnpike going toward King's Lyme—Aling.

The sun was up by this time, the air warm and the sky clear. And it was quiet, still. Church still, the only sound the carriage wheels crunching up the drive that wound around to Aling.

She couldn't breathe. Now that they were that close to the house, she thought she would expire right on the floor of the cab. She couldn't absorb anything except that it was quiet and Aling—the house—was dead ahead of them, its crenellated roofline just visible above the trees.

Slowly, inexorably, the house came into sight. A big stone house, sited low to the ground. Nothing intimidating about Aling, if it weren't your father you were about to confront.

The drive wound in a circle to the front door. There was not a sound as the carriage pulled to a stop. Just that still peacefulness. Nothing at all to be afraid of.

She looked at Charles. His expression was grim.

"Come in with me?"

"We'll see."

The carriage drew up to the door. There were two steps leading up to the highly polished front doors. The windows on the first floor were low to the foundation. Everything about the house seemed as if the architect had wanted to minimize its grand scale.

But grand it was nevertheless, with twelve full windows marching along the second floor alone, and that smooth swath of lawn around which the drive curved.

"Welcome to Aling," Charles said, getting out of the carriage and coming around to her side.

"Come." He held out his hand. She took it, her own cold and trembling, her eyes locked with his, reading— what?

The enigma of the man. The strength of his hand, the vigor of his body, now denied to her. If that was the price for this moment, she didn't want to pay it. Now she was here, surely she could make changes.

He leaned forward suddenly and his lips touched hers. He meant it to be reassuring. He meant it to be a connection between them, that he understood and nothing more.

And certainly nothing carnal.

And yet it jolted him, just rocked him to the ground to feel the softness of her lips against his in such a decidedly nonsexual way.

Because the promise was there. And the heat. And her scent. And the memory of all they had done and everything still yet to be done. All there in the touch of her lips, in the faint sound at the back of her throat as he pulled away.

And then she was out of the carriage somehow and the door was in front of her, and she couldn't move to save her life.

Don't make anything of it. It was a kiss good-bye, nothing more, nothing less. The kind of thing that moves the earth, and yet when you look at it, nothing changes. Just you, because of everything that was, and everything that will not be.

It was still early. Perhaps even too early to pay a call, she thought, desperately trying not to think about the kiss. They'd left Wexley before eight o'clock, so it couldn't be much past nine. Not a good time for visitors. Probably a very rude time for visitors to call.

"It's way too early, isn't it? Can't we come back later?"

"I overestimated how much time it would take to get here," Charles said blandly. "We might as well go in. Are you ready?"

"No." Not ready for her father, not nearly ready for that soul-destroying kiss.

"Good." Charles turned to the driver. "We'll be but a few minutes."

"No never mind on me as long as the tick is running," he muttered. "Take your time."

Then Charles stepped up to the door and rang the bell. It was a sonorous thing, tolling like a church bell, loud enough to wake the dead.

"Not even a servant to come to the door?" she murmured. "How odd. But then, it is early and nobody receives callers at this hour. Even I know that. Truly, Charles, we should come back later."

He rang the bell again.

And again no one came.

"Do you suppose—" He tried the door. It was unlatched and swung open easily. Too easily. Which made him very uneasy. "Well, now—"

"Now I've become Alice," Georgiana said, trying to get a glimpse inside. It was dark, the reception hallway, and she could see nothing beyond Charles's shoulder. She wondered what he could see.

"Then I'll go down the rabbit hole," Charles said. "You stay here."

That, in fact, would have been easier. But not after that kiss. And it was her father. And now she was wildly curious to know why there were no servants to answer the door.

She gathered up what little courage she could muster. "I'll come."

Charles led the way. They entered a broad hallway that

was sparsely but elegantly furnished with a thick Turkish carpet, a highly polished center table, and a crystal chandelier.

There were doors all around the hall, and not easy to tell which led to the hallway, the stairs, or the parlor.

And it was so quiet. Too quiet. As if the household staff had all been given the day off.

An impossibility. And Charles didn't like the further thought that occurred to him. "I suppose we'll just try one and see what happens . . ." he said, choosing the one directly opposite the front door.

That proved to lead out to the main hallway, also similarly carpeted, and furnished with console tables and paintings. There were more doors along this hall and Charles walked back and forth across the hall, opening them.

"The parlor. The dining room. Another parlor. The breakfast room. The library. The morning room. Aren't you wondering why *no one* has come to challenge our being here? The billiard room . . ." He stepped inside that room for a moment, and then disappeared.

Georgiana edged into the room after him.

"Georgiana?"

Oh God—"I'm here."

"I found him . . . Don't come any farther."

"What does that mean?"

"What you think it means. He's in his office, back beyond the billiard room. You do not want to see him. What you want to do is slowly and calmly walk out of here, and get into the carriage. Tell the driver I'll be along in a minute, that we made a mistake, that this is the wrong house after all, and I'm making amends with the butler. Are you clear?"

"Yes."

"Good. Do it." He listened for a moment, he heard her

footsteps receding, and then he looked back down at the body. What remained of Henry Maitland, drowning in his own blood, just like Lydia.

Brutal, senseless, amoral act, and for what? He couldn't conceive of a sane reason to murder Henry Maitland. Not one damned reason, and yet dead he was. And for certain by the same merciless hand that had taken his mother's life.

The wheel of fate—didn't things always come full circle? He was fatalistic enough to believe it, and to trust that instinct yesterday that compelled him to journey here early and fast.

He just had to make sure there was no sign that someone had discovered the body or that anyone had been there at all.

But that was the point of the game, wasn't it?

Was it? What was he thinking?

The carriage tracks were a problem, but nothing he could solve in the next five minutes. He merely needed to make sure he hadn't stepped in the blood or was tracking any of it out of the room. He hadn't touched anything, or inadvertently bumped into anything.

All he needed to do was close all the doors.

The point of the game . . .

Interesting thought, that.

He pulled the hallway door closed behind him.

What had they done with the servants? There was not a soul, not a sound. As if everyone had been drugged . . .

No.

Maybe. He paused at the door and looked around. What if he checked the servants' quarters? Or was that what he was meant to do after finding the horrific scene in the office?

Anyone would be curious, with the door open and a body in a back room, and not a servant in sight.

He was ravenously curious, and wary at the same time.

This scene had been meticulously played out for them. The only variable element was the fact they were here so early.

What if they had come later? During calling hours? What if he hadn't had that gut feeling? What if they'd just stumbled onto the still dead house. The missing servants. The mutilated body. What if they'd gone to the servants' quarters as anyone would, trying to find someone, trying to find an explanation?

He closed the front door behind him. It was tempting to think about looking for answers. But that was part of the game, human nature, natural curiosity.

His adversary didn't deem him worthy. Had fully expected that he and Georgiana would fall right into the trap.

He climbed into the carriage. "Back to Wexley then," he called up to the driver. And to Georgiana, "We're not going to talk."

She started to protest, and he silenced her, whispering in her ear: "He's gone, Georgiana. Everything else can wait."

He could just see the house over her shoulder as they drew farther and farther away. Silent house. Deadly house. Tool of the devil. Vanishing finally behind a hedge of yews.

So now there were two impossible things to be dealt with: their unexpectedly life-shifting kiss, and the vicious murder of Henry Maitland, and the fact that the two things were now inextricably linked forever.

He wondered if she were thinking about that. It seemed all of a piece suddenly: it had been exactly like looking at the scene of Lydia's murder. The blood. The cruelty. The fact he had been the one to find the body.

Could Moreton have made the supposition that he would happen upon the murder scene first? He had contrived it so it would be eminently likely.

The man was a genius. And more than that, utterly without conscience. He had decided he wanted something and he was systematically going about getting it. It was clearer than clear now that Moreton wanted Olivia, and Moreton wanted Aling, and all of it was almost within his grasp.

Except that he and Georgiana had come too soon. Found the body too early. Left with barely a trace. Would not be there when presumably Moreton planned to find them with the body, which would have been so incriminating and so hard to explain away.

Moreton would have been the one to call the constable, and *they*, together, would have discovered the servants, stupefied and drunkenly unaware, in their beds in their quarters.

By all that was holy, the man was insidious. And depraved. There was no one to stop him, not in Bliss River, and not here, if he could have gotten Georgiana out of the way.

After all, he would have explained, Olivia and he had just come in from South Africa. They'd debarked in Greybourne the previous day, and had traveled up to Medwyn only this morning to be met, on arriving there, by this shocking sight. Henry hadn't even known his wife was about to return, Olivia would have told them, and she would have been overcome and possibly fainted.

And they'd have believed her too, since she hadn't been at Aling for more than twenty years, and had no reason at all to want to do her husband any harm.

And Moreton. Well, she would tell them, he was just an old friend, escorting her, keeping her safe on the journey.

That probably would have been their story. And if Moreton could have caught him and Georgiana with the body, all to the good. Then all the loose ends would have been tied up, and there would have been nothing to stop him from marrying Olivia after a prudent amount of time.

In fact, there still was nothing to stop him. He would just convince the authorities that an unsolved murder had nothing to do with *him*.

But why? Why now? Why England after all those extravagantly dissolute years in his libertine kingdom in the Valley?

What snake had slithered into his Eden?

He turned the thought upside down. A snake? Or a blight in the garden? Something intrusive, disruptive . . .

Dear bloody hell . . .

A creeping fungus—*Him*. A pestilence, a scourge.

By all that was bloody sacred, he was the catalyst for everything that had gone wrong.

Chapter Twenty

A nd now it all made some kind of twisted sense, every piece of the puzzle having some value, some reason— at least in Moreton's eyes.

"He's going to come after us, you know."

It had been a fraught journey back to Wexley. Charles hadn't been in the least forthcoming during the trip, and Georgiana had no idea what he was thinking. She had been dissolved in secret silent tears anyway, mourning all the years gone and all the years to come that she would never know the man who was her father.

They couldn't have talked anyway, with the driver listening avidly, and a possible witness to their having gone to Aling, and Charles hadn't nearly finished coming to grips with the notion of his own culpability.

So in all, it was a deadly and silent trip back to Miss Elmina's boardinghouse, with Georgiana huddled in the corner, shaking with silent sobs, and him staring stoically out the carriage window.

He had just aired his conjectures about Moreton, and Georgiana was skeptical at best, and beyond thinking *him* rational about it at this point.

Moreton didn't want *them*. Moreton wanted—well, who knew what Moreton wanted, really?

"Let me say it again," Charles said emphatically, "we were meant to find the body, and he was going to corner us with it, in the office. He could have made an excellent case that you killed your father, and that I helped you. That would have gotten us both out of the way, and he would have successfully committed yet another murder. He must feel invincible right now."

She ran a weary hand over her swollen eyes. "But why? This doesn't make sense. There's nothing here he needs or wants, and Aling is a liability for a man like him."

"Absolutely. But fate handed him something he didn't expect . . ."

"I think *you* believe in fate too much," she said waspishly.

He let that comment ride in the air for a moment, and then he said, "Me."

Oh, that was too much. Now *he* bore the burden of Moreton's perfidious deeds? *"What?"*

"Me. It occurs to me that none of this would have happened had I not come to Bliss River. It's so clear now: the minute my mother recognized me, she was bound to die. That was what gave Moreton the impetus to come to England and the idea he might want Aling. Even if he would have to commit two murders to do it. But he had two likely suspects on whom he could pin those two murders."

"Who? *Us?* No." She covered her eyes and rocked back and forth. "No."

"Olivia is free to remarry now. That was the whole point. For him to marry her and disable you. They will come after us, Georgiana. Moreton will be very precise about how much you hated your father and how you had come back to England to confront him. Olivia will run through a litany of hateful things you might have said about him and how you had always resented his leaving you in Bliss River. They will want to question you. Not soon. But sometime, after they investigate further, they will."

"You're scaring me."

"He's a frightening man, Moreton; there's absolutely no moral underpinning there. Yet, he can be so personable, one tends to underestimate him. But he is here in England, and he will marry Olivia and they will take over Aling."

Dear heaven, what an improbability. Those two dissolute libertines shackled in a conventional marriage, living a conventional life at Aling? It was impossible to conceive.

"They won't."

"They will. Who's to stop them? There's no other family apart from you. You're the only thing standing in their way."

"He didn't have any brothers or sisters," she said slowly, trying to dredge up what little she knew of inheritance factors. "But Olivia wouldn't inherit either"—she stopped abruptly as the next thought almost took her breath away. "Barring any sons, Aling comes to me—"

That floored him. He hadn't even considered that possibility, knew less than she did about how estates were passed. "Good God." He immediately conceived a half-dozen other scenarios based on that fact. "I daresay he never thought about returning to England at all before I arrived, and he killed Lydia. And then you disappeared too—" He thought about that for a moment. And there it was: Georgiana's leaving the Valley was the key.

"Do you see? He fully expected to execute me and go on as usual in the Valley. But we got away—you got away . . ." The succeeding thought was so chilling he almost did not want to voice it. "Georgiana—he killed your father not because he wants Olivia. Olivia can give him nothing now. He'll kill Olivia, too. He killed your father because he wants to marry you."

"He can't do that." That was her first thought. He was her uncle, after all. He was prohibited from doing that. "I would never . . . How could he possibly? Uncles can't . . ."

"Firstly, no one knows he's your uncle. And secondly, I don't think he knew. This was purely his taking advantage of unforeseen circumstances. He had no idea, no plan until I came into the picture. It was an opportunity pure and simple. Killing Lydia freed him. Your father's death freed the estate so you could inherit. And he will find a way to have all three murders linked to me."

"But why? *Why?*"

"I don't know. Maybe it's as simple as he couldn't go on the way he was going in the Valley. He's getting older, and a man's vigor diminishes after time. Perhaps an estate and a fertile young woman are enough to entice a man like that to get an heir, to leave something behind besides a legacy of lust. Whatever it is, he's into it so deep, he will take it to the end. So we need a plan. We need to go on the offense."

"This whole theory of yours is an offense. And I'm too tired to make plans." More than tired. Her head was whirling with all the theories and the notion that everything that happened hinged on his having come to the Valley.

"We have no choice. We can't wait on this; otherwise, he will be lying in wait for you wherever you turn, and I might not be around to protect you. We need to be visible; the more visible, the more impossible for him to pull you down. We have to establish ourselves immediately in society and make him come to us."

Georgiana had had enough. This was verging on dementia. She'd been traveling all this while, seducing—and loving it—a man who might be certifiably insane. "This is crazy, ridiculous. You're sunstruck."

"In this weather?" Charles asked, amused.

"Well, *cadi,* we have no camels to trade for an invitation into my father's social set."

"Well, my *lady,* it is not only your family who trades with that social set. A prince of the desert who breeds winning horse stock has some cachet among them."

"Indeed, and is that how you style yourself?"

"That, my lady of the valley, is what I *am.*"

"And I am what I am, is that what you're saying?"

He pulled back on every impulse to just ignore her. It would be easier on both of them if he did. She was indeed what she was and that would never change, even if the queen of courtesans were tricked out like a lady. For a minute though, he let himself believe she could be a queen. For a kiss, he might even capitulate to her. The ache was always there, the erection incessant, and the kiss earlier that day had shifted the bedrock under his feet.

It was a kiss on which promises were made. Even to someone like her.

It didn't lessen the danger though.

"I am saying," he said patiently, "that we don't have a lot of time or money. We need to get ourselves in place, fast."

She felt the heat drain from the air around them. She felt worn out, and dislocated. Moreton's evil could not be this all-pervasive, and yet—and yet, they'd come thousands of miles, her father was dead and she *was* the presumptive heir.

Whatever had been between them was hardly important at this point.

If he was right. If Moreton was after them.

"How do we do this?"

"You could marry me." He threw that out as casually as a puff of air. He wasn't even sure he meant to say that, or something else. But there it was, floating, resonating, the fastest and easiest solution to prevent Moreton from harming her.

He thought it made the most sense of anything since this misbegotten adventure had begun.

And she laughed. She just burst out and laughed and laughed and laughed.

Stupid! Gullible! She'd been living in a fog all these weeks with him.

And now, suddenly and with those words, everything became clear. Bright and clear and irrevocable. So much so, she wished she hadn't given away all her power because those things came so hard won.

No matter . . . there were other ways, other means. And by no means would he trick her into marriage. She might be easy to blindside, but she wasn't that naive.

"Ah, Charles. Dear, dear *cadi*—now we finally come to it. Now we have the truth—and the truth is that, in fact, there has always been more than one plan. And that you, too, saw an opportunity, didn't you? An opportunity for a foreigner like yourself to marry and inherit a country estate . . . You are the next in line, but you know that already, don't you, Charles? You spent enough time in England to be aware of such things. I daresay you did some research on that order before you came to Bliss River."

"Georgiana . . ."

"Oh, I don't believe you've thought beyond finding a way to coerce me into marriage, *cadi*. In spite of who and what I am. You would never otherwise marry someone like me. But it now becomes crystal clear why you were so willing to shoulder the burden of taking me with you. You were gunning for an estate and meantime you could have all the sex you could handle besides. Cousins can marry, but you knew that, too."

"Georgiana . . ."

She waved him off. Treacherous bastard. She didn't know how she was going to survive this, but she would. Even after so many deaths—including her heart . . .

She'd never believe for a moment he hadn't thought of that connection, of that possibility. Nevertheless, he tried again. "If we were to marry, he wouldn't come after you. He'd have to kill me first."

"If we were to marry," she spat, "it might be too tempting for *you* . . ."

He saw her point instantly. "Bloody goddamn hell . . ."

"You weren't above plotting your mother's demise—"

"Well, I've learned a goddamn lot about myself since then; I would never have killed her. My *mother?*"

"We can't ever know. We only know that Moreton did murder her, and so now we come to the bargaining point."

"Is there one?" he asked grimly.

"I think so. Your mission isn't yet done, *cadi*. The queen must be protected at all costs."

Oh, yes, now she was royalty, icy and imperious, her mind working like a steel trap, snapping on every angle.

"Go on."

"We will *pretend* to be married. With none of the sexual privilege that entails except as it provides security for myself and the estate until Moreton is brought to justice."

"That may never happen, Georgiana."

Her expression grew hard. She lifted her chin.

"Then I'll just have to kill him myself."

By now, she thought, her father's death had to have been reported.

Or had it?

"That should not affect our plan," Charles said.

"What was our plan?" Georgiana asked. He didn't have a plan, short of marrying her and then their entrenching themselves as ostentatiously as possible in London. And even then, there was no telling whether that would lure Moreton away from Aling.

"To establish ourselves in London."

"Which takes a lot of money."

"Indeed, and I have no problem with securing an advance on breeding futures from my friends here. I do have friends in England, Georgiana. I do have some reputation as a breeder and a gentleman, no matter how *foreign* I may look. This is not as impossible as it seems."

"What seems impossible is Moreton's manipulating everything the way you think he did. As opposed to the way you did, which makes perfect sense."

His face closed. There was no talking to the queen about any of this now. Her conclusions were set in stone and it would take dynamite to destroy them.

"I assure you, he did. And he's probably looking for you right now."

"And you did, and you've got me. So it's time to be married in public, *cadi*. I'm ready. When do we start?"

He started by contacting a gentleman who had been a classmate at Oxford, who was pleased to welcome him and his wife to dinner on the succeeding night, even on such short notice.

It was the horses, of course. It wasn't that far from Ascot opening day, and they were always on the lookout for fine horseflesh. How fortuitous that Charles had landed in London just now. They would have so much to talk about at dinner the following night.

"We came up from Greybourne not three days ago," Charles told him. "We've leased a house in Hyde Park, and on for the Season. Fortunate we arrived now, wouldn't you say?"

Indeed, his host would say. In March, everyone would descend for the Little Season and there wouldn't be a place to let anywhere.

Charles got the house next, a small, nicely respectable, two-bedroom town home at the edge of Hyde Park. Then he set up a line of credit at Harrod's, all on the strength of his name, and guarantees from his host. Risky things both, on the face of it, but sportsmen were gamblers, too, no one more so than that gentleman, a fact Charles had counted on.

Next then, Georgiana.

"We're going to a dinner party. You need appropriate clothes."

So he had done it. Why had she thought he couldn't? Charles Elliott could do anything. He had a life beyond anything he had yet revealed to her, and he'd still wanted Aling besides.

There were too many surprises, too soon. She wondered if he had thought she wouldn't get onto him at some point. Or that the sting of betrayal wouldn't go deep.

"No clothes would be more my taste," she muttered. Those tight constricting clothes on top of it. God, she hated these garments. Hated the idea of going out among society with him and having to meet new people and behave in a proscribed way.

His dark eyes glinted. "We're on the attack, my lady. You will do nothing to upset the boat."

"No," she retorted, "I will dutifully steam into the harbor, and contrive somehow to stay afloat."

And in the end, it was easier than she thought. She only had to look beautiful, say nothing (not that she could, so tightly was she bound into that dress), let herself be led to table by one or another talkative man, and let Charles take the lead.

He was very good at dinner table conversation, which all centered around his—his!—fictional adventures in South Africa. The company hung on his every word, breathless as he recounted his highly romanticized escape from the Valley, populated now with cannibalistic heathens who had taken her captive as well.

The fairy tale story of how they met—

The company heaved a collective romantic sigh.

And how they'd gotten married—in Sierra Leone—and they were here doing business before returning to South America.

This was the story all his friends would put out, and that Moreton would be hard put to deny.

There were a dozen men and their wives seated around the luxuriously appointed town house dining room table, and every one of the women saw herself in that romantic fiction that Charles had created.

Every one of them wanted to be *her*, Georgiana, racing for her life from the killers in the valley.

"A toast to Charles and his bride," the host called out, and the men stood up. "To Charles and Georgiana . . . May all the years of your marriage be an adventure."

The men stood. "Hear, hear—" They drank; the women clapped.

Charles stood and bowed, and motioned to Georgiana.

"Give up South America and come back to England to live," his host proposed, and that engendered another toast. "By God, Charles. You could find something in Essex or Kent and set up a breeding farm here. Import your ponies; they are spectacular. But we need you here."

Another round of applause, and then the host stood up, the women rose as well, and one by one filed into the adjacent drawing room.

And so the evening went, with the women discussing the inconsequentials of their daily life and the latest gossip, and Georgiana sitting back quietly to listen in her beautiful bronze-colored silk with the voluminous sleeves and brown velvet bow.

This was how proper society went on. There was no suggestion there would be anything more than coffee and dessert to follow, and then everyone would return to their respective and respectable homes.

No promenades, no assignations, no expectations. Everything private, respectful and revered.

Ah, too late for any of that now that she deduced the true purpose of Charles's generosity. There was nothing left to the story but to vanquish Moreton.

And then what, for her? A return to the Valley, perhaps? Where else could she fit? What else did she know how to do?

Or she could go to Aling. After all the blood was washed away, after all the memories faded, she could go to Aling and start all over again.

Could she? Without Charles and with all the explanations that would entail? It didn't bear thinking about—not yet, at any rate.

But she had that choice: she *could* go to Aling . . .

They returned to the little town house on Hyde Park at midnight.

"This is but the first strike," Charles said, taking her wrap. "Everything I said will be bruited all over the city by tomorrow. Everyone will know that we are here, why we are here, and how we got here. There will be no way for Moreton to countervent that."

"And then what?"

There was no getting around this part. "We wait."

And while they waited, Charles conducted business. Once word got around he was in London, there was no end to the number of inquiries about his stock and the possibility of his starting a horse farm in England.

There were even offers to bankroll him, and to structure the business to sell shares in it. It was god-awful tempting, and not in the least what he had thought would happen when they got to England.

It was the window, at long last, to a life with some normalcy, some hope of a future. A life to share with someone.

Someone who thought him capable of murder.

No, Moreton's game must be played to its end.

And so they waited. There were invitations to the homes of various friends and acquaintances. There were balls and parties, dinners and hunts and the theater, all things so vastly foreign to Georgiana that all she could do was marvel.

He spared no expense to showcase her in these settings. After all, the advances were coming in thick and fast. And everyone was charmed by his beautiful, refined wife who was so quiet and serene.

And everyone was interested in his ponies. And he was beginning to become interested in the idea of staying in England.

That, and the idea of really being married to Georgiana. Of having a family, a farm, a life. Her.

Because Georgiana in England was the queen he always imagined her to be. Beautiful, elegant, sensual. *Dressed.* Even with the mandate that he never touch her again.

It was folly. He couldn't live in that tiny house with her without wanting her.

But not being able to have her was the penance that must be paid. For all his failings, for all his destructive desires, and the life he'd led before Georgiana, he must pay penance now.

So he made himself content to be her escort, her protector, her husband in all ways but one. Because the thing would be over soon. Moreton was cracking, and the nightmare he had created would have to finally come to an end.

"Well, Moreton seems to have gone to ground," Georgiana said several days later. "And there's been nothing in the London papers about my father. You think, if an Honorable were reported deceased, it would be in the paper."

They were sitting in the little morning room at the back of the Hyde Park house. He'd hired a housekeeper, a cook, and one maid. The maid was serving them a light breakfast of tea, toast, jam, eggs, and fruit, as Georgiana rifled through the paper.

Charles had wondered, too. Moreton had been unconscionably quiet since the murder. Since they had slipped out of his hands. What would a man like Moreton do if he were thwarted?

But he already knew, and he was loathe to even say it.

He said it. "Maybe . . . no one knows he's dead." And maybe Olivia was dead, too.

Georgiana looked away. "Even Moreton wouldn't be that cruel."

"He's that cruel and that clever, Georgiana. We've gone public, and we're supposedly married. He knows he can't get at us here. He wants us to come to him."

Chapter Twenty-one

The tension escalated, especially between them.

She needed him, and it was the worst thing, now that she had exposed his secret agenda. It was always between them.

But so were the sensual memories of their journey, and all the things they had done that she could not forget.

Moreton was the enemy, the evil to be vanquished. Charles was merely the opportunist he had painted Moreton out to be.

It was hard to live with that nevertheless. And with all the little flicking memories of what had gone on between them. Like when she would catch a glimpse of him in the morning, nearly undressed. Or the sight of him through his half-closed bedroom door, sprawled out naked in his bed.

Did she prowl the town house looking to ignite something? Looking for an excuse?

She hadn't changed that much.

Life in London was a veritable banquet, once she got used to the clothes and corsets, and the fact that sex was not the primary activity and the center of everyone's world.

But the habits of Bliss River were more ingrained than she had ever imagined, and a strong resilient man could be forgiven anything in the heat of a woman's need.

But Moreton's presence at Aling overshadowed everything. It brought the depravity of Bliss River to London. It pervaded the simplest moments of contentment. It invaded her soul.

Of course, she couldn't give in to her desires. If she did, Moreton would win. And all of his sins would go unavenged.

So they waited. One day gone, with Charles immersed in starting up his business. There was no dearth of parties interested in investing in profitable ponies, he discovered, and it was taking no time at all to accumulate a book.

Neither did they hear news of Henry Maitland's death. "He hasn't reported it," Charles said. "It's the only conclusion. His plans went awry, and he's waiting for one of us to break."

The second day gone. They attended the theater with some of Charles's friends, ensconced in a box, where during the *entr'acte,* their hosts left them to procure some refreshments.

"Well, well, well, here are my pretties," a voice said from the curtained archway. Charles jumped up as Moreton appeared on the threshold. "Sit down, my boy; don't make a scene. I came to applaud you. You are a worthy adversary, Charles Elliott, married to Miss Georgiana of Bliss River—and *not*. Married, I mean. You foiled my little plan very nicely. I salute you. And I came to chide you, Georgie. You haven't come to visit your mother. Olivia has been expecting you these many days, and here you sit as if you never had a mother at all."

"I don't have a mother," Georgiana spat.

"Ungrateful wretch. It's the least you can do after all the trouble you've caused her. Bring her to Aling, Charles. Olivia is waiting and we can settle everything then . . ."

He whirled. The curtain dropped and Charles leaped after him, but Moreton had vanished, like a magician, into thin air.

"And now what?" Georgiana demanded the next morning.

They were seated in the parlor, Charles by the window with a pad of paper and pencil in hand, and Georgiana by the fireplace, which couldn't generate enough heat to warm her up after last night.

Nevertheless, with them together like this and the world closed out, she felt curiously safe for the moment, and curious altogether about what Charles meant to do about Moreton.

"Last night was his preemptive strike," Charles said, sketching something on the paper.

"You think Moreton plans things? How did he find us? How did he know the marriage is a fake?"

"We've been public enough with the details, Georgiana. I told you word would get around quickly, and he certainly wouldn't have believed the story of our wedding in Sierra Leone. And he did have time to check the churches in the surrounding area. He had to. If you *were* married . . ."

"I'd be dead," she interpolated.

"There would be no point to that except to clean house," Charles murmured. "But still and all, Olivia is at Aling."

"Yes, and probably dancing on my father's grave."

"It's not that simple, *khanum*. He will kill her. We could save her."

She was stunned by his use of that name, her tent name. She didn't want to save anything but the ferocious pleasures she could not forget.

Except she couldn't forget his betrayal either.

"I don't want to save her. I don't care."

"She's your mother," Charles said gently.

"I seem to recall, *cadi,* that you were not above wanting to murder *your* mother."

"I wouldn't have done it, Georgiana. I couldn't have done it. And whatever either of our mothers did or did not do, neither of them should pay for it with their lives."

"I don't believe you. I don't. My mother conspired in the death of my father, was complicit in fostering the hedonistic lifestyle of Bliss River, and sacrificed her own daughter to it without a qualm. What should I rescue her from? Her sins and her vices?"

"She's your mother. She gave you life, and for that alone, *khanum—*"

She hated his using that name, hated him arousing memories she'd sooner forget, hated that stoic forgiveness that would extend even to her depraved mother.

"As your mother gave you life," she hissed, "and you fully meant to take hers—"

He ignored that. "We can save her."

"From what? For what? She's wallowed in Moreton's ooze for so many years she wouldn't know where to begin again."

"She's your mother. And he will kill her."

"You are so sure." She was furious that he was so certain, and that he thought Olivia was worth saving.

"He has no need of her now."

"But he was only baiting you. He doesn't need to kill her, and we don't have to walk into his trap."

"I didn't intend to." He turned the page on which he'd been sketching so she could see it. On it, he had drawn the first-floor plan at Aling, as viewed from the front door. The reception room. All the doors. The hallway. All the rooms they had seen. "She probably wouldn't be secreted in any of the public rooms. She's probably in one of the bedrooms. However many there are. It should be a simple matter to sneak in and find her."

"When?" she asked, her voice heavy.

"Tomorrow, first light, just as before."

"Damn you, you are going to do this. Why? Tell me *why.*"

He put down the pad. "Because on my mother's soul, *khanum,* I can't let him kill her sister, too."

He had thought it all out. Not one more life would be sacrificed to Bliss River. And with this one act, he would wash away his own sins in his thirst for redemption. And he would vanquish Moreton, too. Moreton would not win, and with that, perhaps, he could finally forgive himself.

"Then you *will* go, *cadi,* but not without me."

Fog shrouded the landscape, drifting in the bushes and trees, obscuring the road. It was so early, it hadn't burned off yet, and the sound of the horses' hooves was eerie in the fogbound stillness as Charles guided the carriage on the road to King's Lyme.

It took no time to breach the gates of Aling, and place the carriage behind the yew bushes out of sight of the house. It remained only for them to quiet the horses, and, keeping low, to take the direction opposite the drive, along the hedges toward the back of the house.

"Oh my God, look at the house," Georgiana whispered. "There must be dozens of rooms on the upper floors."

Charles was counting. "Twelve double windows. Not too many. I don't see any extensions or ells at the back from here. No separate kitchen wing. Deadly damned quiet though." That, and the eerie creeping fog.

"What about the servants?"

"I have a feeling they will be nowhere around. He's waiting, Georgiana. He knows we're going to come."

That was her feeling, too. But surely Moreton was not that devious. He couldn't know what the trigger would be that finally brought them here.

And yet, it was so still, so quiet, even at this hour when a gardener or a stable boy might be awake and on the job. The fog drifted across the lawn as if it had a life of its own.

"I don't like this."

"We have to run for the side of the house now. Get as close as you can to the rear wall." Charles set off, his body as low to the ground as he could comfortably run, and disappeared into the mist.

Georgiana girded herself as Charles was swallowed into the foggy swath, and followed him a moment later. Followed his whispers.

"Here, here."

She felt her way toward the wall, and then toward him, several yards away.

He grabbed her hand. "Here, now. Look. Two doors. Some windows. Flatten yourself against the wall and come with me."

She was so cold from fear she thought she would crack into shards, whereas he seemed so used to doing things like this. Still more things she didn't know about him.

"If the doors won't open?"

"We'll break a window."

He was so confident. She was so scared. They inched their way down the wall, and he tried the first door. "Locked."

"Good." Sneaking into Aling this way . . . maybe Moreton had manipulated that, too?

"Shhh." He held still for a moment, listening. There was nothing to hear, just the still matte silence of the rolling fog. "All right. Next door then."

It felt like hours, edging down that back wall toward the second door. Aling was a large square house, more appreciable now that they were taking the measure of the back wall.

"Don't move. I've got the knob."

They listened again. Not a sound. The thick, moist, faintly sour scent of the fog enveloped them.

He turned the knob. Pushed. A small protesting creak of the hinges, and then he whirled her in. The scent was stronger here, more metallic. He closed the door with barely a sound.

The silence was nerve-racking. Georgiana could hear Charles groping his way carefully around, trying to grasp where they were. "It's an anteroom; the walls are stone. It doesn't seem to be a storeroom, and there's another door over here. Take my hand."

His hand warm, still, in spite of the foggy cold. He was leading her blind, step by tiny step, relying on his senses to give him direction.

"Got it. Stand back."

A shard of light . . . his shadow moving across to the opposite side of the door. "Kitchen. Come."

They darted inside. Here at least there were windows. One of the three or four, they guessed, they had seen on the entrance door wall outside.

A still stronger scent pervaded the room. And just enough light to avoid crashing into tables and pots that were strewn all over. And more doors. One to the pantry, one to a storeroom, one to the hall.

Charles let a breath. "This is familiar territory. This is the hallway from the reception room. God, something smells. We'll go in the interior rooms. The office is this way." He led the way into the small room, which was dominated by a desk that had been pulled over the spot where a big blot of blood had stained and seeped into the floor.

Georgiana averted her eyes, and followed him into the

billiard room, the dining room, and from there, into the hall, and the ornate staircase that wound upward seemingly without any support.

"To the bedrooms then," Charles said, and began taking the steps two at a time, ignoring that malodorous scent, with Georgiana just behind him.

The stairs gave onto a long hallway with six doors on either side.

"A lot of bedrooms," Georgiana murmured. "And no servants."

"The most likely thing is, he sent them away. No witnesses. So let's not waste time." He thrust open the first door, to the right. Empty. And to the left—empty. And on, down the hallway, with the foul odor seeming to envelop them—every stiffly stuffily furnished bedroom empty.

"Damn. Empty—empty—she's not here; she's not there."

He slammed the doors closed as they went down the hall, his fury mounting as he realized what they would find. And it was too late to shield Georgiana as they approached the twelfth bedroom.

The odor here was nauseating. Georgiana gagged.

"Cover your nose. Don't come in with me."

He pushed open the door. The stench hit him like a wall. Death incarnate rampant in the room, and Georgiana, disregarding his orders, too close behind him.

God, that lunatic didn't have a shred of decency in him.

He should have expected this. He should have known. He put his arm out to bar her way, to prevent her from seeing anything further.

But she saw anyway.

The bodies. The dead, decaying bodies propped side by side on the stuffy four-poster bed. Olivia reunited with her husband at last—in death.

"Go on in, my pretties." Moreton's voice, behind them,

slicing through their horror. "It's about time you came to visit your mother, Georgie. Go on in and say hello."

How did one move, how did one keep from coughing and choking and acting as if this wasn't the most grisly sight in the world? How could Moreton act as if everything were normal?

Something poked her ribs. She stumbled forward, into Charles so that he was forced to move farther into the room, and she fell on the floor. She rolled away from the awful sight on the bed, and started choking again as she caught sight of the pistol in Moreton's hand.

He waved it at her, seemingly oblivious to the foul stench that pervaded the room.

"Olivia is very happy about our impending marriage, aren't you, my dear? And she's so happy we're all finally together at Aling." He leaned against the doorframe, the gun dangling from his finger, effectively blocking any escape.

"Or so she would have told you, if you'd come sooner. You should have come sooner, Charles. Damn your eyes. I couldn't wait any longer. I had to kill her. That damned infernal woman, thinking we would actually have this delicious life together running Aling as a brothel. I must say though I was very convincing. She bought that fiction in the blink of an eye. Stupid woman. Well, she's paid for that now, and you, Charles, are going to hang for it. And Georgie and I are getting married. It's as simple as that, and I'm damned furious that it took this long. Georgie!! Stop that coughing!"

"I can't. Can't we go in the hallway at least? I need some fresh air."

"Oh, I don't think so, Georgie. We have a few things to get done in here. And I like your submissive attitude; there's nothing like a willing woman at your feet."

She choked again, at his words this time, as she eyed the

distance between them. "What? What else could you possibly want to do here?"

"I want Olivia to bear witness to the fact that you're here and we will be married. I posted the banns, you know. Yes, it was ill-considered of me to do it without your knowledge. When Olivia found out, she was livid, but the priest is willing to perform the ceremony without the requisite wait. That's why I killed her anyway. She found out, and she didn't want me to marry you at all."

"You can have Aling. You don't need me," Georgiana said desperately between coughs, as she tried to slither toward him. If she could just distract him, just move in tiny increments, get near his legs, topple him over somehow.

"Oh you're so wrong about that, Georgie. How else would I attract all those wealthy studs to our little enterprise? It makes such sense, a bawdy house in the country. All the privacy, discretion, and decadence that money can buy. And my delicious young wife, the mound mistress. Oh, they'll buy it. They'll come in droves. I can hardly wait. All that money. All those stallions plowing you. Don't move any closer, Georgie dear, or I'll shoot you. I know exactly what you're up to."

"Charles—" Georgiana whispered, looking up into his dispassionate eyes, and gagging once again.

"That's a very appropriate response, Georgie. He's useless. Always has been. Couldn't save Lydia. Won't save you. I'll kill him first anyway. Dead or alive, he will be convicted for murder."

She gagged again, and Moreton reached down and yanked her to her feet. "Don't move, pretty lady." He reached down again, for a coil of rope at his feet. "It's too bad, but I have to tie you up, so I can take care of Charles. On second thought, I like the idea of having you tied up and at my mercy."

She felt the life drain from her limbs, and she couldn't

take the stench much longer. But there was no reasoning with a madman. Charles was too far away from him, and Moreton could get off a shot in an instant if Charles moved a muscle.

She was the one who had a chance of disabling him. One chance. The only chance.

"Just cooperate, Georgie. It won't be that bad."

"What do you want me to do?" she whispered.

"Just turn around. Just let me get Charles out of the way."

The gun was on her. The death-odor was powerful, heartstopping. Charles was still as a statue three feet behind her. And there was another two feet between her and Moreton, and the gun.

"All right. I'll do what you want." He'd like that. Whatever the madman with the gun wanted was fine with her.

She pivoted on her right foot, and swung the left one, suddenly, sharply hard against his shin.

His leg buckled as she ducked to one side and Charles dove into him, like a bullet, and they went down hard, as the gun flew into the air and landed on the bed.

Oh God, she couldn't reach it, not from where she was hunched beside the bed. She'd have to reach over those bodies to the foot rail. She'd have to touch them, feel them dissolve against her skin.

She felt faint. She gagged again.

She had to get the gun. She had to stop Moreton, who was fighting with superhuman strength. If he got loose, if he got the gun, they would both be dead.

He shoved at Charles, Charles toppled backward, and Georgiana scrambled over him to the foot of the bed.

Moreton was a step behind her. She jumped onto the mattress, over the desiccated corpses, her fragility, her scruples, her fears, and covered the gun with her body.

"Now, Georgie—" Moreton panted, and a minute later Charles jumped him and sent him crashing down to the floor.

She backed off the bed with the gun in her hands. Both hands. Her hands weren't even shaking. She felt a calmness, a certainty that finally something was right.

She pointed it at Moreton, who was pinned at the foot of the bed by Charles's large body.

Charles climbed off him, and Moreton levered himself up. "You can't kill me, Georgie. You don't have the taste for it."

"Oh, I could kill you, Moreton." She leveled the gun at him. "I can count three reasons I should." Her voice was calm, so calm, but for some reason, the tears started then.

She cocked the trigger as they streamed down her face. "I *want* to kill you." She squeezed, and the shot went close, so close he looked stunned.

"Goddamn it, Georgie, I *made* you. You can't kill me."

"*What?*" He couldn't mean what she thought he meant. He said it to rattle her. To get her upset. Dear, dear God—

Everything shifted. *Kill him now.* She squeezed and the shot grazed his shoulder.

"Jesus, Georgie—"

"You made me? *You* made me? *This* is what you made—" She waved the gun. "You are going to die.

"Think, Georgie, why do you think your father left Bliss River? Why do you think he abandoned you?"

"Because you *made* me?" She felt close to the edge now, felt the blood of the madman coursing through her veins.

"The minute she stepped foot in the valley, Olivia was a pig in heat," Moreton said desperately. "Wallowed everywhere, with everyone and got knocked up soon after."

"Oh, that's so nice to know, and you don't want to die? Just for that, I'll kill you." She shot again, and the bullet hit the wall behind him.

"The man who fucked my mother is going to die." She pulled again, and Moreton ducked and howled and backed away.

"Georgie—don't—"

I am the child of my father. The bloodlust swamped her, enfolded her, seeping into the enveloping scent of death, into her suppurating soul.

"Georgie." He was pleading now.

"Tell *them,* you bastard. I am the child of my father. You tell them, Moreton. Beg their forgiveness."

She fired again and he stepped back still farther. And now his back was to the window, and he was facing the bed.

It was right that her parents were the last thing he should see. She was the child of her father, after all. He was the one who made her. The tears kept coming. She couldn't understand why the tears kept coming and why she suddenly felt bereft.

Moreton saw it, saw that shearing moment of weakness, and lunged at her.

"The man who killed my father is going to die," she whispered, and fired again, sending him to his death.

Epilogue

Charles had taken care of everything. The newspaper report put it all very succinctly:

The death of the Honorable Henry Maitland of Aling, Medwyn, Kent, still remains a mystery. The servants, who had been given an unusual weekend off by Olivia Maitland, who had just returned from South Africa after many years' residence there, found the decaying body of Sir Henry, and his wife, together in a bedroom, as well as that of an unidentified stranger who had been shot. The murder weapon was found on the scene. The authorities estimate that Sir Henry had been dead for almost two weeks, and that Mrs. Maitland and the stranger had died within the past two or three days.

Attempts to locate Sir Henry's daughter, who was thought to have been living with her mother in South Africa, have been unsuccessful.

* * *

I am my father's daughter.

It was a fitting end to the story of Bliss River. She was either the spawn of Lucifer or a child of the Valley, and either way, Henry Maitland had never been her father, even if he had contributed his seed.

That alone was a stunning realization. Moreton had won, in the end.

There was nothing left to do but go to the authorities. Charles advised against it.

"Let them find you," Charles said. "Give them time to cook up their own theory. At a minimum, they will find that Moreton came to Aling with Olivia. The servants will testify that they visited your father, that they had a lot of words. That your father took an unexpected trip, and that Olivia generously gave them a lot of time off. They will conclude that Olivia and Moreton conspired to murder your father, and that Moreton killed Olivia and then, perhaps, in remorse, killed himself. Unfortunately, any testimony about Moreton will contradict that idea. It's the only sticking point; after all, he was on the verge of getting what he wanted."

"Me," Georgiana said dryly.

"Yes. And at that point, they will find you."

"Of course, they'll find me," she murmured, her voice odd. "I can't expect to have shot a man and live a long and happy life."

"But you absolutely can," Charles said. "Never forget, Moreton was coming after you. You had just told him you'd gotten married, and he was utterly distraught—"

Georgiana looked up sharply.

"Out of his mind distraught and far stronger than you. I was too far away to help you. You had the gun and you had no other choice, Georgiana. None. He meant to attack you, kill you, even. That's the story, and I'm your witness. And if you ever testified to what he did in Bliss River, you'd be a national hero."

"Oh." That simple. That complete. They never saw the other bodies. And there was always Bliss River, if things should get tricky.

"Well." She blinked. She still wasn't over having taken someone's life, even a monster like Moreton. Still couldn't quite comprehend that her mother was dead.

And, once the hurtle of going to the authorities was clear, she would be free. Whatever that meant. She would never be free. Her history and Bliss River would pulse inside her till the end of her days.

But she'd be free . . . Free to do what?

Everything must come to an end. And Charles was still with her, now, protective and solicitous both. Charles, in fact, seemed to have all the answers. "So where have I been all this time that they couldn't find me, Charles?"

He held out his hand. "You've gone to South America, where you really will marry me."

She wasn't even shocked. He wanted that. He wanted her.

Was there ever any other choice after he had marked her and claimed her all that time ago? Her petal-rimmed breast, the paint not faded yet, was the constant reminder of every erotic moment she had spent with him.

Not even Moreton could crush that.

Or the horror they had just gone through.

No other man met his measure. She knew that now. And no other man could live with the litany of her sins.

And he was the only man who could ever hold her, contain her, and make her beg. She would forever be *khanum* and he was her *cadi*.

Marry him . . . for real—

A life together, for real. A home, a farm, a family. Corsets and constraints.

And a tent, their private world, a world with no restraints.

They sailed for South America later that week.

There, she discovered that he was wealthy in his own right, that he had stud farms and land and money all his own, and that she need never see Aling again if she didn't want to.

He would now hire managers for his farms, and import his stud stock to England for his investors, and buy land in the English countryside and a fresh new place for them to live.

The things that were possible outside Bliss River—not least a future, with him.

It sounded like a plan.

"But you need not marry me," she pointed out. "Everyone believed that we were, except Moreton."

"We will show every possible authentication of our union," Charles said. "I will have nothing less."

"You really want Aling." The last thing to clear up.

"For God's sake, Georgiana. Hang Aling. Sell Aling if you want. I'm not a gentleman, no one knows that better than you—"

She stared at him. *The things that were possible. Things other people did, like get married. Have families.*

He stared at her. She was so beautiful, his queen. And she'd come through so much. And come so far. And in the end, she was everything he wanted, and life without having her was no life at all.

He was so close to her now. A breath away.

Things lovers did—like sometimes—

He settled his mouth on hers.

"You can run naked through the house if that's your desire," he whispered against her lips. "You need never put on clothes."

"My favorite mode of dress—" she sighed, opening her mouth to him, that sweet little feeling unfurling inside.

"Good. God, I want you." He wanted to devour her. He knew every inch of her body but her mouth. Every part of her, but her kisses. He couldn't get enough of her. His whole body vibrated with it, and found that answering resonance in her.

This was different. This was because they both had changed.

He felt as if they had finally walked together into clean sweet air, that everything was bright and fresh and they were entering a world where two sinners were free to start over.

Had he not sinned as much as she?

"There are no just impediments, Charles."

"There are a damned lot of clothes," he muttered.

"I can remedy that, *cadi.*"

He pulled away from her lips reluctantly. "Do you know what, *khanum?* We're going to do this right, with all due tradition: no fucking until after the wedding."

"Not possible," she murmured.

"Anything is possible." Except his towering erection. That might not last for many more days. No, minutes at this rate, with those kisses. "It's only a matter of days. And I didn't say no kissing . . ."

Ah, the kissing. The sweet tender ravenous kissing. She would never get enough of the kissing.

She opened her mouth joyfully to receive him. She knew where kissing led.